THE
PRINCE
OF
BERLIN

Also by Dan Sherman

THE MOLE
RIDDLE
SWANN
KING JAGUAR
DYNASTY OF SPIES
THE WHITE MANDARIN

THE PRINCE OF BERLIN

by
DAN SHERMAN

ARBOR HOUSE
New York

FOR MANON

We got a little carried away by the Cold War.
—anonymous CIA officer who took early retirement

PART ONE
THE DISAPPEARANCE

CHAPTER
ONE

HARRY ROSE DISAPPEARED on a Thursday, the second Thursday in October. It was an unnatural time reminiscent of that first autumn after the war. There were night winds at dawn, a river mist in the market square and a deeper hint of winter. Later, residents would also recall that the week had been filled with unsettling events "as if the entire city were askew." On Sunday a mutilated dog had been found in the park. On Wednesday there was lightning but no thunder. Came Thursday, and in the exhausted afternoon Harry Rose simply disappeared.

It would never be clear exactly who had been the first to notice Harry's absence. Ordinarily those failing to respond to the morning call were immediately placed on report. But Harry had never regularly attended staff muster, and although this was technically a breach of station regulations, no one had had the heart to discipline him. So Harry more or less kept his own hours. He was not formally attached to an active section, nor accountable to the department head. Generally he would just wander in around ten o'clock. He never ate with the others. He always brought a sandwich and a carton of milk.

It was not until the following Tuesday that a written alert concerning Harry's disappearance was circulated. Precisely how his absence could have gone unnoticed for five days was never fully determined, but apparently there had always been some confusion as to who was responsible for the irregular ones. Then too it was generally known that Harry's health was not so good.

Typical of the negligence associated with these early moves, the first attempts to locate Rose were very feeble indeed. By Wednesday responsibility for the case had fallen to station security and an improbable young man named Guy Campbell. Initially Campbell's only effort to contact Harry had been to telephone the man's home. Of course there was no reply.

Later that same morning Campbell spoke with a woman from the registry, who supposedly knew Rose better than the others. She reported that Harry had often spent the summer with relatives and suggested that Campbell contact them. This, Campbell attempted to do, but he found no reference for an extended family in the station directory. A brief conversation with Harry's nominal senior confirmed that since the death of his wife, Harry had no one: no children, no friends.

It was not until Friday that Campbell actually visited Harry's home. He left in the afternoon, but because the roads had been blocked by a disarmament rally he did not reach the house until early evening. By then another river fog had moved in from the southwest. Except for an occasional wandering bus the suburbs were deserted.

The house was larger than Campbell had expected. The steepled outline rose well above the surrounding trees. The outer wall was high, gray stone blackened with ivy. By the hawthorns stood a rotting gazebo and half-timbered gables. In the wake of a passing car there was nothing but darkness and the ticking of wet leaves.

14

Campbell circled the house twice, testing the locks, then entered through a window. There were only night sounds: settling floorboards, a dripping faucet, wind under the door. He waited, letting the room come to him out of the darkness. Above a grand piano hung a seascape in muted tones. There was an empty bottle of gin on the mantle, a vase of dead geraniums on the table.

How long Campbell remained he would never clearly remember. Later, when asked to describe his visit, he would tell how he had calmly stalked from room to room, examining stray papers, peering into closets, noting the contents of drawers. None of this was true. In fact he spent no more than twenty minutes in that house and all he would recall was the still gaze of a woman's portrait, a ticking clock and the oddest sense of someone watching.

Later that same evening he found himself drinking and did not know why. Still later he began his initial summary of the Rose case. In the end this summary would comprise nine typewritten pages and a photocopy of Harry's personal file. It was routed from Berlin on a Friday and reached Langley, Virginia on a Monday.

Three days after the arrival of the Campbell summary two men who would ultimately share responsibility for the Rose case were alerted and briefed on the details. These men were Lyle Severson from counterintelligence and George Clay, the effective head of the European sphere. Both men had been with the agency for decades and their involvement in the case underscored its importance. Whatever else might eventually be said about the search for Harry Rose, no one would claim that those in charge had taken the disappearance lightly.

As with others of his generation Clay had originally entered the clandestine service at the start of the Second World War. Those who knew him from that era said that even before the German defeat he had been a strong, vocal critic of the Soviets. He was also

15

said to have personally dealt with Stalin at Potsdam and disliked the man intensely. At the war's end Clay stayed on with the service as the regional director for the Rhineland-Palantinate. There he was remembered as a fierce in-fighter with a volatile temper.

Clay had been vacationing in Geneva when word of the disappearance reached him through the diplomatic route. He had arrived from Brussels after twelve days at the October war games. In Zurich he joined a German girl named Kristian Haas. Photographs from their last afternoon together showed them posing on the west shore: he, a fairly stocky figure with cropped gray hair; she, slender and very blond.

Following word of the disappearance, Clay left Geneva on an evening flight, landed in Virginia on a Tuesday afternoon. By now more than two hundred pages of documentation concerning Harry Rose had been drawn from the Langley vaults. Also included was a photograph of Rose from 1962. On reading this material Clay telephoned Lyle Severson's home on the edge of an older suburb.

Like Clay, Lyle Severson had also entered the service at the start of the war. Stories of his early years varied, but all agreed he had had a hard war with the loss of his bride, his health and much of his faith in what he referred to as a higher justice. Also like Clay, Severson had remained in the service through that transitory period of the late forties. He was a frail man with pale gray eyes and long features. He did not take the death, or disappearance, of agents well.

It was eight o'clock in the evening when Clay arrived at Severson's home. Severson was waiting in an oval room above the garden. All afternoon there had been intermittent rain, and Clay came back with a black mackintosh over his arm. Severson wore corduroy trousers that his daughter had given him years ago. There was a fire in the grate, brandy on a table, odors of coffee and the smell of damp earth.

"I suppose we should talk about Harry Rose," Severson said softly.

Clay had moved to the far wall and an etching of a schooner in high seas. "I don't know what there is to talk about, Lyle. The man has been giving this agency trouble for twenty-five years. You think I'm surprised that he's finally gone dirty?"

"But he *was* good. You have to admit that he *was* very good."

"Erratic. He was good on the political front, but you couldn't trust his strategic estimates."

"You mean nuclear strategic?"

"Yes, nuclear."

Severson had picked up a fountain pen, toying with the cap. "And they used to say that his people were very loyal to him, didn't they?"

"Hitler's were loyal to him too, weren't they?"

Clay had moved back to the table, poured a glass of brandy, drank it, poured another. "I'm going to send a man in, Lyle."

Severson ran his hand across his mouth. "Who? That boy I met the other day?"

"Jerry Mace? No, not him. I was thinking of using Alex Petty. Remember him? Thin? Fair hair? Good-looking?"

Severson shook his head. He had never been able to remember them all. He did not even know where Clay got them. Or how he kept them loyal.

"Look, if you've got someone better in mind . . . "

Severson shrugged, "What about Charlie Wilde?"

Clay had moved to another etching: boats along a dark canal. "What about him?"

"Well, he knew Harry, didn't he? Knew him better than anyone."

"That was years ago, he's an old man now."

Severson had drawn back the curtains. There were the lights of passing cars through the trees. "Look at it this way. You can send in your boy Petty and he may or may not get lucky. But if Harry

17

Rose is still in the zone Charlie will find him."

"And you'd prefer it if Wilde found him, is that it?"

Severson sighed. "You never liked Rose, did you?"

"Not particularly."

"Well, I did. Of course I didn't know him well, not as well as you, but I liked him. I mean he definitely had a way about him, didn't he?"

"He was a crook."

"Oh, I suppose, but still he had the way about him. You can't deny that."

Their final moments together were spent at the edge of Severson's garden. Here along the hedgerows lay the scattered debris of an earlier wind. There was an oblique view through the trees of a back street lined with parked cars.

"Have you been there recently?" Severson asked.

"Where?"

"Berlin?"

"I was there a few months ago."

"But you didn't seen Harry?"

"It was a rough trip, Lyle. I had two days to pave the way for a counterforce budget."

"What about that young lady of yours? How is she?"

"Kristian? She's fine. Why?"

"Does she still live in Berlin?"

"Yeah."

"Very pretty girl, isn't she?"

"Lyle, what the hell are you driving at?"

Severson had torn off a strand of ivy. Now it lay coiled at their feet. "Oh, I don't know. I just wonder about the disparity."

"What disparity?"

"In lifestyle. That is, you've done very well, while Harry . . ."

"So?"

"So perhaps it's jealousy. Perhaps it's frustration. I understand that tactically you've never seen eye-to-eye with him. I mean he

18

never much liked the idea of a—how shall I put it? A European theater force?"

"Lyle, what's your point?"

"Oh, no point really. I'm just trying to understand."

"Understand what?"

"The motivation. I mean, after all these years, why defect now?"

When Clay had gone, Lyle walked back into his house and sat down in a burlap chair by a reading lamp. An hour passed. It was raining again. Earlier he had rummaged through a box of old photographs, but he had not found one of Harry Rose. Still, he remembered the man well enough from 1956.

Alex Petty was a slender man with light hair and delicate features. Before joining the European desk he had been posted in the East: Macao, Hong Kong, Vientiane—all tough assignments. On his return to Langley he studied weapons systems analysis in Brussels, then surfaced in Rome under the shallow cover of a Rockefeller grant. From Rome he moved to northern Greece and a rushed tour of the Balkans. Between the continent and Langley there had also been London, where he was generally regarded as distant and unreadable, but perfectly suited to the trade.

Petty met Clay in a restaurant seven miles west of the Fairfax County line. The bar was filled with travelers left stranded by the rain. Beyond lay a stretch of open highway to the railroad line. Petty arrived in a beige linen suit, a gray shirt and thin tie. His hair was longer than others on Clay's staff, but acceptable within the European sphere.

They sat by the window. There were miles of headlights moving south to the city. A drab girl had brought them beer.

"I've had Jerry Mace book you on a Monday flight," said Clay. "I assume that's okay."

Petty shrugged. "Sure. That's okay."

19

"You should also know that you're going to be working with someone else. His name is Charlie Wilde. He's one of Lyle Severson's people—in a manner of speaking."

"Local?"

"No. He used to work with Rose. Severson thought he might be able to help."

"Do you know him?"

"We've met."

"What's his story?"

"Like I said, he used to work with Rose. Then a few years ago Rose sent him over the Wall. It went bad, and he took a bullet in the shoulder. I wouldn't ask him about it if I were you."

"What's his arrangement with us?"

"Nothing formal. Just play him along for whatever he's worth. He's an old man. He won't last the whole run."

Past a wasted yard two children were waiting by the road on the fender of a Chevrolet: a boy in black leather, a girl in a torn jumper.

"So what's he like?" Petty asked suddenly.

"Who? Wilde?"

"No, Rose."

Clay shook his head. He had also turned to watch the northbound tracks. "I haven't seen him in years."

"Do you think he crossed the border?"

"It wouldn't surprise me."

"Who's been handling the case?"

"A guy named Campbell. Station security."

"According to the file, Rose had a wife. What do you know about her?"

"Not much. Rose picked her up in Germany after the war. She died a few years back, natural causes."

"Kids?"

"No."

A woman in a red dress kept watching Petty from the doorway.

20

There were sounds of a passing train, then laughter from the kitchen.

"Why do you think he did it?" Petty asked.

Clay shrugged. "Why do any of them do it? Money? Women? Politics? I'd say someone bought Rose. He always spent more than he had."

"I gather he wasn't too happy about the tactical side of things."

"What do you mean?"

"Nuclear."

"Who told you that?"

"It's in the file. He wanted to go on record for a cutback."

Clay turned in his chair to the window. There was nearly a mile of undisturbed railroad track to the swamp. "I want you to remember something when you're over there," he said. "You're going to hear a lot about how Rose used to run things in the old days, a lot of weird stories from a lot of weird people. I want you to try and ignore it. You understand what I'm saying? Just find him, and ignore the rest. You're good at ignoring things, so just keep it up."

Afterward Petty accompanied Clay to the parking lot. Farther on Petty passed Jerry Mace, glaring from behind the windshield of a Cadillac. Once, months ago, Petty had been paired with Mace on the night course at Langley and had almost killed the man. Now they rarely spoke, except in the presence of Clay.

Two days after the involvement of Alex Petty, Severson took a morning flight to Tampa, landed in the afternoon, then caught a bus to St. Petersburg. Charlie Wilde was waiting at the station. Severson saw him first through a break in the disembarking crowd. Wilde stood unsmiling by a fountain, in dark glasses and a tropical suit.

Like Lyle, Wilde was a thin man with white hair and long features. His eyes were also pale gray. At the start of his retirement

21

he had purchased a duplex and four acres in an older section along the shore. There were cypress groves to the south, a long view of the bay to the west. Here, too, the days had been marked by an intermittent rain.

Wilde's house stood above a seawall at the end of a beaten path. There were palms to the water, a crumbling wharf, a half-submerged dinghy among the reeds. Inside there were odors of cigarettes and rotting wood. Lyle sat in a rocker. Wilde faced him on the window box. The first moments were taut, filled with a pointless exchange about the weather and life along the Florida coast. Severson kept glancing at the objects around him—driftwood, a rock, a slab of shale.

Finally Wilde said, "I always knew this would happen."

"Knew what, Charlie?"

"That you or someone like you would eventually come to see me about Harry."

"Why do you say that?"

"Well, he was always more or less an outlaw, wasn't he? Always on the edge to a certain degree."

Severson had risen, turned to the window. Here too there were headlights on a distant bridge. "They tell me that Harry had strong feelings about the escalation. Is that true, Charlie?"

Wilde shrugged. "He never believed in the deterrence theory, if that's what you mean."

"Is that why he hated George Clay?"

"Oh, I don't know. I'm not sure that he ever really hated Clay so much as the Clay mentality. The Russians build this, we build that . . . I think there just came a point when Harry stopped believing—"

"You don't think he defected, do you?"

"No."

"Then what happened to him, Charlie? Tell me what could have happened to him."

Two women were moving between the seawall and a line of

22

palms. One of them seemed to be limping, the other dragging a stick.

Severson said, "I imagine that you've already guessed that Clay is sending in a man. Very smooth little cobra by the name of Petty."

"So?"

"So do I have to tell you what will happen if Clay finds him first?"

Wilde had also turned to watch the women, although by now they were fairly indistinct against the water. "I can't promise that I'll find him, Lyle."

"I realize that."

"And I'll need a passport."

"It's been taken care of."

"And I don't want to have to work with anyone. This Petty, for example. What's the deal with him?"

"No deal, Charlie. Let him do your leg work, that's all. He needn't even stay through the end."

"And Clay?"

"I'll do my best to keep Clay out of it. I promise."

Wilde managed to unearth two inconsequential letters from 1968 and a photograph of Rose on the balcony of a cabaret. Later there was rain again, and the unexpected sounds of passing ships. Severson spent the last six hours in a rented room, then caught an early flight from Tampa.

Now all that remained were the final preparations. On the last day before departure Petty wandered down to the Langley vaults where the bulk of the dead files were kept. The librarian was a nervous boy whom Petty remembered vaguely from the year before.

The master index held seven references to Harry Rose, but the actual files were relatively thin. There were three letters of recommendation, a medical voucher and a loyalty pledge, presumably in Harry's own hand. The service record contained only twelve sheets with minimal notations. Apparently Rose had fought an undistinguished war in a propaganda unit outside of London. He was, however, rated in hand-to-hand and small arms. Also, he was Jewish.

Attached to these pages were two entries relating to placement in the zone, and a receipt for three hundred redeemable barter unit certificates. The only other article of consequence was a photograph, obviously decades old and never intended for the Langley record.

Here Rose appeared as a dark boy against a descending landscape of Berlin rubble. His face was lean, but undeniably handsome. The features were even, strong, and with the shadow of the cap across his eyes, almost Oriental. On the obliterated horizon stood the remains of a clock tower and a gray cathedral.

Wilde's preparations were no less random. On the last day before departure he too returned in a haphazard way to the past and the Harry Rose he once knew very well. There were letters in a coffee tin, photographs in an envelope, even a drawing that some woman had done: a reflective portrait of Rose in the doorway of what looked like a brothel. "Things may go under," Rose had once written, "but you and I will survive, maybe win." And years later in another note: "Be quiet, Charlie, and swallow defeat. There's always tomorrow."

There were remnants of a lifetime with Harry scattered everywhere in Wilde's cramped room. Under the rolltop was a book, the second of two volumes on cabalistic thought. On the wall was an etching stolen from a house outside of Dachau. From Harry's first days in Berlin, two silver candlesticks confiscated from a tank commander. From a later era, a nine-point proposal for bilateral arms reduction. Then another of Harry's favorite books: *Alchemy and the Jewish Tradition.*

24

Harry Rose. There were moments when it seemed to Wilde that he had never really known the man. Specific memories were no help. There was a contemplative Harry watching the city from a window on the Kanstrasse, a cynical Harry with diamonds under the floorboards. There was an intense Harry feeding a clip of an automatic rifle, and a secret Harry who really believed in magic. There was also a private Harry for friends, and a public Harry for the city. But like an object in a darkened room he kept changing, depending upon what you thought you saw. By the spring of 1946, much of Berlin was afraid of him. By the fall of 1980, even his own people had forgotten him.

CHAPTER
TWO

ALEX PETTY REACHED Berlin on a Thursday, two weeks after Harry Rose's disappearance. En route he spent a night in Hamburg with a girl he had known from before. They dined on the Rahausplatz among the canals. She discussed the placements of the new Pershing II's. He was exhausted and did not have much to say. Afterward they walked east past abandoned quays through a neighborhood of cheap shops and factories. In the end he returned to her apartment, but slept badly on the couch.

There was rain in Berlin and another disarmament rally disturbing traffic from the airport. After waiting for a long time, Petty was finally given a room in a small hotel near a radio tower. He registered under the name of Alarie. From the window there was a cramped view of a nightclub and the corrugated roof of a service garage. After drinking in his room for a while he fell asleep. When he rose again and lifted the blinds he saw that the rain had stopped, but a yellow fog had descended. It was four o'clock in the afternoon.

There was no formality to the actual start of the search. In the morning Petty ordered coffee and an egg. Then he rented a black Audi from an office six blocks from his hotel. When he returned, he telephoned the acting head of Berlin Security. An hour later he met Guy Campbell in a blank room at the station.

The Berlin station stood in a quiet district on the suburban edge of the Grunewald. Supposedly it had originally been built by an industrialist as a villa for his family. The surrounding grounds comprised several wooded acres encircled by a high stone wall and chain link. Although damaged in the war, the balconies had been restored, also the molding and gabled windows. Then too, there were the trees, quite a number of them planted during those determined years after the blockade.

From a distance Campbell vaguely reminded Petty of that pale librarian from the Langley vaults. The boy was tall and very thin. There was an unnatural pallor to his complexion. His hair was red, receding from the forehead. He was dressed badly in a suit that he must have purchased locally. As Petty approached, Campbell studied him without comment, but it was clear from his eyes that he was uneasy.

"I've heard a lot about you," Campbell said.

"Yeah?"

"From George."

They had left the blank room and were moving down a narrow corridor. There was a distant clack of a typewriter, hushed voices, footsteps on the linoleum.

"If I had known you were coming, I would have sent someone to meet you. Would have at least saved you the cab fare. Did you get stuck in a rally? It's been going on for weeks. I imagine it's got George concerned, what with the Bonn conference coming up."

"I wouldn't know."

Campbell's office lay at the end of the corridor. It was a bleak, triangular room that might have once been a nursery. An oval window with an iron grill looked out to the courtyard.

"Is that where he lived?" Petty nodded to the trees.

"Rose? Yes. He's got a house on the other side of the park."

"You've been there?"

"I took a look. One of those old neogothic things. Almost as large as this place."

"Where did he get the money?"

"Money?"

"For the house."

"Oh, well, he's lived there for years. Probably picked it up for a song right after the war."

Petty stepped back to the window. He was running his fingers along the sill. "Even so, there's the upkeep, isn't there? Gardeners. Painting."

Petty was looking down at the courtyard below. "So why don't you tell me about him, Campbell?"

"What do you want to know?"

"Who were his friends?"

"None to speak of."

"None?"

"Well, everyone knew him, of course, but he liked to keep to himself. He read a lot. History. Other stuff."

"They say he's been around for a long time."

"That's right. He was one of the first, the last of his kind."

"Freewheeling type? I understand he was actually here since the war," Petty said.

"Yes."

"Isn't that a little unusual? I mean for someone to stay on at one station for so long?"

Campbell picked up a cigarette lighter. He began turning it over and over. "Apparently there was a time when Rose was considered invaluable to the station. Then he just sort of entrenched himself."

"How?"

29

"Look, I'm not responsible for that end of things. Placements are made in Langley."

"But the duty roster is drawn up here."

"So?"

"So what did Harry do for a living?"

"Historical."

"What's that supposed to mean?"

"He worked in archives."

"That must have kept him real busy."

"As a matter of fact it did. The files are always on call. Both Operations and the Special Branch couldn't function without them."

"And that's what Rose was doing? Research?"

"Well, he knew the territory, didn't he?"

"How so?"

"You're talking about material that goes back maybe thirty years. There's a lot on the occupation, a lot on the Russians, a lot on the nuclear thing. From what I gather, it was all Harry's world."

"So they stuck him down in the basement pushing paper, is that it?"

"As a matter of fact I think he volunteered for the job, but you'll have to ask about that downstairs."

Before descending again Petty stepped out on the balcony to smoke a cigarette. Behind him through a french window lay a room in renovation. An electronic sweep of the walls had left suspended dust in the sunlight, plaster rubble on the floorboards.

It was nearly four o'clock when Petty left the station. He drove east, following a map that Campbell had drawn on the back of an envelope. Beyond the suburbs the streets were littered with handbills from an earlier rally. A black dove had been spray-painted on the wall of a department store, a mushroom cloud in lipstick

30

had been drawn on the windshield of a limousine. Closer to the park there was evidence of sporadic violence: broken glass and police vans.

Like Campbell before him, Petty saw the house from a distance: the twin spires above the pines, a length of gothic molding. Also the neighborhood was very still with only random traffic and intermittent wind.

He entered as Campbell had entered, reaching through a broken pane of glass to unlatch the window. There were only sounds of dripping taps. Even the clocks had stopped. He began with the drawers, sliding them open, drawing out papers. There was an unpaid telephone bill, a stack of receipts from local shops. He glanced at them briefly, then slipped them into his coat. In a bureau by the entrance hall there were matchbooks, a stamp collector's catalogue and the frayed strap from a wristwatch. Then there were the empty drawers, quite a number of them that Rose had obviously cleared before he left.

There were moments, moving through this house when Petty had the oddest image of himself submerging into water. Several rooms were filled with underwater shapes of looming furniture, palm leaves reflected in mirrors. There were magazines in an upstairs room: Der Spiegel, Newsweek, Le Point. On the cover of one was a mushroom cloud rising from a wasted city. There were similar articles in the foreign journals with photographs of the Trident missiles against a German landscape, demonstrations in the streets. Then there were the books, dozens of them: *The Light of Moses Luzzatto, Documents of the Soul, Alchemie in Mittealter.* Only the bedroom was neutral in pastels and with a view across the park to the city.

In all, Petty spent more than three hours in that house, but left with relatively nothing. There were only those receipts from the neighborhood shops, that telephone bill and a few handwritten notes that appeared to be the basis for an intraagency piece on European tactical options. There were also photographs, one of

31

Rose in later years and what must have been an early portrait of his wife. She appeared standing on a bridge against the winter trees, slight, remarkably pretty.

After leaving the house, Petty drove randomly until he reached a tawdry district of cabarets and cellar clubs. From here he wandered on foot, peering into cheap shop windows. He was tired, hungry, but more than anything he wanted a drink. By nightfall the streets were filled with others like himself, youths with no place in particular to go.

There was also rain on the afternoon that Charlie Wilde arrived. It was a cold rain, the first of the season, and mixing with the wind the air was shattering. Later another yellow fog descended, slowing traffic to the city, leaving travelers stranded indefinitely. The airport in particular reminded Wilde of that phobic period after the war with all the aircraft half-buried in mist.

The hotel that Wilde had chosen lay in a suburb not far from the station. He was given a room facing the park. There was a view of a long avenue between the beeches. For a while he sat on the bed. Then he walked to the window and shut the curtains. Earlier he had been drinking white wine. Then he had a whiskey in a bar adjacent to the runway. When the valet came with his luggage he ordered another whiskey, toward dusk another.

When he finished drinking he slipped off his shoes and stretched out on the bed. There was a water stain on the ceiling that looked vaguely like a dog. All day he had been afraid the night would come to this: a rented room, an empty glass, German voices in the corridor. In other cities when he could not sleep he took long walks. But he did not think he could face Berlin in the darkness. So he waited, lying very still on the bed. Twenty minutes passed, then an hour. It was particularly bad just before dawn.

Unlike Petty, Charlie Wilde did not meet Campbell at the station. They met in a cafe. The ceiling was low with heavy beams. The walls were whitewashed brick. Wilde arrived early and took a corner table where the light was poor and he knew that he could not be seen. Campbell arrived a few minutes later, hesitating in the doorway.

"I'd like to thank you for meeting me here," Wilde said. "I hope it wasn't too much trouble."

"No, sir, no trouble."

"Still, you must be tired of it all by now."

"Tired of what, sir?"

"Harry Rose."

Campbell smiled. He was dressed like other young agency officers that Wilde had met: a moderately priced blazer, brown slacks, an unobtrusive tie. Wilde on the other hand wore what he had always worn in these German autumns: a raincoat and a tropical suit.

"I wonder if you'd mind terribly going over what you told George Clay's boy?" Wilde said.

"Well, sir, we didn't discuss much. He asked about Mr. Rose's position, and I told him that Mr. Rose worked in archives."

"What else?"

"He also asked about Mr. Rose's friends."

"And you told him?"

"I told him that Mr. Rose didn't have any friends, not at least that I knew of."

"Anything else?"

"Not really, sir. I told him that Mr. Rose has been helping the tactical research. Then he went down to Mr. Rose's house."

"And you haven't spoken with Petty since?"

"No, sir."

Wilde was silent for a moment. There was a charcoal sketch of Albert Einstein on the wall, another of Peter Lorre. There were also portraits of student leaders who had recently made names for themselves in the disarmament movement. Wilde recognized their faces from the newspapers.

Finally he said, "Did you know him at all, Guy?"

"You mean Mr. Rose?"

"Yes."

"No, sir, not really. He kept pretty much to himself."

"Still, you must have formed some sort of an opinion."

"Well, sir, to be honest I guess I felt kind of sorry for him."

"Sorry?"

"Well, he'd been around for so long, and then to end up in archives like that . . . I don't know. I suppose it just didn't seem right."

"Do you know much about his past?"

"Only that he was one of the first out here, and he had a pretty rough time of it a few years back."

"Did you know that he and I were once very close?"

"Yes, sir. I did."

They left the cafe, moving slowly between black trees and an iron-gray apartment block. There were students milling on the concrete, children on a balcony. I feel like I never left this place, Wilde thought. Maybe I've always been here. He asked, "What did you think of him?"

"Sir?"

"Alex Petty."

"Oh. Well, I suppose he was capable enough."

"Tough?"

"Yes, sir. I guess you could say that."

"Do you know where I could find him?"

"I believe he's at the station, or at least he was when I left. Shall I take you there?"

Campbell had left his Chevrolet parked beside a gum tree. There were wet leaves plastered on the windshield. While Wilde waited for Campbell to unlock the door he saw two boys watching from across a footbridge. One of them held a camera with a telephoto lens. A moment later they were gone.

There was nothing special in Wilde's first meeting with Petty. Wilde found the boy, as he thought of him, in a third-floor room

34

adjacent to the station registry. Like other offices along the corridor, a team from renovations had left the place in shambles. The linoleum had been stripped to the floorboards. There were gaping holes in the ceiling and walls. Petty was standing by a filing cabinet. He wore a cotton suit—simple, but Italian and expensive. There was an unlit cigarette between his lips and a fountain pen in his right hand.

"Mr. Petty?"

Petty nodded slowly. He was watching Wilde's hands.

"My name is Charlie—"

"I know who you are. How do you do?"

They sat on packing crates. Petty had still not lit his cigarette. Wilde was facing the flat light from the window. Dust hung in the air.

"So how is George?" Wilde asked.

"He's fine."

"I understand that he's the last word on the tactical end."

"He heads the European Desk, if that's what you mean."

"Do you work for him exclusively?"

"I help with local problems."

"And that's what this is? A local problem?"

"You could say that."

There was a pause while Petty withdrew a matchbook and lit his cigarette. As Wilde looked on he noticed that every movement was very precise. Good or bad? Who knew?

"I hear you've already been out to the house," Wilde said.

"That's right."

"What did you find?"

"Nothing much. He seemed to know what he was doing. There were a lot of empty drawers."

"And his office downstairs?"

"Same thing."

"Have you spoken with the people around here?"

An ash fell to the floor. "They don't know anything."

35

There was another momentary pause while Petty extinguished the cigarette. Again a careful gesture.

"I assume George told you that I used to know Harry Rose pretty well," Wilde said.

"He mentioned it."

"But you don't see that as being particularly relevant, is that it?"

Petty smiled. "No, I'm afraid I don't."

"Care to tell me why?"

"Oh, I think the facts are clear enough. After a lifetime of service the man winds up pushing papers around a basement. Now, obviously he had to have felt a certain amount of . . . frustration."

Wilde rose, crossed the room and unlatched a window. The air was cooler now. "Come here," he said. "Come here, I want to show you something."

Petty hesitated, then also moved to the window. Now they were both facing a gray vision of the city under clouds.

"Do you see that?"

"See what?"

"That. Berlin."

"What about it?"

"There was a time when Harry Rose controlled damn near all of it."

"What do you mean?"

"I mean that in a very basic way this city belonged to him."

"So?"

"I just thought you should know that." Then Wilde turned and moved off. It was noon, and the station was silent, except for a solitary typewriter on the second floor.

CHAPTER
THREE

TOWARD DUSK WILDE went down to the motor pool and signed
a requisition slip for a gray Volkswagen with untraceable license
plates. Then he drove east along the Grunewald following a half-
remembered route to Harry's home. He entered as the others had
entered, circling the grounds twice, then slipping in through an
unlatched window. It was the blue hour, muted with fog and a
premature darkness in the city.

He began by simply wandering, examining those objects which
seemed most familiar. There was that piano that no one ever
played, those Dresden figurines. He had never intended to make
a concentrated search. There was no point. Harry Rose had never
been one to leave secrets lying around.

After about thirty minutes of aimless inspection Wilde sat down
in a chair by a dying plant. There was a bottle of brandy on the
table. He knew that if he stayed much longer he would drink it,

so he poured it down the drain. Remembering was not difficult. The trick was to face it.

Whenever Wilde thought about how it all began he thought about those closing months of the war and the countryside west of London where he first saw Harry Rose. It had been early autumn, the second week in October. Wilde had come to London by way of New York, then caught a military truck to the edge of Wiltshire. Travel was slow behind the convoys. It was 1945, but the landscape was still blacked out and deserted.

The Wiltshire facility consisted of a sprawling estate on the edge of a mustard field. It was locally known as Griffen Hall. Half a mile down the lane were shuttered cottages where the staff was housed. Beyond lay open grassland and dark elms. There were long twilights here, leaving standing stones in black relief.

There were nine Wiltshire units destined for the German occupation and a role in the postwar world. The European Advisory Commission maintained a staff of twenty, and there were seventeen from the scientific sector. Beneath division command were twelve representatives from the Office of Strategic Services and several quiet teams from the private sphere: Standard Oil, General Electric, International Telephone and Telegraph. At twenty-two, Wilde was among the youngest.

In later years Wilde came to call these months his salad days, and often looked back to Wiltshire for some seed of understanding to all that eventually happened in Berlin. Before Wiltshire he had vaguely heard of difficulties with the Russians, rumors of trouble in Potsdam, unexpressed resentment in the Balkans. Apparently Churchill had never liked Stalin much, nor had Harry Truman. But it wasn't until Wilde had joined the Griffen staff that he actually began to sense the shape of things—a Soviet threat, a divided Europe, the atomic bomb.

Of those nine units bound for the occupation, six were actively concerned with the Soviets, two with atomic experimentation. As for Wilde, he had originally requested an administrative post with a vision of helping refugees, particularly children, preferably in France. But within a week of his arrival he found himself among lists of German heavy-water plants, radio intercepts from Stalingrad. He was often lonely at night, often left wondering what happened to the war with the *Germans?*

There was a wind the first night Wilde saw Harry, a warm wind, the first of the season. Earlier, Wilde had wandered out across the downs to the spine of a hill. From here was an unobstructed view of the holly groves and a ruined kirk. As he was returning along the deep lane he noticed that the crows had fled. Within an hour the wind had risen from the south. When he returned to his cottage he found Harry Rose sitting on the davenport.

There were two canvas bags on the step, a raincoat on the peg. The curtains had been drawn apart leaving parallel shadows on the brick. There was a bottle of gin on the windowsill. From the doorway Wilde saw only a silhouette and the glowing tip of a thin cigar.

He said, "Hello. Who are you?"

And that casual reply, "Oh, didn't they tell you? I'm your new roommate."

"Well, you're sitting on my bed."

"You mean you actually sleep on this?"

"And that's my bottle."

"Sorry. Let me pour you a drink."

They spoke for several hours the first night, but Wilde learned next to nothing about the man. When asked how he had come to be at Griffen, Rose gave only the sketchiest story of a recruitment from an advertising firm in Boston. When asked about his education, Harry's reply was equally vague. And there were discrepancies about Harry's age—he was either eighteen, nineteen or twenty-five, depending on how one chose to calculate from the varying things he said.

39

Harry's physical appearance added to the aura of mystery. His complexion was dark, suggesting a Mediterranean parentage, but the eyes seemed almost Asian. The fingers were long, slender. The features were strong, some might say striking. There was a certain grace to his movements, his voice was soft and even.

Among Harry's personal possessions, Wilde found only four revealing items: a pack of Tarot cards, an annotated translation of the Cabala, Einstein's treatise on nuclear physics and a stiletto with a spring blade. There were no magazines, no novels, no photographs of loved ones or letters from home. Even Harry's wristwatch was G.I., government issue.

There was a rumor from these early days—Wilde never found out who started it—that Harry was actually the son of a dispossessed monarch. No kidding. Those who subscribed to this theory claimed that the name Rose was only an alias, probably a play on the actual title. As for Harry's nationality, all agreed that he was either Greek or Rumanian, but had been extensively educated in America. When Wilde eventually questioned Harry about the rumor, he received no clear answer one way or another. A few days later, however, he discovered that Rose was probably short for Rosenbau, because Harry was a Jew.

Among others, whether at meals or relaxing with a beer, Harry remained aloof. He did not participate in the Christmas pageant, nor the New Year's celebration. Neither did he take part in the Griffen sporting events: softball, football, a string of soccer matches with the British. On the combat course it was a different story. Nobody knew where Harry had learned to fight with a knife. He did not talk about it.

From the beginning Harry exhibited an exceptional flair for the so-called secret life. Initially he served in Analysis, deciphering fragments from the Soviet sphere. From Analysis he moved to Operations, where he monitored the Red networks throughout the Balkans. Finally he was transferred to the Central Planning board, where they said he had been born for the game, what with his wonderfully devious mind and all.

There were only two incidents from this early period which stood out in Wilde's mind as particularly revealing of the inner Harry Rose. The first occurred in March, not long after Harry's arrival. At the heart of this incident lay some sixty pages relating to the extermination of German Jews. This had not been the first time such material had circulated among the Griffen staff, but never had the details appeared so graphically. There were seven pages of laboratory analyses on hydrogen cyanide, thirty-nine pages of correspondence concerning the transportation of corpses and the subsequent processing to caustic soda. There were also photographs that obviously had been taken in secret.

Response to the material was fairly uniform . . . all deeply, properly disturbed, women in particular. Harry, however, seemed unaffected. His only public comment concerned a technical point. He could not understand how the photographer had achieved such definition.

But later, much later, he was seen walking out at the edge of the oaks. He wore boots and a yellow slicker. By midnight there was rain and high wind, but Harry had still not returned. Wilde waited several hours in the cottage, then fell asleep. He was finally awakened shortly before dawn by a light in the kitchen. Through a half-open door he saw Harry's profile. The man was fixed at the table, motionless. There was a pencil in his hand, a crumpled sheet of paper in another. After about ten minutes his lips began to move but there was no sound.

When Wilde awoke in the morning Harry was sleeping on the camp bed. The boots and the slicker lay on the floor. There was a broken glass in the kitchen, blood in the sink. The sleeve of Harry's jacket had been cut with a knife. There were strands of hair in an ashtray. On the crumpled sheet of paper underneath the

41

table, Wilde found fragments of mathematical notations, a drawing of a wheel with radiating spokes, another of a hanged man.

For days Wilde carried that scrap of paper in his wallet, occasionally taking it out to study the more intriguing symbols. He was particularly fascinated by what may have been Einstein's equation and a reference to the rain of blood from Exodus. Then one Tuesday afternoon, without knowing quite why, he shredded it, just as in the years to come he would eventually shred dozens of Harry's stray papers.

The second incident which Wilde recalled as telltale of the essential Harry Rose occurred in April, the trailing days of the war. The incident concerned one of the more controversial projects at Griffen: the recruitment of those German officers with detailed knowledge of Soviet networks. Although individual cases varied, most of those Germans enlisted were still actively part of the Nazi effort. In return for their agreement to help deal with the Soviets at the war's end, they were promised modest financial reward and, if needed, immunity from Allied military prosecution. Code-named Hammer, the physical line from London to Berlin ran through Zurich. As sectional head of central routing, Charlie Wilde's involvement began rather early, but always remained peripheral. He knew the fundamental direction, but not the ends.

As for Harry, his involvement began casually enough on a Wednesday afternoon. Earlier there had been a rain of shooting stars, and he and Wilde had strolled out across the downs in the hope of sighting another. As always, Harry wore his yellow slicker. A freak cold spell had frozen the smaller ponds.

"I need a favor, Charlie."

"Favor?" Wilde was still watching the sky.

"I need a little peek at the Hammer list."

Wilde stopped. "Jesus, Harry."

"It'll only take a minute, I need to verify something."

"What?"

42

"Well, it's a little hard to explain. Let's just say that I've got something going on the side."

"Harry, that stuff is locked up tight."

"But you've got access, don't you?"

"Yeah, but—"

"Trust me, Charlie, just trust me."

Other requests followed. By the end of two weeks Harry was regularly receiving transcripts of the Hammer alerts. By the end of three weeks he was receiving copies of all Hammer outstation memos. Wilde made two discreet inquiries regarding Harry's relationship with the project, but no one knew anything. Which meant that either Harry's involvement was extraordinarily confidential or else he had snowed the entire division.

On a Friday the end of the Hammer affair came very suddenly. At the center of events was the murder, in Switzerland, of a German officer named Bruno Kessler. Like other Hammer assets Kessler had originally entered Switzerland to discuss the terms of his agreement with Griffen representatives. Also like others he had crossed the border from Bavaria, entirely alone. His death from sniper fire north of Basel was attributed to members of the Polish resistance, but exactly how the Poles had known Kessler's route and schedule was never fully determined. There were those who believed that Kessler's death had been precipitated by a leak in Berlin. Others blamed the Zurich team. Only Wilde, however, thought about asking Harry Rose.

In all Wilde spent two days quietly investigating Kessler's murder. It was Tuesday when he finally confronted Harry. Earlier there had been reports that the German resistance had collapsed in Vienna and Zhukov had broken from the Oder. Harry had spent the afternoon with a girl from the clerical pool. He returned to the cottage vaguely drunk at seven o'clock in the evening.

Wilde began obliquely with a reference to Kessler's death and the subsequent London inquiry. Harry had opened another bottle of beer and picked up a deck of playing cards. As Wilde continued

43

prodding, Harry started laying out the cards on the cot. Eventually there were two lines of hearts descending from the ace.

Wilde said, "Look, Harry, you can be straight with me."

"About what, Charlie?" Now laying down a line of diamonds.

"About Kessler."

"What about him?"

"I know that you had something to do with what happened to him."

Rose had picked up the jack of clubs, then another ace. He had still not looked at Wilde.

"Two weeks ago you asked me for the Hammer list. Then you asked me for the background files. Then you wanted to know the drop schedules. Come on, Harry, I'm not that stupid."

"Never thought you were, Charlie."

"So why don't you just tell me what the hell you did?"

Harry stood up and moved to the window. There were rows of empty beer bottles on the ledge, cigarette butts in a jar, a waiting van beyond the trees.

"Tell me, Charlie, how much do you know about Kessler? I mean about his record in Poland. I mean about the seven hundred people he had gassed in a bus outside of Poznan."

"Harry, what are you talking about?"

"I'm talking about the fact that Bruno Kessler was a fucking animal. Okay?"

Later that evening Harry opened a bottle of gin, laid two glasses on the table. By midnight they were both fairly drunk, talking about an uncertain future, peace and women. At one point Wilde asked why Harry had volunteered for the occupation. Rose replied that he hated the Germans, very much.

There were two months in London before departure to Berlin, and through the first Wilde saw Harry only intermittently. They met on the first Sunday after the war for a drink and a meal in a chophouse near Kensington. Harry arrived with a typewritten pamphlet entitled "Black Market Theory" and the first of two volumes on the sack of Rome. He talked about the victory and little else. Women kept looking at him. Afterward they walked for an hour in the rain. The streets were filled with demobilized soldiers, most of them looking for prostitutes.

The last months were spent in debriefings held in the basement of a converted hospital on the West End. There were more than thirty in attendance, an odd assortment of medical teams, four intelligence units and then again those representatives from the private sector: Westinghouse, General Electric, Chrysler.

The instructor was a humorless officer from the Commission. He spoke in clipped, direct sentences. On the first evening he explained the dominant governing structure that was to be applied to Greater Berlin with an Allied Kommandatura under the general direction of a Control Council. The second evening's lecture was devoted to health hazards and housing. There was a description of the inhabitants and their expected relationship with Allied administrators. It was noted that many of the citizens still appeared to be in a state of shock. Young women appeared particularly affected. Also noted were health hazards connected with the unburied dead, disruption of sewage facilities, starvation and rats. Although the Russian soldier had officially been given only two days of unrestricted rape, incidents of sexual assault still remained inordinately high. All were advised to boil the water before drinking.

Finally there were three specialized briefings for those within the clandestine services. Now the talk of the Soviets became extensive, details regarding the intelligence apparatus and the potential value of surviving German networks. There was also a discussion about the remnants of the German technological sector with an emphasis on telemetry, the rocket sites and atomic research. They kept referring to the bomb as "the development."

On one of the last evenings there was a conversation which

Wilde often thought about in later years. It took place in a drab room Wilde had rented the month before. The walls were brown. Hot water cost a shilling. It was Sunday, gray in the morning, clearing at night. Harry appeared shortly after nine o'clock with a bottle of wine, that torn canvas bag and a newspaper under his arm.

Wilde cleared the remains of his dinner: sardines, an apple, beer, then laid two glasses on the table, uncorked the wine. Harry had begun to straighten his tie in a cracked mirror.

"Do you think about it much?" Wilde asked.

"Think about what?"

"Berlin."

"Sure I think about it."

"Do you ever think that maybe it's kind of crazy? I mean while everyone else is going home, starting new lives, we're going to be stuck in some bomb crater playing tag with the Russians."

Harry had still not moved away from the mirror. There was lipstick on his collar, grass stains on his trousers. Beneath the cigarettes and gin his clothing smelled faintly of a woman's perfume.

Finally he said, "Listen to me, Charlie. The Russians are just our excuse for being there. They've got nothing to do with the truth of it."

"Huh?"

"To the victor belong the spoils. Remember that. You can't get the spoils unless you're part of the occupation, and I definitely intend to get my share of the spoils."

"Harry, what spoils? The country is a goddamn ruin."

"We'll see."

Once again the evening ended with a long walk through yellow fog. They eventually found themselves in a club not far from Charing Cross. It was dark. There were no women. At one point Rose told Wilde that the first thing he felt like doing when he got

46

to Berlin was to beat up a German. A German official would be best. Germans . . .

But it did not happen like that.

They arrived in Berlin on a Monday in July, three months after the war. Harry had managed to requisition a house on the southern edge of the Tiergarten. It was large and very ugly with that special imprint of the Reich. All the reichs. There were granite eagles on the gateposts, figures from Teutonic myth cut into the molding. Beyond the outer wall were lines of scorched hawthorns and an open stretch of land where the last battles had been fought. Another roofless villa stood on a rise to the north. There were factory ruins to the south. Past willow mounds lay a tiger tank half submerged in mud. There were always lights in supposedly deserted bunkers.

Closer to the heart of the city were empty boulevards littered with brick and shattered masonry. Concrete still dangled from the reinforcing rods. On the second afternoon a strong wind brought odors of escaping gas. On the fourth day two Russian soldiers raped a woman and left her in a crater. On the fifth day Wilde found himself in a neighborhood of looted shops. A young girl beckoned from a doorway, lowered the straps of her dress. Wilde looked at her, then emptied his pockets of money, which he gave to her, and turned away.

In the beginning, unlike Harry Rose, Wilde supposed that his feelings toward the Germans were ambivalent. On the one hand there had been new information from the camps: photographs from Buchenwald, medical assessments from Dachau, survivors from Treblinka. On the other hand there were the exhausted eyes of women, children gazing from the blackened window sockets. Over cocktails with officers' wives one occasionally heard a sympathetic word.

Wilde's first real encounter with a German took place on a

Tuesday afternoon, the second week. There had been a reception for a congressional delegation with a garden buffet and chamber music in a gallery. After several hours Wilde had become bored and wandered out to a balcony to smoke a cigarette. There he met one of the servant girls. She was young, slender and her English was remarkably good. In the lamplight from the window her hair was silver-blond, her eyes blue-green.

At first she seemed shy. She told him only that her name was Lotte and that her mother had died of diptheria, her father shot in Barbarosa. Below, the guests had gathered under the chestnut trees. She kept watching them intently, her hands tight on the railing, her lips slightly parted.

Then because he was vaguely drunk, vaguely entranced with her profile: "Tell me something, Lotte. What was it like under Hitler?"

She did not raise her eyes. "Oh, so you're one of those."

"One of those?"

"You think there must have been a reason, but there was no reason. It just happened."

"Did you like Hitler?"

"That used to depend on who was asking the question. Can you understand that?"

"Yes and no. Anyway, I'm asking it."

"The answer is no."

Nine weeks later Wilde saw the girl again. She was waiting by a limousine in the suburbs near the Grunewald. Her hair had been dyed brown, her eyes darkened with mascara. She wore a Star of David around her neck and pretended not to recognize him.

On a day-to-day level attention still mainly focused on the Soviets. There were seven officers attached to the Special Section. Briefings were held on the second floor of the Luft Grau complex. Discussions usually centered on the reliability of former German officers and their potential use as agents in the restrictive Soviet zone. Harry rarely had much to say.

Regarding these early briefings, Wilde recalled only one significant conversation. It came on the heels of a particularly blunt discussion concerning the use of German couriers in the Danzig networks. Wilde and Rose had left the compound at a quarter to six in the evening. Half a mile south lay a stretch of pavement and the ruins of a granary. As always there was a quality to the light that left Wilde uneasy . . . blue-gray, or steel-gray and cold.

"So what do you think?" Wilde asked.

"Think?" Rose had obviously not been listening.

"About what they said. About using Krauts in the Russian zone."

"Oh I suppose it's one way to go."

"Then you approve?"

Rose smiled. For days now he had been intrigued by everything around him: camps of displaced persons, craters filled with rainwater, paper-blown streets. "Let's just say that I can appreciate the reasoning from a financial point of view."

"What do you mean?"

"I mean that I recognize the fact that there's no money, no game either. So obviously now that we've beaten the Germans we have to find another enemy. It's a matter of percentages."

"Come on, Harry, you don't really believe that."

"I do."

"Then what the hell are you getting involved for?"

"I've got my reasons."

Later, even years later, long after the Cold War had become a deeply personal struggle, there would still be these moments of flippancy, as if Harry somehow believed that part of his power depended on keeping others from knowing how he really felt.

Finally there were aspects to life in Berlin that no one fully understood. Engineers from General Motors kept meeting with Germans in the basement of a hospital. Chemists from Switzerland kept coming and going with samples of methedrine. There were rumors of German commando units training with Americans for a war against the Russians. There were also rumors of plague and cannibalism, some of which were true. In the evenings there were dinner parties with the British and the French, where everyone drank and drank and talked about the next war. When sober, boredom was epidemic.

Like so much else in Harry's life, the black market came in a succession of quiet steps. There was no obvious commerce, no definite pattern. A lot had happened even before Wilde knew about it, with cartons of cigarettes in the basement, chocolate, whiskey, Nymphenburg porcelain and etchings by Otto Dix. (If nothing else they could never deny that Harry's taste was impeccable.)

Within the larger scheme this was a settling period. Camps for the displaced had been established on the edge of the city. The interrogation programs had begun. Regulations had been formalized about such matters as abandoned children, fraternization, venereal disease. The days were generally mild with brief spells of rain. Artillery and fallen Stukas had started disappearing from the landscape. Vegetation had begun to cover the northern fortifications.

At this time the visible center of black market trade was the Tiergarten, not that Harry ever personally bartered on that level. Even from the start he worked exclusively through representatives, most of them recruited from a refugee camp under the pretense of building a Baltic network. Eventually there would come a point when Harry's financial concerns were eclipsed by politics, but in the beginning he at least did not seem to care about politics very much.

Although there had been early signs of involvement—strings of wedding bands, unexplained absences, unaccountable money—it was not until mid-August and a week in Freiburg that Wilde began to grasp the scope of Harry's involvement. Ostensibly they had come to Freiburg to photograph a rocket factory, one of the few that the Soviets had missed. They had left Berlin on a Friday, crossed the Rhine on a Saturday, entered the Schwarzwald on a

Sunday afternoon. Here there were villages that the war had barely touched, with empty coaching inns, deserted roads and a sense of an older Germany that Harry undoubtedly hated as much as the new.

From the outset of this Freiburg week there were hints of Harry's double life, with telephone calls in the mornings, meetings in the afternoons. On the third evening Wilde found a case of penicillin wedged between the seats of a black Mercedes. On the fourth evening he found at least ten thousand dollars in the lining of Harry's coat, a revolver with a pearl handle underneath the mattress.

Rose had returned late. Wilde had been waiting for hours. Their rooms overlooked a cobbled square. There were river bells distorted in the fog. When Harry entered he poured two glasses of whiskey, then moved to the window and drew the curtains. For days now he had not stopped watching the streets.

"Don't you think it's about time you told me what's going on?" Wilde said.

"Going on?" Rose had not turned away from the window.

"Come on, Harry. I think you know what I'm talking about."

Rose had let the curtain fall, laid his glass aside to light another cigarette. "Yes, I suppose I do."

"So how about it? Are you going to stop?"

"Stop? Why should I want to stop?"

"Because it's wrong."

"Wrong? Do you mean ethically? Legally?"

"I mean *wrong.*"

After a long beat Harry said, "Considering what's happened in this country, what this country has done . . . you think that's relevant?"

What Wilde would eventually see as the end of the beginning came very suddenly in November. By now Harry's organization resembled nothing less than a spider's web. The structure was thin and

51

only visible from certain angles. The extended ends had been spun into a dozen provisional offices. Harry talked some about a political statement, and by the end of July there was an awful lot of money.

And with the money came elements of a lifestyle that would always be associated with Rose. In August Harry spent a weekend in Switzerland with a girl from the Frankfurt Command. Ten days later an inquiry concerning his activities was dropped. On another line there were also gifts to members of Central Command: a string of pearls for the wife of a British officer, two landscapes by Moritz von Schwind, another black Mercedes.

Through these weeks Wilde's view of the man remained oblique. There were moments when Harry appeared to be just another postwar hustler, then again there were moments when he was definitely something else. By this time more than fifty young men and women had been added to the payroll, all fiercely loyal, all former misfits of the Reich. Generally their days began early in the Tiergarten or else along the Kurfürstendamm. Harry usually met them in the evenings on the pretext of debriefing agents from the zone.

Until November Harry had rarely talked about the Soviets, except in reference to his nominal duties with the special service. He *appeared* to see them as a market for cameras and wristwatches.

But then came that Sunday and the first cold spell of the year. By six o'clock the sky was black, by nine the gutters frozen. Earlier there had been a series of telephone calls, but Wilde heard only fragments of what was said. Afterward Rose grew unusually reticent, chain-smoking, continually gazing out the window.

"You're in trouble, aren't you?" Wilde said.

Rose had been chewing on a toothpick. The room was unlit. There were playing cards scattered on a piano bench. "Trouble is a very imprecise term."

"Come on, Harry. You don't have to play games with me. What the hell is going on?"

Rose had picked up a jack of clubs, tossed it onto an ace. "I think the Russians are trying to put the squeeze on me."

"What do you mean?"

"Yesterday they beat up one of my couriers. This afternoon they raped a girl."

"Jesus! Why?"

"Don't know. Maybe they want to close me down, or maybe they just want a piece of the action."

"So what are you going to do?" Wilde had moved to a bottle of brandy. "Harry, I think we better talk about this."

"There's nothing to talk about, Charlie. My people expect me to do something. They *expect* it."

Toward midnight Wilde was awakened by gunshots or else the sound of a backfiring truck. In the morning he found Harry sitting on the fender of his jeep with sunglasses and a Colt revolver.

Three days followed with no further discussion about the Russians. Wilde saw Harry only occasionally, and then they talked of nothing. On Thursday there was a dinner party in the French zone. Harry arrived late, obviously exhausted, possibly drunk. He spent the night chatting with a Polish girl, then left alone.

On Friday there was rain, then another white fog from the river. Wilde spent the morning interviewing refugees from the Eastern zone. Harry telephoned at four o'clock. They met in one of the surviving cafes between a back street and a ruined bank. Harry had arrived in a Volkswagen that Wilde had never seen before. He carried a raincoat over his arm.

"I need your help, Charlie."

"What for?"

"Just come on with me."

"Where?"

"Charlie, just come with me."

They drove east, then northeast to another roofless district.

53

When they reached the edge of the Soviet zone Harry stopped the car, lit a cigarette. There were odors of scorched timber, disinfectant, something like nitrate. Wilde had turned at the sound of a truck. When he looked again Harry had a gun in his hand, that tiny French pistol with a pearl grip.

"I want you to take this," Rose said, then pulled back the bolt, inserted a magazine.

"Harry, what the hell is going on?"

"Just take the gun."

"What for?"

"This is where the Russians have been hitting my people."

"So?"

"I've got a girl coming through in a little while, and I think they're going to try and make another hit."

"Jesus, Harry. Don't you think we should—"

"Charlie, just take the gun."

Wilde watched from the blown window of a trolley station. It was five o'clock, the gray hour. A wind had scattered papers across the boulevard. Harry had left between ranks of gutted tenements. Wilde saw him pause to toss away his cigarette, then lost him in the shadows.

Now there were only the evening sounds of deserted streets; a jeep along a steel bridge, papers still stirring on the concrete. For a long while Wilde hardly moved, except to wipe his hands across his trousers. He was cold, definitely frightened. He could not recall if Harry had flipped the safety off.

The girl appeared at a quarter to six, Wilde saw her first from a distance. She was young, slender, walking briskly from the rubble mounds. She wore a man's coat buttoned to the neck. There was a canvas bag across her shoulder. Wilde was fairly certain he had seen her before but could not remember where.

Then he saw the Russians.

There were three, two in overcoats with automatic rifles, an officer along a side street. One was thin, very young. The others

54

were indistinct. They stopped the girl in the center of the boulevard, forced her to kneel on the bricks. While the boy kept his rifle leveled, the other two rummaged through her bag. There was a camera, another smaller object that Wilde could not identify. The officer was speaking. The girl kept shaking her head. Now the officer moved closer, knotted his fist in her hair. The boy had lowered his rifle, looked away. The other had lifted the girl's skirt, bent to slap her thigh. There was silence, then muffled laughter.

Until Harry emerged from a doorway.

Wilde had rarely seen him so casual, his hands in the pockets of his raincoat. At twenty feet he stopped, faced the Russians, nodded, then shrugged. The officer still held the girl's hair. There were voices, fragments of Russian, German, a little broken English. Harry said something about the east. As the voices grew louder, Harry remained motionless. He had not even taken his hands out of his pockets.

Next there were only the unreal impressions of an accident . . . the officer raising a black automatic, Harry firing twice from his raincoat, then firing again as the second Russian tried to bring his rifle up. The officer crumbled in stages. The other reeled off, clutching his throat. The boy had let his rifle clatter to the pavement, backing off slowly. "Harry, don't," Wilde called out. Rose did not respond. He was still fixed: back straight, arm at his side, the revolver leveled at the boy. For the love of God Harry don't . . . As if Harry had ever really believed in anything except himself.

And he shot, but into the air. So there were only the slow impressions of the boy's receding footsteps, the hysterical girl among the litter of junk jewelry, binoculars, two cameras and what may have been a pair of boots.

Given the political sentiments of that November in Berlin, response to the shooting was fairly predictable. There were two formal Soviet complaints and a smug reply from the Frankfurt

55

Command. Rose was informed that regardless of Russian demands he would not be punished for what was judged a defensive posture in a Western zone. Washington was also said to have been supportive.

Civilian response was no less predictable. In cellar clubs along the Kurfürstendamm it was said that Harry had actually killed twelve Russian soldiers in defense of twenty German children. Stories from the outlying districts were equally enthusiastic. The making of a legend.

At first there was a quiet period following the incident, with a week in a cottage northeast of Lubeck, another week along the Baltic. Rose spoke of the shooting only once, and then in reference to a bad dream. The days were mostly spent recovering from nights of hard drinking . . . Wilde among the sand dunes, Rose by an open window with a book entitled *The Splendor of Israel Spinoza.*

Finally there were repercussions that even Harry could not have foreseen: letters from burgeoning anticommunist groups, an invitation to speak in Hamburg. A Frankfurt memorandum from October called him a reliable fixture among the citizenry. In a photograph from December he appeared as the prominent figure among the dozen cabaret girls.

Also two Dresden figurines, a gift from that girl he had saved. In later years he would be given others, some of which were lost or broken but those two he always kept: a maiden and a shepherd with a missing arm. They were on the mantle when Charlie Wilde finally left Berlin in 1976, and they were still there when he returned in the wake of Harry Rose's disappearance.

CHAPTER
FOUR

ALEX PETTY HAD also turned to the past. He had begun on
Friday with the early correspondence from 1946, emerged on a
Monday in the late afternoon. The newspapers carried photographs of another disarmament rally. The rain had broken with
a heat wave from nowhere. He took a crosstown bus to the Kurfürstendamm and an older section of cabarets. Something was
different, but nothing had changed.

The nightclub lay down a tiled alley. The marquee had been
riddled with a pellet gun. An iron staircase led to the door. Inside
it was dark. The chairs had been stacked on the tables. There were
plastic palms along the walls, photographs of nudes. Two women
in gold halters were lounging on the stage. One of them kept
twirling a disconnected microphone.

"I'm looking for the proprietor," Petty said in German.

The girl with the microphone smiled. "Are you English?"

"American."

"Too bad."

"What about the proprietor? Is he around?"

She pointed with the microphone to another iron staircase. "Up there."

At the top of the stairs was a green door, half-glazed. The name Kurt Grimm had been stenciled in black script. There was music from the hallway: a sultry voice singing, "I need you so bad that it hurts all the time." Petty knocked lightly, then louder. A man's voice told him to enter. The music stopped.

The office was virtually bare with only a row of steel cabinets, two vinyl chairs and a window with venetian blinds. Kurt Grimm sat behind a plastic desk. He was a large man with black hair and thick features. Petty guessed he was fifty. He wore a pale blue suit, blue tie. His wristwatch was Swiss and expensive.

"My name is Petty," Petty said. "I believe we have someone in common."

Grimm had been sorting through a stack of child porno photographs. "Who is this friend?"

"Harry Rose."

For a moment there was no response. "Who are you, please?"

Petty lit a cigarette. "George Clay sent me. It seems that Harry has disappeared."

"So?"

"I thought you might be able to help me find him."

"How?"

"I understand that you used to work with Harry."

"This is old history."

"Not so old considering—"

"Considering what?"

"That nothing changes all that much. I mean, the game."

The music had started again, drifting softly from the corridor. This time the voice was a man's and the song was about a winter in Berlin.

"Anything you can tell me would help," Petty said.

58

"What can I tell you? Once upon a time I do a little work for Harry. I run a little money. I run a little merchandise."

"According to the file you were also part of the Fury team. You worked the Russian zone for eight years until George Clay closed the network down."

"So?"

"So have you seen Harry recently?"

"What? You think Harry Rose comes in a place like this?"

"How about on the streets? In one of the old cafes? They say that Harry used to keep in touch with all his—"

"Okay, maybe I saw him . . . maybe a few weeks ago."

"Where was that?"

"A club. The Last Exit."

"What did you talk about?"

Grimm shrugged. "Politics, the world, God, everything. Harry was always crazy. Genius maybe, but crazy."

"Why do you say that?"

"You ever hear his ideas?"

"What ideas?"

"About magic, atom bombs. About politics, about dreams. Not that it was *all* crazy, because Harry also had the gift. I have seen it with my own eyes."

"The gift?"

"You know, like a gypsy. He could do things. Lots of things. He could make people dream crazy dreams. He could make them love him, make them scared for no reason. Lots of things."

A woman's face appeared in the doorway. Her skin was pale, eyes dark. She started to speak, Grimm waved her away.

Then Petty asked suddenly, "Did Harry ever talk about the Russians?"

Grimm smirked. "Ah. So now we get to the point."

"One in particular. His name was Boris Tatlin. Did Harry ever talk about him?"

"Sure, he talked about him."

59

"What did he *say?*"

"Lots of things. Tatlin is a big wheel in Moscow now. So what? In the old days he was just another bad boy. He even tried to kill me once. Too bad he missed, huh?"

"What would you say if I told you that Harry might have gone over?"

"Gone over?"

"The Wall."

"Listen to me, I'm no longer political. I'm a businessman. These spy stories are finished for me. You follow?"

Petty nodded. "Sure, I follow, but—"

"Maybe Harry takes a little trip. Maybe he goes over the Wall. I don't know. I know it's all finished for me, though. Once a long time ago people used to say, 'Hey, there goes Kurt. He's the right arm of the famous Harry Rose.' Whatever I wanted I could get. And if I couldn't get it, Harry would get it for me. But that's all over now. You follow?"

Strains of a violin and an old song that Petty had heard before and as usual couldn't identify. "One more question. It's about George Clay . . . Why didn't Harry like him?"

Grimm shook his head. "Who knows? Maybe political, maybe the secret stuff. Like atom bombs. Harry thought maybe some day George Clay might blow everything up to little bits."

"How well did you know George?"

"Me? Not too well."

"Did you like him?"

"I liked his lady, Kristian Haas. Very beautiful girl. Very talented. Also very expensive. You ever seen her?"

"No."

"Too bad. You'd like her. Everybody likes her."

As Petty was leaving, another woman's face appeared in the doorway, drained like the first. And two boys in a half-opened door. Both wore leather jackets and blue jeans. One of them held

60

a camera with a long lens. As Petty approached they stepped back and shut the door.

It was well past the closing hour when Petty returned to the station. Guy Campbell was waiting for him in another renovated office on the second floor. The wall clock had stopped. The telephone was off the hook. Campbell was sitting at a typewriter but not typing.

"George Clay called," he said. "He wants to know how it's going."

Petty had moved to the window. There were only the lights from the nightshift, sentry lights along the perimeter. "What time did he call?"

"Six o'clock."

"What did you tell him?"

"Nothing. It's your case, not mine."

From the second floor Petty took the backstairs down to the archives. The basement was cold, colder than on any of the previous days. A bulb had burned out in the corridor. He found a coffee cup left over from the morning, washed it out and drank from the tap. The water tasted like copper.

He began with the peripheral entries. Half the series had been eaten by dry rot, another damaged when a pipe had burst in 1976. Mostly there were letters: Harry Rose to the Frankfurt Command concerning the status of displaced persons, Harry Rose to Allied Control regarding Soviet intrusions into the Western zone. Three formal protests had been lodged in response to the rape of a Polish girl mistaken for a German. And twenty-two pages on the coming of the nuclear age.

There was a summary at the end of the first series, but still no definite perspective on events. It seemed that by the winter of 1946 Harry Rose had been the focal point of several issues, but the man himself remained obscure. He was living well, but no one knew quite how. His networks were extraordinarily successful, but no one knew quite why. Later when George Clay began talking on and on about "delivery systems," "throw-weight" and "payload," Rose wrote quiet appeals for moderation. Not that the man was by any means a bleeding heart. Here too the record was unmistakably clear. By the end of 1949 Harry had won control of the entire zone, running seven ruthless networks out of a suite he had furnished from black market profits.

It was nearly midnight when Petty finally left the station. He was tired, but did not think he could sleep; hungry, but he did not want to eat. Earlier he had told himself he would stay away from alcohol, but by two o'clock in the morning he was sitting in his room with another bottle. His last thoughts before falling asleep were that regardless of what either Langley or Clay wanted to believe, he was convinced the key to Harry Rose's disappearance lay in the past. The issues weren't minor. Loss of personal influence, jealousy, money—none of these was it, he was pretty sure. What was it was this damned city, this everlasting cold war, and something about nuclear politics that no one ever talked about.

Wilde also descended to the archives from a concrete staircase that was very rarely used. There was music along the corridor, German voices on the radio. He brought nothing but a sandwich wrapped in cellophane, coffee and an apple. There were signs of Harry everywhere.

He had to use a stepladder to reach the earliest entries, a trolley to carry them back to the reading table. The first file was green, bound in canvas. The spine had been reinforced with masking tape. There were warning labels on the title page, an illegible signature in black ink. From the window above came sounds from the courtyard: an idling truck, high heels on the gravel.

As Wilde had suspected, the initial files were lean. There were references to the larger issues but not the larger pattern. There was the sequence, but not the meaning. Wilde's own name appeared twice in the opening summary, then came Harry, then George Clay, then the Russians. Miscellaneous notes followed, including twelve pages from Rose to Clay: "You have my sympathy, George. It must be no easy matter convincing people that peace and freedom can only exist on the edge of total war." Ten years later in the mid-fifties the theme had still not changed. While George Clay wrote about a missile gap, Harry disagreed, from a penthouse above the Grunewald.

Wilde could recall only one conversation with Clay from this time. It had taken place on the cusp of the first hard winter. Clay had entered the city the evening before. Wilde kept missing him at parties all over the zone. Finally they met at a French reception in Reinickendorf. It was late, but not yet dark; cold, but the rainwater had still not frozen. Beyond the compound gates lay a particularly wasted street with tank tracks in the asphalt, a line of withered chestnuts. Wilde had stepped out to a balcony. Clay was sitting among the potted palms. They had both been drinking flat champagne.

Clay said, "So where's your famous Harry Rose?"

"Hamburg." Which was a lie. Rose had been in Paris with a woman for over a week.

"Too bad. I was looking forward to seeing him. But on the other hand maybe it's better this way. Gives us a chance to talk—alone."

"Talk to me? About what?"

"Your career."

"Huh?" As if life in Berlin could ever be called a career.

"Now, I don't mean to imply that Harry hasn't been doing a first-rate job here, but the man's a maverick. If he doesn't start playing with the rest of the team he's going to fall, and I'd hate to see you fall with him. You understand what I'm saying, Charlie?"

"Sure," although in that autumn of 1946 who would have ever thought that Harry Rose could fall?

Records were by no means precise concerning Harry's ascendency, but in the third volume there was a collection of letters unlike any before them. Most had been typed on Harry's portable Remington. All were unsigned. There were dozens of references to forgotten details, the landscape and the cities. The tone throughout was dry, detached, mostly understated. Finally there were twelve handwritten pages describing the events of late November and the trailing days of autumn. It was essentially a bad time. Penicillin was out of sight, belladonna very scarce.

By now there were more than eighty young men and women running merchandise for Rose throughout the zone. Among the later recruits were nineteen survivors from Auschwitz. Profits from these days were still high. There was a lot that could not be converted to cash until the spring, a lot that went out in bribes. Then, too, November was a kind of turning point. More than once Harry simply gave things away: potatoes, canned fruit, cigarettes. When Wilde eventually questioned him about twenty pounds of missing chocolate Rose became evasive, reticent. He claimed that there was no such thing as a gift in Berlin. There were only investments. But by early December he had taken to referring to neighborhoods of the zone as "my people."

And in turn there were a lot of Germans who had come to think possessively of Harry Rose. There were gifts over Christmas left on the doorstep of that Tiergarten house: a fountain pen, a spoon, pressed roses in a scrap of cellophane. There were also roses in black paint on the Zehlendorf walls, roses as far east as the Brandenburg Gate, as far west as the Teltow Canal.

Vielen Dank, Herr Rose. Vielen Dank.

Harry Rose, black marketeer, spy, Robin Hood . . . ?

But if November had marked a turning point for Harry and the Germans, then December was the point of no return as far as it went with the Russians. There were two outstanding conferences in January, both held in a farmhouse near Spandau. Among those present were representatives from London, Paris, George Clay from the Frankfurt Command, Lyle Severson from Washington. Topics of discussion ranged from the details of physical surveillance to the broader questions of Soviet encroachment. Harry spoke on the maintenance of courier lines and recruitment among the itinerant Poles. Severson spoke on the liabilities of political manipulation. George Clay delivered a terse address on power-projection in a political vacuum.

Years later, from the isolation of a Florida bay, Wilde would write that these seven days in January of 1947 had in their fashion been the beginning. George Clay had come with photographs of Hiroshima, the crude scenario of a preemptive Moscow strike. There were comprehensive briefings on Soviet rocketry and the prolonged effects of radioactive exposure. But on a deeper, more personal level the real beginning had not been January, but February and the advent of a man named Boris Tatlin.

Like others from the Soviet camp Boris Tatlin appeared suddenly, seemingly from nowhere. Early attempts to reconstruct his life were feeble. Apparently he had been one of two hundred officers dispatched from Moscow to the West. He was young, very tall with dark eyes, black hair. He wore his hair with no part; the effect was definitely Eastern. In later notes Harry Rose would describe him as a shadow-man, and the worst sort of technician.

Wilde and Tatlin met for the first time on a Friday, the first week of February. There had been a series of municipal talks concerning influenza, then a reception near Spandau in the evening. Wilde had arrived early from a discussion of rocket sites in Wilmerdorf. Tatlin had obviously been watching the door.

"I understand that you are a close friend and associate of Harry Rose."

"I work with him, yes."

"It must be very stimulating."

Wilde shrugged. "You could say that."

"But also dangerous?"

"Dangerous?"

"Well, surely in the process of making so many devoted friends, Harry Rose has also made a great many enemies."

Later when Harry arrived with a Swedish girl and a raincoat on his shoulders, Tatlin was still waiting by the buffet table. Wilde heard only snatches of their conversation, but beneath the exchange of amenities was an obvious reference to those Russian soldiers that Harry had shot in October.

Afterward Rose and Wilde wandered out to a frozen garden. By then the evening had pretty much run down with talk of diptheria, electrical failures and an outbreak of suicides in Marienfelde. There were guests withdrawing along the flagstones, the exhaust from departing limousines.

"So what did you think of him?"

"Tatlin?"

Rose nodded, turned to watch a woman in a Spanish cape. "I think you should try and find out more about him."

"Anything in particular?"

"How about what he's *really* doing here?"

Still later Rose spent another hour in his bedroom on the telephone. Again Wilde heard only the more obvious references to Tatlin and another confrontation at the border.

By the second week in February more than two hundred pages detailing the structure of the Soviet intelligence mission in Berlin had been compiled and forwarded to the Frankfurt Command. Of particular interest were photographs of a very young Tatlin in Spain and the floor plans of the NKVD establishment in Prenzlauer. Also of note were the incidental items concerning Tatlin's private life: He neither drank nor smoked, and he did not eat meat.

Following these initial inquiries there were three relatively placid weeks of windless cold and a tour of Renebeurg, where Harry met with refugees from Danzig. Then on Sunday in the late afternoon there was a telephone call from the Reinkickendorf watch.

An hour after the call Wilde found Rose chain-smoking at the kitchen table. There were wadded scraps of paper on the floor, a broken pencil in an ashtray.

"Are you going to tell me what happened?" Wilde said.

Rose lit another cigarette. "Tatlin just grabbed one of our people out of Wedding."

"What do you mean?"

"Shot him in the leg, threw him in a car."

"How do you know it was Tatlin?"

"I know."

"But there's half a dozen—"

"It was Tatlin."

"Are they pressing charges?"

"Of course not. It's all unofficial. They won't even admit that they've got him."

"Who is it?"

"That Rosen kid. Karl Rosen."

"But he's just a courier. Why would they—"

"Because he's seventeen years old. He spent nineteen months in a camp, and he's a Jew. Now do you understand? Tatlin did it because he knew it would hurt. The bastard just wanted to hurt me."

There was whiskey in a cupboard, two glasses by the sink. Wilde poured the drinks.

"Harry, I know someone in—"

"Forget it. I'm not negotiating on his terms. I'm negotiating on mine."

"What do you mean?"

"Find out where he's weak, Charlie. Find out who his friends are."

"Harry . . ."

"And get me one of the Potsdammer kids, someone who can shoot."

Twice that night Wilde woke to the sounds of Harry moving

67

through the house, maybe looking for something else to drink. In the morning he found Rose asleep on a velveteen sofa with another empty bottle on the floor, cigarette butts in an abalone shell, a record still turning on the gramophone. There was also one of those books: *Notes from Macroprosopus*.

Between Tuesday and Thursday Wilde saw Rose only once, and then only for an hour in a shell-pitted yard off the autobahn. Wilde had spent the previous afternoon sifting through transcriptions of Soviet radio traffic. Rose did not say what he had been doing, where he had been sleeping. The cold did not seem to affect him.

"I want to talk to the British," he said.

"Yeah?"

"Tell them I need one of their people in Pankow to watch Tatlin for a night."

"Harry, I don't know if they're going to go for that. They don't like—"

"Charlie, listen to me. Tatlin has been seeing someone. I've got to find out who."

Past a sheet of frozen rainwater lay an overturned truck, stumps of trees that had been cut for fuel.

"You know Frankfurt is starting to wonder what's going on," Wilde said.

"So?"

"So I'm going to have to tell them something."

"So tell them something."

"Like what?"

"I don't care, just keep them off my back for a few more days. I need a few more days."

In the evening Wilde returned to the Luft Grau complex, sent another cable of half lies to Frankfurt, did not wait around for the reply. Toward midnight he found himself in Siemensstadt with two British officers he had vaguely known from Griffen. Like so many others, six months in Berlin had left them drained. He told them only: "Look, Harry needs a favor." It was half past three in the morning before he finally got to sleep.

On Saturday Rose appeared again, somehow thinner, darker than Wilde had ever seen him. They met in a room above the featureless wreckage along the Friedrichstrasse. There was a table but only one chair, nothing on the walls except strips of charred paper. The floorboards and ceiling had been riddled from an explosion below. There were two Hungarian boys watching from a burnt-out lock-smith's shop. Wilde had asked who they were, but Rose had ignored him.

What he said was, "You know, at first I wasn't sure, Charlie. I mean it could have been anything."

"What are you talking about?"

"Tatlin."

"What about him?"

Without answering Rose withdrew a buff envelope from the inside of his coat. There were seven photographs obviously taken from a distance. The first showed an indistinct couple descending a flight of concrete steps. There was another of a woman walking beneath a trestle, a man possibly waiting for her by a fountain. Finally there were two precise shots of the same woman emerging from a limousine. She was young, slender. Her hair was dark, her eyes lost in the shadow of an attentive chauffeur.

Wilde laid the photographs on the table, ran his hand across his mouth. "Who is she, Harry? Tatlin's wife?"

"Girl friend. Her name is Anna Falk. She's a Pole, I think. Tatlin sees her twice a week on the sly."

"Oh, Harry, what's the point? You're going to pick her up and trade her back for that Rosen kid, is that it?"

"More or less. Those two boys down there will be coming with us to run interference. I don't expect too much trouble."

"But where's it going to end? You hit Tatlin, Tatlin hits you

69

back. Tell me where it's going to end."

Toward dusk a chilled wind from the south brought odors of ruptured sewers. Wilde had gathered newspapers from the staircase, tore a leg off a chair, then lit a fire in a wastebasket. Harry had brought some whiskey, a bit of sausage. The two Hungarian boys were still waiting in the locksmith's shop.

They left at nightfall along a southeastern route that Wilde had never taken before. Rose drove his gray Volkswagen. The two Hungarians followed in a battered Mercedes. There was a sawed-off shotgun taped beneath the dashboard, shells in the glove compartment. Troops were moving randomly all along the Leipziger.

They passed into the Russian zone at the Friedrichsban, where rumors of typhoid had kept the patrols away. Twice Wilde had asked questions, and again Rose avoided answering him. Here too there were lingering odors of disinfectant, long blocks of plowed brick heaps. Rose had been chewing on an unlit cigar. He kept only one hand on the wheel.

North of the rubble on Unter den Linden lay a neighborhood of black side streets and empty shops. Rose coasted to a stop beneath a line of hacked trees, the Mercedes in the shadow of a water tower. Ahead the road dipped to a row of brick flats pitted from stray shrapnel. There were lights in upper windows, music drifting from a radio.

"She lives in there," Rose said quietly.

"What's her name, Harry? I forgot her name."

"Anna Falk."

There were pigeons beneath the rainspouts, a voice from the radio.

"She's not with him tonight. He's in Dresden with some tough guy from Moscow."

"But how do you know she's alone? Harry, what if she's not alone?"

Rose slid the shotgun from under the dashboard, dropped in two shells, laid it on Wilde's knees. A six-pointed star had been cut into the stock, also someone's name: *Rudy.*

"All you got to do is cover us, Charlie."

"I thought you said she's alone."

There was music again, the faint strains of a Polish rhapsody mixing with a breeze. Rose had lit a match, stepped out of the car. One of the Hungarian boys was waiting by an iron gate. Rose must have spoken. The boy nodded, pulled a knit cap over his ears. There was a moment when both were firmly etched against a streetlamp. Then they climbed a flight of stairs and were gone.

It was cold. Wilde had scarcely felt it as he rolled down the window, laid the barrel of the shotgun on the door. One elbow rested on the steering column, a leg was jammed against the hand brake. When the music stopped there was nothing but stray papers blown across the street.

Then a woman's breaking scream.

Rose appeared first, then the Hungarian leading the girl by a locked arm. The Mercedes had moved out of the shadow, the tires slipping in the rainwater, a rear door swinging open. She was much younger than Wilde had expected, more beautiful than her photograph suggested. When they had her in the car they told her to get down behind the driver's seat. When the car had pulled away, Rose was left on the curb, brushing something off his sleeve.

They brought her to Steglitz, half a mile south of the border canals. A crumbling farmhouse, smelling of cats. There were no carpets, only stone. The damp seemed to come from the walls. Surrounding the farm were low hills under bracken, patches of untended forest. The roads were pitted with cart tracks. The fences were down. The fields had lain fallow since the war.

It was nearly midnight when Wilde arrived. He was tired but he did not believe he could sleep. One of the Hungarian boys was drinking whiskey on a window box. Harry was in a bedroom with the girl. There was a tiled oven in the hall, but no one had been able to light it. Eventually Wilde built a fire with stuffing from a rotting chair. Earlier he had heard the girl crying, but with Rose she was quiet.

Toward dawn Wilde fell asleep on a narrow bed off the kitchen. He woke up to the distant moo of an unmilked cow, the sound of boiling water. Snow still lay in the shadows. There were hoofprints leading to a granary. Rose was smoking on the porch. His eyes were ringed with red. He had not shaved.

"Do you want some coffee?" Wilde asked.

Rose pointed to an empty tin cup on the railing. "Already had some. Thanks."

"How about an egg?"

Rose shook his head.

Another Hungarian boy was moving slowly from the cattle shed, absently dragging a stick in the snow.

"So what's she like?" Wilde asked suddenly.

"Scared."

"Did she talk at all?"

"A little."

"About Tatlin?"

"No."

"How long do you think it'll take before he bites?"

"Three, maybe four days."

"And then what?"

"Then we negotiate."

"So we should have Rosen back by the end of the week, is that right?"

"Maybe."

The wind had shifted. A second storm may have been building in the north.

"She's very pretty, isn't she?" Wilde said. "Anna Falk. She's a very pretty girl."

72

"I suppose."

"Is she nice?"

"What do you mean?"

"I mean is she nice?"

"How should I know?"

"Well you were with her half the night. I should think that by now—"

"Charlie, forget about her. She's part of an exchange. Nothing more."

But in the late morning, while searching for something to read, Wilde happened to catch a glimpse of her through a half-open door at the end of the hall. She was standing by a window, her face reflected in the glass, black hair falling past her shoulders, hands like a child's. Her eyes were soft. One arm rested on the sill. Her dress was torn at the seam. She did not wear shoes.

Four days followed. Wilde spent them waiting, mostly alone. He worked afternoons at Luft Grau, drank in the evenings. He spoke with Rose twice, but Rose had little to say beyond the fact that there had been contact, which meant the ball was in Tatlin's court. Also there had apparently been a letter: handwritten, less than a page, Harry's elaborate signature at the bottom. Wilde never saw it but he imagined that it was fairly brief: "Want Karl Rosen . . . Have Anna Falk," or something to that effect. Then, too, Rose may have also sent along an article of the girl's clothing. Those missing shoes, for example? It was Sunday when the affair finally crumbled to an end, another Sunday of lingering snow. Wilde had gotten up late, after drinking until midnight. He did not reach Steglitz until noon. Harry was waiting for him in the kitchen. There was more whiskey on the table, ashes in the basin, the smell of burnt paper.

Rose only said, "It's over, Charlie."

"What do you mean?"

"They shot Karl Rosen last night."

Wilde stood up, walked to the window. Both Hungarian boys were sitting on the porch. Obviously they hadn't been told.

"Harry, I'm sorry, I'm truly sorry."

Rose nodded. He hadn't moved his eyes, his hands. "So am I."

"Do you know what happened?"

"Apparently he tried to escape. He hit a guard and they shot him. They're calling it an accident. The notice says he tried to steal a truck."

"What about the girl? Tatlin must know that he won't get her back now."

"Seems he still wants to make a deal. He contacted the Kreuzberg watch this morning, told them that he had nothing to do with what happened to Karl, told them he'd make it up to me."

"How?"

"Don't know, don't care. Says he wants to appeal to my compassion as an officer and a Jew. Nice touch."

Wilde found a clean glass, poured himself a drink. "What are you going to do?"

Rose shook his head. "We could put her through the wringer, see what comes out. She might be able to tell us something."

"And then what?"

"Send her back to Tatlin. In a box."

"Harry, she's just a kid—"

"So was Karl Rosen."

By nightfall Wilde had still not left the kitchen. He had begun to drink seriously when Rose and the two Hungarians had entered the girl's room. He had shut the door when the voices had grown louder. He heard little or nothing after that, but he imagined too much. He turned the radio on—an adagio for organ and strings on the armed forces band.

There were several variations on the story concerning Harry Rose and Anna Falk, each scarcely more credible than the next. Wilde's own version held that Harry's ultimate feeling had formed suddenly in a moment of clarity and compassion, a phenomenon not unknown to occur in instances of lengthy interrogation.

Supposedly it had been late, two, three o'clock in the morning. The two Hungarians had been asleep for hours. Rose had been drinking since midnight. There had been still another drab snow. Rose had seen it from a window. When he had finished smoking a cigarette he poured one more glass of gin, then walked slowly down the hallway to the girl.

It was dark and he could not see her face, but he knew that she was watching him. There was a pitcher of water on the floor, an untouched plate of food. She remained rigid while he sat down in the chair, turned her head when he lit a kerosene lamp. After twenty minutes she had begun to cry, after an hour she was nearly hysterical. When he shook her, hard, she lowered her eyes. When he shook her again, slapped her once, she looked at him. For a long time just looked at him, maybe like the way she had looked at Boris Tatlin.

It was a Wednesday when Wilde first saw them together, literally together. He had left Steglitz that first Sunday evening, returned three days later when Rose had not telephoned. In a later account he would say that at first he had feared the worst: the girl dead, Harry ruined. But when he actually reached the farmhouse he found nothing more than an unmade bed, two empty bottles of wine and a stack of dirty dishes. There was coffee on the stove, still lukewarm. Wilde heated it, drank it on the porch.

After about an hour Rose and the girl finally appeared on the spire of a hill above the granary. They were moving between patches of the last snow. Rose walked with his head down. She wore his coat around her shoulders. At fifty yards Rose stopped, said something to her, then continued to descend alone. Wilde met him halfway on the unpaved road, the girl still watching from above.

"Harry?"

Rose bit off the end of another cheap cigar. "I'm okay. How about you?"

"Okay. Where are the Hungarians?"

"Sent them home."

"Oh."

"Didn't need them anymore."

"I see."

There was an awkward silence. Then Rose said, "Look, Charlie, she's a nice girl. She's not what we thought. She knifed some Ivan who tried to rape her, and then Tatlin picked her out of the holding cell. It was him or Siberia."

"Was she able to tell you anything?"

"It's not like that. She spent the war on the Russian border. Her parents were killed in the camps. She drifted in here with the Red Cross. She doesn't even speak Russian."

"So what have you two been talking about?"

"You know, this and that."

"Do you like her?"

"Yeah, I like her."

"Would you like her less if you hadn't stolen her from Boris Tatlin?"

He looked at Wilde, and for one of the two or three times during all the time Wilde knew him, he smiled.

There was a meal in the late afternoon: cabbage, corned beef, more wine. Through it all the girl said almost nothing. Afterward there was coffee and an insipid liqueur. Again conversation remained fairly strained until Rose excused himself on the pretext of finding another cigar.

Then she told Wilde, "He said you were his best friend. Are you?"

Her fingers were tight around the edge of the table, her hair in her eyes. He hadn't seen a more beautiful girl since the end of the war. Since . . . ?

"Yes."

"Is it true what they say about him?"

"What do they say?"

"That he has power, a magic power?"

Wilde shook his head. "I don't know about that."

Toward nightfall there was the strangest southern wind, then a false spring that lasted for days. Rose stayed in Steglitz through the weekend, by which time Anna Falk had become part of his life. In time Wilde came to see that she was a girl who believed in fate instead of history, emotions instead of politics. She read Freud, Oscar Wilde and Mark Twain. She wanted someone to teach her to swim. She didn't say why. At the end of a month she and Harry left the Tiergarten for that estate on the Grunewald. At the end of three months they were married in Monte Carlo—Rose out of uniform, Anna with a dubious Swiss passport. Apparently they also had won a lot of money at the tables.

There was, though, an epilogue to the Anna story. Once more the circumstances were typically postwar Berlin. A Saturday evening, more than fifty allied officers drinking in an off-limits club. Wilde, nothing to do, bored, had come alone and spent an hour at the bar. He was preparing to leave when a very drunk Boris Tatlin slipped onto the stool beside him.

"You have seen Anna?"

"Huh?" He guessed Boris was also pretty drunk.

"Anna? You have seen her?"

"Uh, yeah, I've seen her."

"She is well?"

"She's fine."

"And he is good to her?"

"Yes, he's good to her."

"Does she love him?"

Wilde shrugged.

"You will please give Harry Rose a message from me, okay?"

"Sure," expecting nothing more than some maudlin Russian sentiment.

"Tell him that he is dead."

But given that night, the booze, especially Berlin, Wilde never did get around to telling that to his friend Harry Rose. Who serves up a death sentence to a friend? Or believes it?

CHAPTER
FIVE

BY THE FIFTH day of the preliminary search Alex Petty had finished with the early correspondence, finished with those letters from the middle years. He had gotten up early after waking to the repetitive sound of a stick on the pavement, eaten badly half a mile south of his hotel. There were milling students on the boulevards, forecasts of rain, still another rumor of political disturbance. What had once seemed random now seemed orchestrated.

He reached the station at a quarter to ten, drank a foul cup of coffee on the staircase. Along another corridor of renovated rooms he found a gray man bent under a reading lamp. The man's eyes were red behind thick lenses. There were sheets of printout across the desk. Petty leaned in the doorway. Rain had begun to streak the window panes.

"Mr. Mullen?"

The old man slipped off his glasses. His hands were stained with ink. "You're the other one who's come about Harry Rose?"

Petty nodded. "I wonder if we could talk."

"I don't know what I can tell you. I was never part of Harry's group. I just processed the take."

"They told me that you handled the majority of the product."

"I headed analysis, is that what you mean?"

"And Rose kept you busy?"

"That was a long time ago."

At the end of the corridor was an oblong room. It might once have belonged to a servant. The windows were barred twice, first with wire mesh, then with steel rods. There were collapsible chairs, a half-varnished desk, another disconnected telephone. Mullen had taken off his coat; shabby tweed with a frayed lapel.

Petty rested on the window sill. "You originally came here in 1959, is that right?"

"Yes."

"Who was your ultimate senior?"

"Everything went to the top of the Desk, same as now."

"So you mean it went to George Clay?"

"Yes, it all went to George Clay."

"And your specialty was hardware analysis?"

"We didn't specialize in those days. It was different. You had to handle a little bit of everything."

"But you mainly worked the long-range Soviet stuff, isn't that true?"

"I suppose so."

"What was Harry's product like?"

"How can I possibly answer a question like that?"

"Well, you read it, didn't you? You must have—"

"Okay, it was good."

"Very good?"

"Yes."

"Then what was the problem?"

"I don't know what you mean."

"How come he wound up pushing papers in the basement?"

"You never met him, did you?" Mullen said.

"No."

"Well, he was a pretty strange man."

"In what way?"

"Every way. I suppose you know he was kind of obsessed with the bomb."

"How do you mean?"

"I mean damn near literally obsessed. I think he saw it as a sort of symbol, or something like that. Almost biblical."

"A symbol for what?"

"I don't know. Evil, maybe?" Mullen picked up a pencil, began absently sketching a leafless tree.

Petty had still not moved away from the window. "Tell me something. Why did Rose hate George Clay so much?"

"Who said he hated Clay?"

"Come on, Mullen. It's all over the record."

"Well, maybe Harry had a few crazy ideas. I don't know."

"What ideas?"

"Look, Petty, it's been fifteen years—"

"What *ideas?*"

"That maybe Clay was, you know, fiddling with the estimates. Now don't go—"

"What estimates? Strategic?"

"Maybe . . . and the total of the Soviet offensive capability."

"Why would he want to fiddle with them?"

"I don't know, I only heard rumors."

"So what did the rumors say?"

"Well . . . it went like this . . . you can't push a forty or fifty billion dollar budget through unless you can show that the Reds are willing and able to blow us up. It's the scare factor . . . you want a new bomber, you've got to have a scare factor, a bomber on their side that's better than yours . . ."

"So Clay would change the numbers around, is that it?"

"I didn't *say* that. I only said that Harry might have believed it."

"But was it true?"

"Of course not." He looked hard and directly at Petty when he said it. He was a man looking to retirement.

"How can you be so sure?"

"Look, I think you'd better just leave."

"So Harry could never quite prove it, is that it? I mean he just couldn't quite nail him, could he?"

"Will you *please* get the hell out of here . . . ?"

From the second floor Petty descended to the station cafeteria. There were prewrapped sandwiches on a tray. He took one at random, ate the meat, threw away the bread. Farther across the courtyard someone was watching from a window in the annex. The face was obscured in shadows, but the hands were visible on the iron grill.

Through the remainder of that morning he wandered fairly aimlessly again. What had once been Harry's office had been subdivided years ago, the furniture laid in storage, twenty feet of files processed into the archives.

At a quarter to one in the afternoon he left the station, drove to the heart of the city in the rain.

Past the Kanstrasse he found a dark cafe, ordered a beer and blood sausage. At an adjoining table a British air force officer was talking to a woman about the Pershing II's. Her knuckles were white around her handbag. He used three empty bottles to represent the missile silos. Eighteen months ago George Clay had tossed a plastic model of a Pershing off the balcony of a Holiday Inn: "Behold. I am the destroyer of worlds." It wasn't even funny the first time. George was a true believer, no question. He also knew how to mix holocaust with pleasure.

Along the Kurfürstendamm stood a seven-story tower where Rose had once maintained his extravagant suite, now held by a banking trust. Farther on was a porcelain shop that had once been a steak house where Rose had dined on Thursdays. Beyond stood a rank of nightclubs where Rose had spent three years of Saturday nights. Finally down a side street lay that club where George Clay had recently met his latest in a line of very young, very expensive women. There was a photograph of her beneath the marquee: a perfect blond in gray velvet onstage with a microphone.

Petty returned to the station at a quarter to six. Guy Campbell met him in the foyer. Women from the typing pool kept moving along the staircase above. Once more there were sounds of electric drills. The lights were off in the adjacent halls. Petty followed Campbell to another vacant room with a dismal view of the motor court. There were two black vans waiting on the gravel. Campbell let Petty enter first, then shut the door.

"A Jerry Mace from Clay's office called while you were gone," he said.

"So?"

"So if I were you I'd call him back. He didn't sound too happy."

"Thanks."

"And I'd appreciate it if you'd go a little easier around here."

"Oh?"

"It seems that you've been upsetting some of my people."

"Oh, sorry."

"I'm also going to have to get a progress report for my weekly."

"Your what?"

"Technically you're part of the station now, and I'll need to submit something on what you've been doing."

"Well there hasn't been any progress."

"Fine. I'll pass that along."

By nightfall Petty once again found himself drifting down to archives. Off a corridor beyond shelves lay the alcove where Rose had spent his last fifteen months. Among a collection of correspondence from the spring of 1962 was a typewritten dispatch from Rose to Clay: "You insist on giving truth but don't accept it. So how can there be truth for you?"

Toward nightfall, the fifth day, Wilde also found himself along the Kurfürstendamm, waiting for the rain to stop, in a bookstore near a cinema. Earlier he had met with the last survivor of a Dresden network, spent an hour drinking black espresso, finally left with nothing. Now it was the blue hour, the streets were filled with youth who had probably never heard of Harry Rose.

Half a mile further east he also passed that tower, once Harry's crow's nest, now filled with attorneys, accountants, a coffee bar in the lobby. But years ago up a flight of concrete steps that no longer seemed to be there, Wilde had accompanied Rose to an enormous suite on the seventh floor.

"So what do you think, Charlie boy?"

"Uh, it's nice. It's real nice, Harry." Amid a litter of scorched plaster, fused glass, bits of splintered wood. Even the ceiling had buckled.

"Of course you've got to imagine what it's going to look like when I've finished with it. You'll have your wet bar here, desk goes there . . ."

But as always, Wilde never really could imagine what Harry seemed to see so clearly . . .

All in all it had been a season for dreams. In the spring of 1946 Harry had returned from a week in Frankfurt with a black Cadillac, a sable coat, two sketches by Otto Dix and a tiny Rembrandt: *Woman Bathing.* With a warming spell some semblance of life returned to the city. There were women again in the evenings, children back among the ruins. Venereal disease was up, but overall death had declined.

Politically it was a time of the widening gulf. The Soviets, faced

84

with waning popular support, tried to force an amalgamation between German Communists and Social Democrats. Success was, at best, limited. In August, elections were held according to a temporary constitution. Again the Soviets were left with less than they might have hoped for. As for Rose, Wilde would eventually note that he had never involved himself in this overtly political struggle. But if Rose remained disconnected from an overt war, that spring and summer drew him deeper into a secret war. By June there were thirteen active agencies sparring for secrets in Berlin. The Russians alone maintained three hundred in the field. In August there were nine bodies found floating in the canals, dozens more found in back streets. In September Rose lost a boy near the Alexanderplatz, then another in the men's room of a nightclub off the Unter den Linden. They called this city the "Cold War Capital."

In response to an aggravated assault from the Eastern service, Rose organized teams of refugees, principally those half-mad survivors from Auschwitz and Dachau, but there were also a few Germans and Poles, also left semihuman from the war. Casualties recruited for Harry's legions. Wilde occasionally saw them in the mornings returning from a night patrol. They usually assembled in a courtyard near the Friedrichstrasse, waited for Harry in silence.

And Harry always came to them, sooner or later he came to them all. He was mostly seen in the evenings with the Cadillac, or drinking with Anna on the Tiergarten; associates always bending to whisper in his ear, waiters bringing telephones. Harry does not work, they said. Harry reigns. But just the same, by mid-October he had broken the back of two Red networks in the zone, two more in Bonn, another in Hanover. Until finally Washington had no choice but to grant him formal control of the section with a rather substantial budget, a personal staff of seventeen, and those rooms in that Ku'damn tower.

There was one event from this summer and fall of 1946 that

Wilde had always felt was particularly telling of the period. It began in Charlottenburg the third week in August. Rose and Wilde had attended a dinner party and a piano recital at the residence of a municipal deputy. After the affair Rose suggested that Wilde accompany him back to the Grunewald for a drink. They left in Harry's Cadillac along the Kaiserdamm.

Past the Kanstrasse lay three charred villas, a salt pan, then a long curve to the rubble mounds. Rose had been driving fast but slowed to take a curve when a flatbed truck pulled off the shoulder, blocking the road ahead. As Rose began to apply the brakes two figures emerged from the mud slope. A third slipped out of the truck.

Because the first shot is always unreal, Wilde hardly reacted. He had looked up, questioning. Then another shot sent a spray of glass across the dashboard, still another glanced off the steering column. The rear window had also shattered.

Later, days later, it would occur to Wilde that the snipers had probably expected Rose to turn for the mud slope and into their crossfire. But whether out of instinct or some keener sense, Rose did not turn. He drove straight for the truck, only swerving in the last thirty feet, up the embankment, then back down to the highway beyond. Leaving Wilde with one distinct image he would never forget: Harry Rose grinning wide, that thin cigar still clamped in his jaws, going like hell at a hundred and ten miles per hour.

There was never any question . . . from that first night Harry was set on reprisal, particularly after he and Charlie had returned to the Grunewald and he had seen what they'd done to his car.

"It's definitely going to need a complete paint job."

"Harry, it's just a nick."

It was well past midnight. There were floodlamps burning along the perimeter of the estate, a bottle of brandy on the fender.

"And what about the upholstery? Look what they did to my upholstery."

"Well, you could get a patch or something."

"A patch? Charlie, you don't put a patch on a fucking Cadillac. It's going to have to be redone. That's all there is to it. Not to mention the rear window."

Finally they had both slumped down to the gravel; Harry with his back against the tire, Wilde with the brandy between his knees. It was that serious hour between the false dawn and the real.

"I suppose you realize that we're going to have to even the score," Rose said.

"At five fucking o'clock in the morning?"

"I said we're going to have to make him pay for this."

"Pay? Make who pay?"

"Tatlin. Who do you think?"

"Come on, Harry. You don't have to play that kind of game anymore. Besides, you don't even know for sure that Tatlin was behind it. I mean it could have been one of his Wedding networks acting on their own. Freelancing . . . "

"Immaterial, my dear Charlie. Tatlin is responsible for the actions of his people, just like I'm responsible for the actions of mine."

"So what are you going to do? Almost kill *him?*"

"I haven't decided yet."

Typically the ending was no less conclusive than a bit of plastic stuck to the door of Boris Tatlin's Pankow residence. There were no casualties, but damage was said to have been extensive.

Succeeding months were marked by sporadic violence with arson in Marzahn, an abduction in Lichtenberg, a rash of near-frivolous vandalism. Through most of it Rose remained insouciant, almost jocular. He apparently loved the concept of himself as Robin Hood of the Western zone. Maybe his altruism was a sometime thing, but Sherwood Forest could not have been any more forbidding than Harry's section of Berlin.

Finally even Charlie Wilde would come to admit that there had really only been a few good years before the issues became too intense, the struggle too personal. With the start of the 1949 Berlin Blockade, demands for specific intelligence were such that Harry's networks were virtually stretched to the breaking point. There were two agents killed in July, three in August, three more in November. There was also a story from this period (probably true) that during November when western coal reserves were nearly spent and the airlift appeared to be failing, Rose actually attempted to meet with Tatlin in an effort to end the conflict. Supposedly two notes were passed through unofficial channels. By this time, however, the Russians were very close to the completion of their bomb, and consequently had nothing to discuss.

The bomb: from the beginning Harry must have sensed that life would never be the same, not politically, not emotionally, not any way—never the same. He had been in Paris when Western intelligence learned of the first Soviet test. On his return Wilde found him on the Ku'damm. He was drunk, morose. He kept comparing the bomb to a serpent's egg. Let loose, it would bring everything down, by degrees, whether there was a war or not. Within the same week there were three hectic conferences in Spandau, two extended briefings in Frankfurt. At the end of a month Harry looked as if he had aged at least a year. At the end of two months he talked about insomnia and a recurring dream that gave him fits.

By the end of 1949 Rose was regularly traveling between Frankfurt and Hamburg. If the days were exhausting, the nights were worse. More than once Anna spoke to Wilde about Harry's health. She said that he had not been sleeping, barely eating and she often found him drinking alone. Well, he'd done that before, but . . .

Finally in December Rose spent a week in Washington, conferring with members of the tactical command. He returned on a Friday with sixty pages of a War College estimate on Soviet strength and a kid's notebook filled with some fragments of Einstein's thesis. Once again, Wilde was waiting in the rain. Toward dusk they found themselves in a cafe near the Brandenburg Gate.

There were tanks along the boulevards, rumors of shooting in the north.

Rose laid the estimate on the table. "I suppose you might as well read this crap."

A waitress appeared. Wilde told her to bring coffee but Rose said brandy.

"I want to ask you something, Charlie."

"What's that?"

"Do you think I'm crazy?"

"What?"

"Do you think I'm crazy?"

"No, I don't think you're crazy."

"Good. Then that means they're crazy. You know what they're building now?"

Wilde was looking at Harry's hands, the nails had been bitten to the quick. "What?"

"Fusion bomb. Thermonuclear. It's got a hydrogen core with an extra neutron. They say it'll make the Hiroshima number look like a firecracker. The Russians will probably have one of their own in about two years."

The waitress returned with the brandy.

"Of course it's just the beginning," Rose went on. "Once they've got the bomb they're going to need a delivery system. My guess, from what I've heard and read, is that the Reds will put their money into missiles. Which means that we'll have to put money into missiles too. Which means that . . . How's Anna?"

"She's fine, Harry."

"I don't want you talking to her about this."

Two students had entered the cafe—a girl and a boy. Very fresh. Damn near all-American. Spoils of war. They took a table at the rear. Rose watched them for a moment, then he said, "What makes it so dangerous is that the basic premise is partially true. I mean, the Russians *can* be barbaric, who knows better than we do, but the way we deal with them, it only makes matters worse,

89

reinforces the worst in them, validates the real bastards—like Boris Tatlin. Incidentally the new word in Washington is *containment.*"

"Sounds tame."

"It's supposed to. Don't know who came up with it. Maybe Dean Acheson, maybe even George Clay. Once you buy the theory you can use it to sell anything—little wars, big wars, anything."

"Harry, Anna wanted me to talk to you about getting away for a while."

"Why?"

"She's worried, she thinks you're running yourself into the ground."

Rose had finished his brandy, ordered another. His eyes were still fixed on those students.

"You know, I actually tried to tell them, Charlie. I mean, the obvious . . . that most Russians are no different than we are. I *don't* mean Stalin. But the fact of it is, you can't make them feel pushed into a corner and expect them to lie down. We forget what they went through in the last one . . . Containment. You know where I think it's going to lead? It's pretty obvious, I admit. Doesn't take a genius to figure it . . . we'll get a whole new generation of self-serving bureaucrats, hungry, sold on their own fancy rhetoric. I mean *both* sides of the fence. They have to believe their bull . . . hell, it's their living. That's why they're so dangerous."

When they left the cafe the streets were deserted except for a jeep and a few sentries along the eastern perimeter. When they reached the Grunewald estate Anna was waiting on the gravel drive. Harry took her in his arms, and she began to cry. Wilde left quickly, without saying good-bye.

Four days passed. No word from Rose. Then very late on a Tuesday night he appeared on the doorstep of the Tiergarten house with a black umbrella and a bottle of dry champagne. He wore a cashmere jacket, a pale tie, a dark shirt. Real spiffy. Like he was celebrating something. At first they spoke about nothing beyond the weather and the price of coal. Wilde had opened the bottle of champagne. Rose had lit one of those cigars, then turned to study an angular lithograph of pre-war Vienna.

"You know I came here for a reason, Charlie."

"Never have guessed, Harry."

"I'd like to know where you stand?"

"Huh?"

"About the future."

"Harry, I don't know what you mean."

"I've decided to stay on and I'd like to know that I can count on you."

"Count on me? Count on me for what?"

"To try and stop it. It's going to take a concentrated effort. Hostility is being stirred up by a select group on *both* sides, so I think eventually we'll have to work our way into a position of—"

"Harry, stop *what?* What are you talking about?"

"I'm *talking* about this here Cold War, Charlie. I'm talking about we've got to try to stop it, put an end to it . . . What the hell, who better to . . . ?"

By the spring of 1950 Harry Rose had placed more than a hundred agents in the field with networks as far east as Danzig, as far north as Helsinki. At the heart of these networks were those former refugees that Rose had used for years: Poles, Czechs, Hungarians, dispossessed Germans. In addition to the human resources Rose also made his first substantial use of electronic interception with telephone taps at the switching points, stations in Lichtenberg, wiretaps beneath the Soviet command in Darlshorst. At the end of a year it was said that almost nothing happened in Berlin without Harry knowing it. At the end of two years it was said that nothing happened without his consent.

But if the bulk of Harry's resources were directed East, there were also, it seemed, certain unofficial lines into the West. By the spring of 1952 he appeared to be receiving classified material from a dozen Washington agencies: State Department briefs, Pentagon estimates, even transcriptions of White House conversations.

Wilde gradually had to face that by late 1953 his buddy had actually launched his own peace campaign . . . by using double agents to feed material into Moscow, he was attempting to promote an atmosphere for negotiation. Wilde would later write: "It would seem that Harry is not only trying to figure out Soviet foreign policy. He's trying to help *make* it."

Which would not have been so bad, in official U.S. quarters, except that he was using more or less the same tactics to offset American distrust of the Soviets. When eventually questioned on the subject, Rose fell into his usual evasive mode, saying there had always been certain, you know, gray areas in the secret world. Wilde pointed out to Harry that his private peace campaign wasn't gray, it was purple, for God's sake. He was supposed to be running agents, not an advertising firm for the messiah of peace. For himself.

To which Rose replied: "Trust me, Charlie. Just trust me."

So by winter 1954, Wilde also found himself in a kind of no-man's-land between Harry's brilliance and Harry's obsession, between politics and self-styled morality, between the East and the West. "I suppose we've reached the middle ground," Wilde later wrote. "Me with indecision, Harry with his belief that only he can change the world. Or rather, save it. It's not easy to argue with his logic, though."

Three months after finally settling in Florida Charlie Wilde attempted to reconstruct the middle years in hopes of getting some perspective. At the end of a month he had accumulated more than two hundred pages of handwritten notes and a comprehensive time-track of events. There was much on the advent of the first long-range Soviet bomber, much on the so-called missile gap, but very little on Harry's frustration and even less on the hidden struggle.

No one ever really doubted Harry's obvious talent for the game. "He does seem to have a way of ensuring the loyalty of his people," Severson noted in 1955. While later even George Clay had to admit that Rose was exceptionally good, "with a mind like a sewer rat and an uncanny sense of timing. I hope that he remembers that he's still part of a larger team." Clay wrote in obvious reference to Harry's power, which by 1957 was starting to get a little frightening.

It was in the fall of that year that George Clay first began to cast a long shadow across Harry's world. Rose had recently moved from the Kurfürstendamm tower into the Grunewald estate (taking the largest room for himself with a view across the lake to his own home six miles south). Wilde had been in London with an English girl, a cipher clerk he had met the previous Christmas. When he returned there was Harry, enraged, brooding from the window of his enormous suite.

At the heart of the matter was an incident involving an American naval officer and a pretty German girl, East German, with links to the Soviet intelligence mission. The girl had originally met the American officer in Templehoff on a Saturday evening. After several drinks and small talk, the girl suggested that they move on to more intimate surroundings. The officer obliged her by taking her to his home near the Airlift Memorial. Four hours later the officer caught her trying to crack his personal safe. Rose was telephoned at five A.M. and ordered that the girl be brought to the Grunewald station, where she was interrogated until Rose decided she knew nothing of any real importance. She was just one of a dozen not very experienced women routinely sent hunting by the other side the summer before. Rose had the girl taken to the

Zelhendorf compound and held for eventual trade. She was not to be abused, not physically, not psychologically.

Considering the girl's minimal worth to Western Analysis, the affair would have ended at this point had it not been for the sudden intervention of George Clay. It was a Wednesday when Clay descended from Frankfurt, and immediately on his arrival in Berlin he ordered that the girl be transferred to the Steglitz compound for further questioning, this time under duress.

To justify what was clearly encroaching on Harry's turf, Clay argued that the time had come to teach the Russians a lesson. In truth, it was not so much the Russians that Clay wanted to impress with his clout as the increasingly wayward Harry Rose.

Wilde got involved in it on Thursday after a bad flight in from Rome. He'd entered the station at a quarter to eight in the evening. Rose had been waiting for him since noon.

"Come over here and take a look at this crap," Rose had said.

They'd entered Harry's office, shut the door. There was a rank of black telephones along the wall, a pot of lukewarm coffee, a plate of macaroons. And on the desk a plain folder—bright red and closed.

"Go on, Charlie. Open it."

Inside the folder were sixty-five pages of an interrogator's transcript and a photograph of the girl—face down, one hand chained to the steel frame of a cot. Wilde glanced at the first four pages, then briefly at the photograph.

"Who is she?"

"Astrid Jurgen. She was arrested last Saturday in Templehoff."

"What charge?"

"The usual. She picked up some navy officer, slept with him and then tried to open his wall safe."

"Get anything?"

"Of course not."

"So who worked her over?"

"Take a guess."

"How long has Clay had her?"

"Since Wednesday."

"And she's still on the rack?" Wilde shook his head. "Have you tried talking to Langley?"

"They don't want to know about it. Seems Clay has them convinced she's still holding onto the Kremlin jewels. And then there's the internal side of it."

"Meaning?"

"Meaning Clay would like nothing better than to dig a little gold out of a case I tossed away."

"Have you tried talking to him?"

"Oh, yeah."

"And?"

"It didn't go so well."

There were figures below in a vacant lot, outstation visitors, probably Clay's from the Frankfurt Command. Wilde watched them for a moment, then shut the curtain.

"This Astrid Jurgen, what's her story?"

Rose shrugged. "She's one of Boris Tatlin's girl scouts. He found her in a Dresden camp, had her trained in Leipzig. She doesn't know shit."

"How did they target her?"

"Templehoff network."

"And the navy officer?"

"A jerk. Total jerk."

"So then it's all pretty low-grade, huh?"

"Not low-grade, Charlie, rock-bottom. Worthless trash. Except our glorious George has finally got himself a real live Commie agent and by God he's going to find out what makes her tick."

"You want me to talk to him?"

"Sure, talk to him. Talk to the pompous ass," and he stormed out of his office, leaving Wilde with nothing but that photograph.

The Steglitz compound lay on the western banks of the Tetlow Canal, little more than four prefabricated barracks and a row of concrete bungalows. An unpaved road led from the highway to the outer gates. Behind the last timber gully there were no signs of habitation, not a house, not a church, nothing.

Wilde was kept waiting for more than an hour on a bench beside a corrugated shed. There had been rain, then a wind dispersing the lowland fog. It was nearly six o'clock and dark when George Clay finally saw him.

They met in a cramped shuttered room that smelled faintly of turpentine. There were bunk beds against one wall, a basic desk, two chairs and an electric heater. Clay had poured the Scotch, laid the bottle on the windowsill. Like always, he was dressed casually —beige cardigan, brown corduroys and worn loafers for that nice locker room look.

"So how have you been, Charlie?"

"Fine, just fine."

"Still not married, huh?"

"No."

"Too bad." He grinned.

Clay was facing the window now, rubbing what may have been an injured wrist. "Why do I always feel like I'm walking on thin ice in this city? Like the damn walls have ears, the mirrors eyes?"

Wilde said, "You know, Harry didn't send me here. I came on my own."

"But it's about the girl, isn't it? I mean, you came to talk to me about Astrid Jurgen, didn't you?"

Wilde nodded. "You can't just keep at her, George. It's not right, it's not the way we play it here—"

"What the *hell* is that supposed to mean?"

"It means that Harry and I have to live in this city."

"So?"

"So if you start cutting on Tatlin's kids, he's going to start cutting on ours."

Clay ran his fingers along the venetian blinds, wiped the dust on his trousers. Neat. "Oh, I get it. I'm breaking the rules, spoiling the game. Well, I'm certainly glad you cleared that up for me, Charlie. Wouldn't want to offend Boris, would we? Wouldn't want to upset him, not our good buddy Boris."

"There's also the question of . . . decency."

"Oh, Charlie, don't. Don't give me that bullshit now."

"She's only twenty-two, George. Twenty-two years old."

"Oh, please."

"And she doesn't know anything, not really."

"*Stop* it."

The rain had started again, loud now against the corrugated roof.

"Listen to me, Charlie. That girl was part of an effort to pull the plug on the whole North Atlantic system. It's big and it's rough, and we're not going to stop it by playing patsy with Boris Tatlin. If she doesn't know anything, fine. But I want to make damn sure about it before I let her go."

Wilde wet his lips. "I understand you've been using electricity."

"Stay out of my business, Charlie."

"I suppose you know how Harry feels about electricity."

"Is that a threat, Charlie? Are you threatening me?"

Wilde took a deep breath. "Would it be okay if I saw her?"

Clay was silent for a moment, then shrugged. "You're a real humanitarian, aren't you, Charlie boy?"

Odors of stale food along the corridor, something else like the smell of ozone. The last room was a concrete box with a window cut into the steel door. A cot, a chair, a naked light bulb under wire mesh. The girl lay on her side, one hand still chained above her head, a cotton dress, torn past the thigh. There was a litter of wadded tissue, a bucket of water. He looked at her until she must have sensed him and looked back. He had to turn away.

Outside the rain had stopped and a panel truck waited in the yard. Wilde returned to the city along a northern route where the

97

evening traffic had virtually died. He heard Chopin on the radio. Nice and soothing.

Given the pace of that fall and early winter, Wilde supposed that eventually the girl would have been almost forgotten if it hadn't been for what happened in late November. It was a Monday with new snow. Wilde had spent the morning in Reinickendorf for his weekly exchange with the French. Following coffee and a meaningless discussion on the northeast courier links, he found a warm cafe filled with clerks from the neighboring shops. After twenty minutes leafing through a magazine he suddenly realized that someone was watching from an adjoining table—a man, conspicuous in a homburg and black overcoat.

A woman had been arrested in Dortmund for murdering her husband and children. There were photographs beneath the caption, but turning to another page Wilde saw that the man had risen from his table for what was obviously an approach.

"I wonder if I might have a word with you, sir." In English, with Russian overtones.

"What about?"

"If you would be good enough to step outside."

"Where?"

"Please. This is most important."

Down a cobbled side street was a fountain and an ornamental tree. There were huddled children by a sausage stand. Snow lay in the shadows. Wilde lit a cigarette, watching the man's hands, surrounding doorways, the ends of the street.

"You are Mr. Wilde, associate of Harry Rose?"

Wilde looked at him, glanced briefly to an open window. "Who are you?"

"My name is Anton, but I'm speaking to you now on behalf of someone very important. An official of consequence."

"And what does this official want?"

"An interview—with Harry Rose."

"What about?"

"I am not at liberty to say—"

"Where?"

"East."

"Forget it."

"But you must understand that this official—"

"Tell him that if he wants to meet Harry Rose he comes to Harry's zone."

There was a telephone booth behind a commercial garage. Fifteen minutes later Wilde met an escort in a bar: two Hungarian strangers from Harry's Contemplative Network. By four o'clock that afternoon more than a dozen teams had been alerted from Pankow to Treptow, but it seemed that no one knew anything about a Russian called Anton and his official of consequence.

Harry's first reaction to the story of Wilde's encounter had been less than enthusiastic. Wilde had first brought it up in the evening over whiskey and one of Harry's cheap cigars. By this time Harry's office had achieved its final stage of extravagance with tubular steel and sheets of illuminated glass. There was even a television set, not that Harry ever used it.

"My advice, Charlie, is to drop it."

"Why?"

"Too shady."

"We could be talking about one very disenchanted Red."

"Fine, then you meet him. But not in the East, and for God's sake bring a gun."

Which ended the conversation until eighteen hours later when Wilde was approached a second time. It was late, two, three o'clock in the morning. Earlier Wilde had dined with Rose, then

99

spent a quiet evening reviewing political summaries from Bonn. Toward midnight another storm had broken. He had been asleep an hour when the telephone rang.

"This is Anton."

"Go ahead."

"Would it be possible for my party to meet your party tonight?"

"No."

"Would your party then be agreeable to—"

"My party wants me to conduct the first interview."

In the long silence that followed Wilde heard a brief exchange in Russian, then: "Very well."

There were two intermediate calls from public telephones, then another brief conversation on the steps of the Philharmonic Hall. Finally toward dawn Wilde found himself alone in a room above a bakery less than three hundred yards from the Friedrichstrasse. Only two shabby armchairs, brandy on a table. The floorboards were bare, the windows draped with blackout curtains.

Wilde opened the bottle of brandy, poured himself a glass and sat down. There were no sounds from the street, no sounds from the corridor. After twenty minutes he lit a cigarette, moved to the door, found it was locked. He sat back down, waiting, conscious of what Rose had insisted on from the start—a nine-millimeter semiautomatic, which he had never really learned how to shoot. Footsteps, a turning bolt, then a man looking in from the doorway.

He was slender with fair hair and pale gray eyes, younger than Wilde had expected. His coat was dark blue, definitely Eastern but not the sort of thing one could purchase without some influence. Then too there was the wristwatch, a Rolex and obviously expensive.

"Forgive me for having kept you waiting." In adequate English, with overtones of Russian.

"That's all right."

100

"Perhaps I should also apologize for these accommodations but . . . " He smiled.

They sat for a moment, Wilde examining the label on the bottle, the Russian gazing at his hands.

"Tell me," he said, "have you ever trusted someone when all your experience and training dictate that you do not trust?"

"Sometimes I guess one has no choice."

"Yes, no choice. Which is the position I am in now. I must trust you, although it is clearly against the rules of my profession."

"And your profession?"

"Let us simply say that my name is Ivan Panov and I am not without influence in the Soviet. Also I have access to secrets that would be of great value to Harry Rose."

"And these secrets, Mr. Panov, they are for sale?"

"They are for trade."

"And what do you want in return?"

"A certain person, a person who is currently prisoner in a Western prison camp."

"And her name?"

"Astrid Jurgen."

Wilde had an image of the auburn hair, the wrist tied to the bed frame.

"I'll mention it to Harry Rose," he said. "We'll need some idea of what sort of secret we'll be getting."

"This can be arranged."

"There may be certain problems . . . she isn't under our direct jurisdiction."

"But surely Harry Rose can have her released. Surely Harry Rose can do this."

"Maybe."

Wilde had moved to the window, drawn back the curtain. There were two men standing on the terrace below, maybe the shadow of a third across the snow. "I assume you'd prefer to make the next contact yourself."

101

"This would be best for my own peace of mind, yes."

"I'll leave you with a number, a secure line. Call it tomorrow night."

"Tomorrow night?"

"Yes. I think we should have something for you one way or another by then."

And just before parting: "Mr. Wilde?"

"What?"

"He is a compassionate man, yes? Or can be . . . ?"

Another fragmentary image of the girl, bruises, maybe electrodes . . . "Yes, I'd say he's a compassionate man."

"Then you will tell him something for me, please. Tell him that I love this woman. Okay? You will tell him?"

"Sure, I'll tell him."

They left separately—Panov disappearing down a side street, Wilde into a waiting van with a boy from Harry's Anagram Network.

There were seven hours between first contact and first assessment. Wilde spent the time skimming through profiles of Soviet outstation personnel and a useless directory of the Central Committee that George Clay had had prepared the year before. Also, he slept. Then around three o'clock in the afternoon Rose appeared.

"Tell me about him, Charlie. Ivan Panov."

"Don't know what else there is to tell."

"Well, what's he like? Friendly? Scared? What?"

"I don't know. I guess he was worried."

"But he didn't talk about his relationship with the girl?"

"Only what I've already told you. That he loves her."

"What about his backup? You said you saw someone in the street, right?"

"There were three, that's all I know."

"It looks like we've got the real thing here, Charlie."

"What do you mean?"

102

"Panov. As far as we can tell he's something, all right. Second Directorate right under the Party Committee."

"And the girl?"

"It seems they met in Leipzig eighteen months ago. Panov was out for a night of fun and ended up falling for her, but Tatlin wouldn't let her out of his stable."

There were three tiny dancers on a cabinet, more of those Dresden figurines that Rose had stolen years ago. Wilde picked one up, held it to the light. "So how do I play it from here?"

"Carefully. When do you see him next?"

"He's supposed to call tomorrow night."

"And he's going to bring us a sample of the merchandise?"

"I think so."

"Then tell him that it looks pretty good on this end. Don't sound too enthusiastic, but you can let him know that we're willing to talk."

"What about George Clay?"

"I think he'll cooperate. He may be a bastard, but he's not stupid. And this time he may have been right. Or lucky."

Wilde's second encounter with Panov took place on a Saturday, four miles north of the Tegler See. Again precautions were elaborate, ending with a little brandy in a dismal room.

About the fragment of actual product, the "trade sample," as Rose called it, it was small, a gray envelope folded once and sealed with cellophane. Wilde did not, of course, open it.

After handing the envelope to Wilde, Panov said, "I believe this will show that I'm sincere." After that there was nothing to say and they parted.

Wilde returned to the station, where Panov's "sample" was passed to Analysis for preliminary judgment. Three hours later Rose came down from the second floor and escorted Wilde into the trees behind the motor court.

"Well, you did it, Charlie."

"Huh?"

"Panov's trade sample. It's a partial breakdown of Boris Tatlin's Munich network. Names, signals, fallbacks. If we give him the girl, he's going to hand us Bonn, Frankfurt and Hamburg. Not too bad for a night's work."

"No, not bad," but he sounded listless, almost like he might not have even cared. He still could see the girl . . .

"Interesting, though, that he decided to hit Tatlin's group. I mean, he could have come up with a much less compromising package. He's just about blowing seven Tatlin networks right off the map."

Wilde shook his head, absently kicked a bottle in the grass. "Maybe he wanted to be sure we'd play."

"Maybe. But I think it's personal. I think your friend Panov doesn't like Boris very much. Which could lead to possibilities."

They had come to a clearing and a rise above the outer gates. Sentries were milling by the drive, another black windowless van.

"Harry, I want to ask you something and I want you to tell me the truth."

"Sure." Also watching the sentries, or else the distant morning traffic.

"You're not thinking of burning him, are you? Leading him into the spikes?"

"Of course not."

"Because I won't let you, Harry, not this time."

Rose laid his hand on Wilde's shoulder. "Getting emotionally involved, Charlie?"

"I just don't want to see him hurt, that's all. He came to us straight. So let's play it straight."

"Sure."

"Then I can tell him that it's on."

"Tell him."

"No tricks?"

104

"None."

"And Clay?"

"I've already sent him a brief, but if you want you can go out and talk to him again."

"Me?"

"Well, it's your show, isn't it? Besides, he likes you better than he likes me."

Wilde slept badly in a second floor rest room, normally reserved for the night staff. Toward three o'clock he took a car from the motor pool, stopped in a tavern for sausage and potatoes, but could not seem to eat.

It was half past seven in the evening when Wilde reached the compound. Again they kept him waiting on a bench beside the concrete bungalows. An earlier rain had flooded the yard. Leaves and strewn paper were on the gravel. Another panel truck stood beside the radio shack, a Cadillac beside the iron shed.

After thirty minutes a boy appeared and told Wilde that Clay would see him. Once again the odors in the corridor, muffled voices from behind closed doors.

Clay stood facing the window in the same bare room. He wore a belted raincoat, canvas boots. There was a suitcase in the corner, another bottle of Scotch on the floor. Also, tacked to the wall, a fairly detailed map of Berlin. Crossing points to the Eastern zone had been studded with red-and-blue drawing pins.

"I read your proposal," Clay said without turning around. "Very nice," but there was nothing in his voice, not approval, not enthusiasm, nothing.

"Of course we haven't arranged all the details, but—"

"What details, Charlie?" Still at the window.

"Well, there's the exchange itself, then—"

"No exchange."

"Excuse me?"

"I said there will be no exchange. The terms are unacceptable."

"I don't understand—"

"It's simple. I'm not letting the girl go."

"What?" Looking at Clay's head, his massive neck, cropped hair.

"I'm not letting her go, Charlie."

"Why?"

"Because I think we can get more for her, a hell of a lot more."

"What are you talking about?"

"It's like this, Charlie boy. I think we can up the price. You tell Panov that if he wants the girl he can come over here and get her."

"George, no—"

"George, yes. I want that guy, Charlie. I want him right here, singing his little heart out all about his Kremlin pals. Of course I'll give him the usual benefits—new name, nice house in the country. And that little cunt. But I want him. I want every bit of him."

There was an empty glass on the filing cabinet, and a bottle, one of the cheap local brands.

"Go ahead, Charlie. Help yourself."

Charlie did.

"He's getting off easy, Charlie. If I thought he had the stomach for it, I'd keep him working for us at least another year—in place."

"He won't go for it, George. I can tell by now . . . he's not the defecting type."

"Well, let's see what happens when he starts feeling a little heat."

"What do you mean?"

"That Boris Tatlin would love to know what Ivan has offered us in exchange for his girl friend. I'm sure old Boris would be thrilled to learn that Ivan has been trying to trade his networks for that little cunt. Now you go tell him that, Charlie. Tell your buddy Ivan that if he doesn't come over I'm going to—"

"You can't *do* that, George."

106

"Bring the wrath of old Boris down and blow his ass right out of the water. Tell Panov he's got three days."

He wandered around after that, following the autobahn as far as Wilmersdorf, then to a bar where no one knew him. Toward midnight he attempted to telephone Rose. There was no reply.

This time it was near the Spandau Forest. There was a tavern on the edge of something called the Gnome, a row of abandoned shacks by a railroad line. Panov was waiting. He stood up when Wilde entered. They faced one another from opposite ends of the half-lit room.

"I'm supposed to tell you," Wilde began, but it was already in his eyes, his voice, the way he fumbled with a button on his coat.

After he'd gotten it out, Panov just turned to the window, a lopsided frame with cracked glass. There was a stretch of unused land.

"I have two children. The mother is no longer alive, but there are the two children. So you see that even if I wanted to—"

"And they're in Moscow?"

"Leningrad."

"Well, maybe we could make some sort of arrangement to get them out."

Panov shook his head. "No arrangement, not for someone like me. They'll want to make an example of me as a warning to others."

"But . . . I mean, if they're only children—"

"Children of a defector are not children . . . This George Clay, he's a hard man?"

Wilde nodded, shut his eyes. "He's the prince of fucking darkness."

"One cannot entirely fault him, not by the standards of our profession. In fact, if our roles were reversed I believe I might at

107

least consider applying these same tactics. I know Boris Tatlin would apply them."

Wilde told him, "Listen to me, I'm going to talk to Harry Rose."

"And this will accomplish something? This will save my children? Save Astrid? Me? All this from the remarkable Harry Rose?"

"Just don't do anything until I've talked to him. Understand? Just hang on until I've talked to him."

"Sure, I hang on, Charlie. All my life, I hang on."

Once again they parted in the doorway. Panov tried to make a joke about the rain, neither laughed.

It was not quite dawn when Wilde reached Harry's Grunewald estate. There was a gray light in an upstairs window where Anna had apparently fallen asleep with the television on. He waited in what Harry called the library, among woodcuts by Emil Nolde, a couple of suspect Goyas and a tiny Modigliani. Also those books, scattered all over.

After twenty minutes Anna brought coffee and sesame buns, then Rose appeared in some sort of Oriental bathrobe decorated with interlocking dragons.

"I suppose you realize that you look like hell," he said.

Wilde shrugged. "Same to you. I saw Panov."

"And?"

"It's bad, Harry. Very bad."

They moved out to the garden—Rose still in his outrageous bathrobe, Wilde with one of those sesame buns. When Wilde had finished briefing him, they continued on in silence to the first line of elms, most of them Rose had planted since the war.

"Panov's kids," Rose said. "How old are they?"

"I don't know . . . Harry, listen. Panov isn't coming over. He'll kill himself. He'll shoot it out with Tatlin, but he's not coming over."

"I never expected him to."

"Then you'll talk to Clay?"

"No, that wouldn't accomplish much."

"Then what?"

"I think we can work something out."

"Christ, Harry. He's only got three days before Clay blows him."

"Don't worry, Charlie. Three days should be enough time."

"Enough time for what?"

"Charlie, why don't you go home and get some sleep?"

"Enough time for *what?*"

"I'll see you later, Charlie."

The last night of the Panov affair . . . It was Monday—nine, ten in the morning. Clay had been planning a leisurely afternoon when he received a telephone call from a member of the British team in Spandau. There had been a little mess in Dresden, and only a man with George's experience could settle the matter. Clay had never liked the British, but by two o'clock he found himself in a lively discussion on Soviet rocketry. Following it (in which he impressed them all) Clay was invited to dinner by London's regional director of covert operations—John Kipling.

After a sumptuous meal in Charlottenburg, Kipling suggested that they conclude the evening with a drink in a club called the Fall. When Clay declined the offer on the grounds that he had commitments in Zehlendorf, Kipling confessed that he had been waiting months to hear "the Word according to George Clay." Then too, as an added inducement, Kipling made reference to the fact that the Fall was a particularly entertaining establishment, with some of the city's loveliest and most accessible women.

So they went to the Fall, where the management immediately

honored Clay with a complimentary bottle of champagne, and two exceptionally beautiful girls joined them at one of the better tables. Concerning the girl who eventually attached herself to Clay, all that is really known of her is that she was blond, slender, about twenty. Also, she wore a short red dress, black stockings and spiked heels. When Clay asked her name she told him Rosa, then clung to his shoulder, running her fingers along the edge of his collar.

"Are you important?" she whispered.

"Not really."

"Oh, but I bet you are. I bet you're more important than even Harry Rose," and fell back laughing in his arms, one hand pressed against his thigh.

They left at ten o'clock after mixing cognac with Himbeergeist. Kipling insisted on escorting the girls back to their apartment, and if Clay had reservations he hardly had time to voice them before finding himself alone with Rosa in a lavish room; also in red, also with strategically placed mirrors above the bed.

"Well, what do you think?" toying with the strap of her dress.

"Nice," he said, and turned to examine an etching on the wall, a naked girl on an auction block.

"Oh that." She frowned. "That was a little gift from a cruel friend. Are you cruel too?"

"I don't think so."

"But you're not sure?" She poured him a glass of something. He sat on the edge of the bed to drink it, and she fell across his knees, arched her back, lowering a strap off her shoulder.

After slipping off her incidental dress she more or less posed for him—first kneeling, then reclining, then caressing her breasts. "I think you should hurt me," she whispered, and pulled off his belt . . . "I bet this would hurt." And when she had his trousers off she pulled him on top of her. "Hold me, hold me or I'll get away from you." And she fixed his hands to her wrists, extending her arms above her. *Hold me.* And when she was pinned, submissive

. . . "Yes, this is perfect, perfect. Now don't move, lover . . . "

And the door swung open with a flash of white light and the solarized image of two boys in black leather.

In the photograph Clay looked ridiculously determined above an obviously terrified woman. There was apparently a police report, complete with statements from the girl, her irate husband and a close family friend—who just happened to be a professional photographer and never went anywhere without his camera.

According to their statements Clay allegedly accompanied the young lady to her apartment on the pretext of discussing her possible employment with an American intelligence mission in Berlin. But after learning that her husband would be away for several hours he promptly fell on her "with the intent of rape, perhaps even bodily harm."

As for Rosa's husband, he claimed that after learning that his wife had left a local nightclub in the arms of another man, he immediately rushed home in the company of his friend, the photographer. Upon entering the room—at which point the photograph was taken—there ensued a brief struggle in which Clay was struck twice before being subdued. Immediately following the struggle, three members of the local police force appeared and proceeded to arrest the suspected party. As a footnote to all this, John Kipling was unavailable for comment.

So they took George down to the metropolitan detention center, where his identification was somehow misplaced and he found himself in a holding tank with two drunks and a Hungarian boy under suspicion of manslaughter. When Clay attempted to telephone the station his call was somehow misrouted to a junior clerk, who in accordance with standing orders concerning unsafe lines, pretended not to know him. A second call to the Zehlendorf compound proved equally frustrating, with nothing but the static of a disconnected cable. Finally Clay even attempted to telephone

111

Rose, but although the man was supposed to be everywhere, no one knew where.

Again it was late, one, two o'clock in the morning. Earlier Wilde had fallen asleep with a record still turning on the phonograph, another glass of gin on the floor. When Rose appeared at the door he said, "Get your coat, Charlie. It might get cold." Just beyond the porchlight stood a lean dark boy whom Wilde recalled vaguely from a rough job in Danzig. There was also a driver and an anonymous black van among the trees.

Wilde sat in the back of the van with Rose. They drove west and very fast. Beneath the seat were blankets, a bottle of vodka, whiskey, two automatic rifles and what must have been canisters of tear gas. The dark boy had said something in Polish, and Wilde saw the driver nod and then laugh. There was a brief exchange about cigarettes and chewing gum. Then it seemed that no one had much to say.

"We're going to the compound, aren't we?" Wilde asked.

Rose had taken out a road map, spread it across his knees. "That's right, Charlie, we're going to the compound."

"To get the girl?"

"That's right."

"How?"

"Same muscle, same intimidation."

"What about Clay?"

"Well, I don't think Clay will be around tonight."

The driver stopped the van behind a fire break, fifty yards from the compound gates. There was no moon, and it was very dark. The road ahead was deserted. There were lights in the barracks' windows but nothing along the perimeter, nothing in the yard. When Wilde had taken out a cigarette the boy had told him, "This is very bad time to strike a match, sir." Another soft exchange in Polish, the even softer sounds of cartridges snapping into clips.

The driver and the boy stepped out of the van, their weapons slung across their shoulders. Rose crouched behind the seat to watch them through the windshield. When they had disappeared into the shadows he turned back to Wilde, smiled.

"Those boys," Wilde whispered. "Who the hell are they?"

Rose shrugged. "A couple of guys. The driver's name is Lazarus. The other is Max."

"But they're head-hunters, aren't they? The young one, he blows things up."

"No, Charlie, they're good boys. Maybe a little impulsive, but they're good boys."

"What are they going to do in there?"

"Twist an arm or two, that's all."

"What if someone starts shooting?"

"Don't worry, Charlie. There won't be any shooting."

But there were shots, first two rapid bursts from across the yard, then another from the pines. Rose had slid into the driver's seat. There was the snap of the hand brake, then the sudden clamor of the engine. As the van eased closer to the gates, Wilde saw them —three dark forms stumbling out of the barrack lights, one leading the other, the third stopping to fire over the shoulder.

They'll never make it, Wilde told himself with a momentary vision of them frozen in a spotlight, lifted into the air and tossed aside.

But finally there were no lights, no shots, only a few casual words as the boys climbed into the van again, the girl huddled between them. Someone asked for a cigarette. Wilde felt a hand on his shoulder, the thin cigar between the fingers. Another laughed, bracing himself as the van swung back to the highway. "We did good, huh? Nobody dead, nobody hurt," with an odor of whiskey and a little more laughter.

The girl said nothing. She wore what she had been wearing the day that Wilde had seen her—filthy blouse, torn skirt, no shoes. There were bruises on her legs, a cut along the hairline. When

113

Wilde handed her the vodka, she took a sip, then passed the bottle on. Someone had given her a blanket, and she drew it mechanically around her shoulders.

The last hours were no less casual with coffee on the terrace of the Kreuzberg house, the Brandenberg Concertos on the radio. On arriving, the girl had vanished with some woman into an upstairs room. The others had slipped into the kitchen. An hour before dawn Wilde met Rose in a rather formal English garden. There was a view between the hedgerows of a walled embankment descending to a black canal. It was warm, almost like a summer night.

"We're waiting for Panov, aren't we?" Wilde said.

Rose nodded, lit another cigar.

"When do you expect him?"

"Soon."

"And he's bringing you the Tatlin networks?"

"That's the idea."

"What happens when Clay finds out?"

"Oh, I don't think he'll be too much of a problem."

There was little formality to the actual exchange. Panov arrived at a quarter to six. The girl met him on the flagstone path a few minutes later. Everyone watched while they embraced; she now in a new coat and flat, black shoes, he with a briefcase under his arm.

Harry Rose was there on the balcony, his raincoat in the wind, one more black cigar.

There was even a last conversation. As Wilde was to recall, it happened at dawn while he and Panov were moving a step behind the girl, the driver and Volkswagen waiting on the gravel.

"She is something, you agree?" Panov said quietly. "Astrid."

"Oh yes, no question."

They watched her for a moment . . . her dark legs, a cigarette,

114

an arm now swinging loosely at her side.

"Tell me," Panov said. "Did he talk to her at all?"

"Who?"

"Harry Rose."

Wilde glanced back to the balcony, but Rose had vanished again. "I believe he did, yes."

"And he is something too, yes?"

"Harry? Yes, he's definitely something, all right."

"And long-time friend to you?"

"Yes."

"Then you will speak to him for me? Tell him that I am grateful."

"Yeah, I'll tell him."

"Also Astrid is very grateful."

"I'll tell him that too."

"But also maybe warn him."

"About what?"

"That he is now in most dangerous position of all . . . on middle ground between both sides."

Wilde nodded. There were sounds of departing cars from beyond the gate.

"I refer to both Boris Tatlin and now your George Clay. Did you know that Boris Tatlin is greatly obsessed with Harry Rose?"

"How do you mean?"

"They say that Boris even keeps a special file. All information concerning Harry Rose is placed into this file, and late at night Boris reads it. Over and over, reads it."

"Sounds like a strange way to spend an evening."

"Please, I assure you that Boris is very serious on subject of Harry Rose's destruction. And now also there is this George Clay to deal with."

One of the boys from the Destiny Network appeared from behind the hedgerows. He held up his wrist to indicate that time was growing shorter.

115

"I think Clay will get over it." Not believing that. Not really.

Panov shook his head. "I don't think so. From what I understand of this man I would say that he will not get over it. This is why I say that Harry Rose is on middle ground, very dangerous place."

They had reached the end of the path. There was the driver behind the wheel, Astrid resting in the back seat with vodka and a magazine.

Panov shrugged. "Well, maybe I say good-bye now."

Wilde nodded.

"But you don't forget what I tell you, okay?"

"I won't forget."

"Also, maybe tell Harry that I am his friend now too. One day maybe he needs an important Soviet official"—he smiled—"then he can come and talk to me. You understand?"

"I think I do."

"So if one day he needs something—"

"Yes, I'll tell him," but actually Wilde felt a bit annoyed, as if collectible favors were somehow beneath Harry Rose. He didn't need them . . . or at least it made Wilde feel better to believe that . . .

Within four days after the exchange, Harry Rose prepared a twenty-two-page brief detailing the scope of the now compromised Tatlin networks and probable methods of bleeding them dry. This material was forwarded to Langley on a Wednesday. The first congratulatory phone calls were received on the following Monday.

Tuesday night very late, Rose and Clay were in Rose's office, the compromising photograph on his desk.

"You've got to stop thinking with your dick, George. That's your whole problem. Any time you pick up one of these local girls you're asking for trouble . . . if they don't screw you, their boyfriends will."

"Just cut the crap, Rose, and tell me what it's going to cost."

"Cost? Oh I think . . . " but stopped, and then slowly, "Stay away from Ivan Panov. Don't involve yourself with him, his relationship with me or his relationship with Boris Tatlin."

"And if I do? Just for the sake of argument."

"Then I think you'll find that this little mess you're in will get more complicated. Charges of rape and assault, not to mention publicity. Clear?"

So Rose emerged victorious. By the spring of 1958 more than thirteen Soviet networks had been broken, another four effectively controlled. Offensively this period was no less dramatic with twelve submissions between April and June, all strong, some remarkable.

Among the early June documents were the transcripts of a Comecon discussion on dissent in Hungary, and another appreciation of nuclear deterrence. Eventually there were two drafts of a Baltic naval maneuver that even George Clay could not ignore, and his written acknowledgment remains in the files to this day.

Finally in January an evaluation of station performance concluded that although much of Harry's material could not be corroborated with secondary sources, no other agency mission consistently produced such a wealth of information. Indeed, after an October series on the Soviet tactical stance, it seemed that only George Clay remained unimpressed. "Why does this man's material continually stress Soviet weakness?" he wrote in early November. And Rose responded in late December: "Maybe because we have continually exaggerated their strength."

There was also the last March meeting with Ivan Panov. Originally slated for the Turkish frontier, they ended up in Helsinki in an unfurnished room a few hundred yards from the market square, where they spent some seven hours talking about peace and the reduction of nuclear arms.

Panov, it seemed, described his position in Moscow as tenuous

... "I am the skater on thin ice," he said. "I am the rodent hiding beneath the elephant to escape the tiger." Colorful, Harry thought. Panov went on to say that Boris Tatlin had obviously suspected from the start that his networks were compromised for the sake of Astrid Jurgen. "Perhaps Boris does not fully understand all details," Panov said, "but the man must know I was responsible. If he hasn't moved against me it is only because I have friends of standing." Although no names were specifically mentioned, Harry's later assessments concluded that Panov was probably very close to Yuri Andropov and others well-placed within the KGB. But for how long . . . ?

Rose came to believe "there are two schools of Kremlin thought, those who believe that war with the West is inevitable and those who believe that almost nothing is beyond the diplomatic process. As intelligence officers it is our duty to distinguish between the two, even encourage the growth of one over the other. It is *not* our duty to lump them together into one killer-whole to justify a military budget. What we have been told is the truth, is just not necessarily the truth at all."

Yet on another track, it was also during this time that Harry Rose launched some of his most adventurous operations directly into the heart of Boris Tatlin's world, then beyond into Budapest, Sofia, Prague and the Ukraine. Until there were no obvious boundaries. It was Harry's empire, vast and at the same time disturbing. It occurred to Wilde that Harry's world was like some intricate warren linking two dozen cities from Washington to Moscow. More often than not Wilde found Rose in moods varying between elation and a sort of further out, mysterious rapture. He was also busy as hell on the telephone, and disappearing without explanation.

In all this glow of Harry Rose's hegemony, there was, however, one unsettling incident that winter. It happened in Greece, where Charlie Wilde had prowled around the ruins for a week because both he and Harry felt they needed a rest. From Athens he found a cottage on Mykonos, spent four days photographing windmills, met an English girl. Returning to Athens on Thursday, he found himself stranded between flights in a cocktail lounge. It was four o'clock in the afternoon. He'd just sat down with a magazine and a beer when from out of nowhere—George Clay, slightly drunk.

"What the hell are you doing here, Wilde?"

"Hello, George."

Later Clay would intimate that his mission in Greece was an executive action; Wilde learned that actually he'd been sent to spike a mailbox on a catch-and-carry job.

He did not look well, sweating profusely . . . "So how's Rose?"

"He's fine."

"Still playing six sides against the middle?"

Wilde smiled. "George, we're on the same team."

"Oh? Then how is it every time I take a walk in Berlin I feel like lightning's about to strike? And it smells like a rotten rose."

Another flight had been called, leaving empty tables and a few unescorted women at the bar.

"He hurt me, Charlie. Bad."

"I'm sure that wasn't his intention—"

"Oh, bullshit. I may not be a genius, but I know when I've been hurt."

"Well, you've got to admit that you put us in a pretty sticky position, George. I mean concerning Panov."

"So that's it . . . Rose cuts my throat to save some wonderful Russian. Speaking of sides, whose does that put *him* on?"

"I don't think that's the way it was, George."

"Sure, Charlie."

Two flight attendants had entered the bar. Clay glanced at them quickly, took another sip of Scotch. "How does he do it?" Clay said suddenly.

Wilde looked at him. "How does he do what, George?"

"You know—the influence . . . power . . . "

Wilde shrugged. "Luck?"

119

"More like black magic, definitely not luck. He still read those weird books?"

"I guess so."

"What about his crystal ball?"

"Huh?"

"Doesn't he have a fucking crystal ball?"

"No, George, I don't think so."

"Well, too bad. If he had a crystal ball he might be able to see me coming for him." And then taking hold of Wilde's arm, "You think I'm kidding, don't you, Charlie?"

"No, George, I just think you're probably still a little—"

"Because I'm not, Charlie. This one is no joke. One way or another, I'm going to take him down. Five years, ten, sooner or later . . . "

Seven months later Wilde had another chance encounter with Clay, this time in a club in Hamburg called the Dwarf. Again Clay was drinking Scotch, again quite a lot of it. But with the seat of Harry's network only a few hundred miles away, he had less to say.

He did not, however, look any more friendly than he had in Greece.

CHAPTER
SIX

LOCATED AMONG SOME correspondence from April of 1960 were
two congratulatory notes from Lyle Severson to Harry Rose and
a photograph of Ivan Panov stepping from a limousine in Budapest. This material was drawn on a Saturday, the fifth day, passed
to Alex Petty on a Sunday afternoon. Also from that April were
two letters from Rose to Wilde about internal conspiracy. Apparently Wilde had divided that month between London and Paris,
while Rose remained with his power in Berlin.

By Monday Alex Petty realized he was hooked, had passed the
point of no return. He woke up in the morning exhausted but did
not get to the station until early evening. It was the slack hour
between the day shift's departure and the night shift's arrival. On
the third floor Guy Campbell was supposedly waiting for a telephone call. There had been another demonstration in Bonn, possibly violence in Hamburg.

At the end of the second-floor corridor was a hexagonal room with a view of the northern perimeter. Petty entered without knocking. A woman in brown stood facing the window. She was plain, thin, looked about fifty. Her sweater and handbag lay on the chair. There was a paperback romance novel on the desk.

"Losi Fletcher?"

She nodded but did not turn around.

"I'm here about Harry Rose."

"I know."

There were puddles of water where a pipe had burst, a row of dismantled typewriters against the wall.

"I understand you used to be with the department watch."

"That's correct."

"I wonder if I could ask you a little about it?"

"Do I have a choice?"

He offered her a cigarette. She lit it with sharp angular movements.

"I was responsible for the integrity of the internal channels," she said.

"You mean the radio links between here and Washington?"

"And between the outlying stations."

"How many were in the unit?"

"Nine."

"Nine? That's a lot, isn't it?"

She shrugged, looked out the window again. There had been rain clouds for hours but still no rain.

"What was it like working for Harry Rose?"

"I don't know what you mean."

"Well, what was morale like?"

"Fine. It was fine."

"What was his attitude about security?"

"What do you mean by attitude?"

"Well, for example, would you say that he was excessively concerned?"

"Not excessively, no."

"Then why do you think others felt he was?"

"I don't know what you're talking about."

"It's all over the records. Some claim that he was almost paranoid."

"That's absurd."

He waited a moment, watched her. "You know, the odd part is that as far as the records go Rose wasn't so concerned about outside leaks as he was about inside leaks. If you get my point."

"No, sir, I don't get your point."

"Well, I can understand the man being afraid that the Russians might find out what he was doing, but why was he so afraid that Washington would find out?"

By now she was sitting sideways in the chair, knotting a paper napkin around her fingers. He thought her face had become more pale. Maybe not, she was pretty damn pale anyway.

"Did Rose ever talk to you about George Clay?"

"I don't recall."

"But you know that there had been trouble between them."

"I suppose."

"Do you know what it was about?"

"No."

"But you must have heard talk."

"I never listened."

A telephone had begun to ring from a room across the corridor. It rang a long time before it stopped.

"What do you think of George Clay?"

"I don't know him very well."

"Have you ever met his girl friend?"

She turned then. "What?"

"The singer. Kristian Haas. Have you ever met her?"

"Why would I have met her? I'm not on everybody's preferred guest list."

He thanked her, left her still by the window, shut the door behind him. Past what had once been the infirmary there were

123

more puddles where that pipe had burst. It seemed that the lights along the staircase had also shorted out. He entered archives from the rear along a path between the radio shacks and generators. There was a new odor of liquid soap, a notice on the stucco: "Kittens available for a good home."

As always the first moments among the records were a little disconcerting. There were dozens of seemingly contradictory themes. By the winter of 1962 Rose was running seven networks into the heart of the Soviet command while continuing to call for a cessation of hostility. A political summary from 1963 noted that Soviet military expenditures were bound to increase, while Rose still asked Washington to seek new diplomatic channels. There were four not very clear notes from Rose to Charlie Wilde with references to deceit in high places and arrogance and power.

Later volumes held only minor variations to the earlier themes. In 1965 Rose submitted some fifty pages about the emptiness of an unchecked nuclear building. In 1966 he noted that there were parties on both sides who fed on one another's rhetorical excess: "The bomb has changed everything except our way of thinking."

From 1967 there were glimpses of an elusive Rose that Petty had seen before, a Rose who appeared to be everywhere, then nowhere at all. Once Petty had left his corner of the archives in search of a misplaced ledger. Past a bolted door that led to the boiler room he thought he saw a figure drifting between the shelves. Closer he of course found nothing more than the reflection of a light from the courtyard, but damn it, he *felt* like Harry Rose was close by. Reconstructed to life from the damn archives. Twice Petty had awakened with an impression of Harry in his room, at the foot of the bed. The features may not have been too clear but even after coffee and a cigarette Petty could still remember the eyes.

Later, for the enhantment of his damnable visions, there were two photographs from the spring of 1968—Rose in sunglasses and then again on the steps of the Sylter Hof Hotel. Petty put them both in his pocket, although he felt like burning them.

Campbell was waiting at the top of the stairs, his hands in his pockets, a manila folder under his arm. He smelled of cologne. How appropriate, Petty thought. The smell of the city. There were also tiny golf clubs on Campbell's tie, initials on his belt buckle.

He said, "I thought I told you to stay away from my people." Petty shrugged.

"You just have to keep pushing them, don't you? You can't keep away from them."

Petty ran his hand across his mouth. "Is there something you want to tell me, Campbell?"

"Yes, there's something I want to tell you. If you don't stop bothering my people I'm going to ask George Clay to take you off this case."

"Fine, do it," and continued slowly down the corridor past janitors smoking on landing, idle typists, a woman just staring out the window. Along a gravel path two boys were probing under the fender of a van. A third seemed to be watching from the steps of the annex, then receded as Petty drew closer.

Petty reached the Kurfürstendamm at ten o'clock, the night-club at a quarter of eleven. The Last Exit. There were students milling under the marquee, a line of motorbikes at the curb. Bricks along the passage to the bar had been spray-painted with the names of itinerant performers: Bruno Taut and the Leopards, Moon Martin, The Spike, The Mind Police.

Then Kristian Haas in red.

He saw her first from the doorway, just beyond the footlights. She wore a lavender dress, cut to the thigh. One hand held a microphone, the other a glass of red wine. Behind her stood a pencil-thin guitar player, clearly drunk, and a drummer in high-heeled boots. She glanced to the left, wet her lips, then very slowly:

I'm on the fire, fire, firing line,
And you're next, the next in line,
So run your fingers through my hair,
I don't worry, I don't care . . .

In perfect English and a wry whiskey voice.

He only got one really good look at her—center stage in the spotlight, a coy gesture to the crowd, the strap of her dress off her shoulder. She had a kind of child's face, with exquisite eyes and a sly smile that made him wonder what she was doing with a guy like George Clay.

He left after that, first in search of a quiet place to drink, then in search of some kind of perspective on the last phase of Harry Rose's reign. Toward midnight he found himself in his room again, with bourbon and a yellow pad of random notes. By two o'clock he was numb but still not drunk. By three he was dead tired, but still couldn't sleep. Afraid to?

Charlie Wilde had also gotten up late on Monday after a restless Sunday night. In Templehoff there had been a woman who had briefly worked with Rose in 1969. Wilde met her in a park. She did not have much to say. From Templehoff he returned to the Grunewald and a restaurant where he thought they might remember him. Toward nine o'clock he drifted back to the station and a last collection of documents he had been avoiding for a week. It was cold again. If it did not rain there was bound to be a frost.

There was a letter from the winter of 1961, handwritten on Harry's rather ostentatious stationery, postmarked Geneva: "Charlie, this city is full of pigs, but Anna seems to like the snow. As for myself there's little to say. I keep thinking that we are getting near to some kind of an end."

Beneath these pages lay fragments of forgotten operations, a telegram from Frankfurt concerning the failure in Vienna, a sheaf

126

of miscellaneous notes. Then in an unbound folder secured with rubber bands he found what he supposed had been waiting for him from the start: ninety-eight pages on what amounted to the decline and fall of Harry Rose . . . .

As it happened, Charlie Wilde had been in Greece when construction had begun on the Wall. On his return, Harry met him at the terminal in Templehoff. They'd dined near the Airlift Memorial then toured the northern border, photographing deathstrips, fakir beds and trip-alarms. Through it all Rose was calm, almost jocular. He kept insisting that the Wall was tactically crude and politically meaningless. In this, as it turned out, he was wrong.

The Wall . . . sometimes Wilde would spend a whole evening just looking at it. On bad nights reception teams would wait for hours only to lose an agent thirty-five feet from the Western ridge. By the end of two months a mythology had developed about safe routes, covers and crossing schedules. A footnote from these days was that by 1963 Harry had established four trails into Pankow and a tunnel into Lichtenberg, but the cost was high. Very high. There were people dying, and Harry never really came to terms with it. In a letter from December he wrote that "we live in a time when reality is not something to be faced."

In succeeding letters through the months that followed the tone stayed unchanged. "It's a damn cruel war," he wrote. He had no use for the later historians. He traveled with Anna whenever he could; twice to Jerusalem, several times to the south of France. And if there were periods of great success, the success no longer brought him pleasure. Wilde remembered an oddly distant Harry, alternatively obsessed with what he felt was duplicity in high places and the prospect of nuclear war. Put them beside each other and they seemed to go together . . . .

Wilde often found himself focusing on a week in the autumn of 1966. He'd left Berlin on a Tuesday, landed in Virginia the following afternoon. He spent a night with Lyle Severson, then drove on to attend the October war games.

A premise for those games was that a Soviet-backed contingent of East German forces had engaged an American battalion near the Tegler See. Faced with a devastating defeat, the Western commander employed a tactical nuclear weapon on Eastern troop concentrations. This first nuclear strike prompted a retaliatory strike on a NATO base outside of Hamburg. By the fifth day of play, escalation had reached an intercontinental level.

Wilde spent much of the time with a magazine in a waiting room. In the evenings he generally drank alone in one of the southside bars, or else in his room off-campus. Occasionally he found himself talking to strangers, but refrained from telephoning Harry.

When he returned he again met Rose in Templehoff, and they again dined near the Airlift Memorial. There had been rain for days, and no escaping the cold. Wilde felt like he had a low fever. Harry appeared tired, pale.

Rose said, "So how did you do?"

"What?"

"The games. Did you win?"

"I was disqualified."

"Did you see George Clay?"

"Yeah, I saw him."

"Did he ask about me?"

"No."

A Turkish girl had emerged from the kitchen with beer and a plate of sausages. She put the food on the table without a word. Friendship City.

After a brief silence Rose said, "I assume you now understand what I've been talking about all these years. I mean the mentality of people like George Clay. Did they tell you about the throw-weight gap?"

"The *what*?"

"Throw-weight gap. It's the newest thing . . . supposedly the Russians are going to have a bigger stick by the end of the decade. George Clay has written and written about it. He wants to send somebody on tour to talk about it." A sip of beer. "Not that the Russians are any less crazy. This very moment the Kremlin is carrying on about target-vulnerability, as if the whole goddamn continent isn't vulnerable enough. Fucking maniacs . . . I've got to get a handle on them, Charlie . . . "

"Who, Harry. Get a handle on who?"

"The hardcore. The missileniks . . . I've got to find some way to cut them out of the game, cut away their crap. Then it should just be a question of convincing one side to buy it, because if one side buys it the other side will buy it too. Have to. Or don't you agree?"

Wilde looked at him. "Agree? Agree with what? Harry, what specifically are you talking about?"

"Peace, Charlie. I am specifically talking about peace, however unfashionable it might be."

After that meeting Wilde came down with a raging fever that lasted a week. When he finally returned to the station he found that Rose was once again consumed with the day-to-day of spying, and so life had more or less returned to normal. By mid-winter there were four new networks between Dresden and Prague. By spring a fifth network had blossomed in Budapest, then a sixth along the Baltic Sea.

During these days Rose rarely talked about anything beyond the immediate concerns of the station. But even in silence there were hints of the deeper feelings, undercurrents. And these were leaving him increasingly disconnected from the mainstream of the intelligence community. Emotionally, ideologically—the man was gradually disconnecting. . . .

In July of 1964 Boris Tatlin left Berlin for Moscow to assume

129

command of the First Directorate and the physical penetration of Western targets. Not long after the appointment, Harry Rose received a copy of a Langley psychological profile in which Tatlin was described as "an exceedingly devious man with the tenacity of a bulldog." For days that profile remained unread on Harry's desk until finally Wilde had it shredded. Such news from home wasn't worth the cost of the shredding.

Nine months later Tatlin's specter appeared again when George Clay landed in Berlin for a series of special briefings on Soviet activity in Germany. After the briefing Wilde found Rose sitting by a third-floor window amid a litter of cigarette ash. There was a bottle of gin on the sill, a photograph of Tatlin from 1956. Wilde entered the room without knocking, picked up the bottle, found a clean glass.

"You know what they're trying to do, don't you, Charlie?"

"What's that, Harry?"

It was cold, with a draft from the stairway and the fire escape.

"They're trying to make him into a goddamn legend to justify their excesses."

"Harry, please—"

"It's classic. You keep exaggerating the success of your enemy until you've got everyone, including yourself, believing that the only way to win, to beat him, is to adopt his methods. And of course the Reds are playing the same game. You should read the kind of crap they write about us."

Rose got up from his chair, poured another glass of gin, went to stand directly over Tatlin's photograph, head cocked to one side. "They're one and the same, aren't they, Charlie? Clay and Tatlin. Same mentality, same motivation. It's a horror show where the creeps have all the lines, and everyone has forgotten that there was supposed to have been a happy ending. I mean, we beat the fucking Germans, didn't we? So where's the payoff? Sure, the Russians have a dirty, vicious oligarchy that's run by a bunch of shits, frightened men. But that doesn't mean we have to get ready

130

to kill two hundred million people . . . ”

"Let me take you home, Harry. It's late. Let me just run you home."

Anna met them at the door of the Grunewald estate, a coat thrown over her nightgown. She asked Wilde in, he said no thanks. By midnight he found himself in a small cafe beside a steel bridge some eighty yards from the eastern wall. There were sentries underneath the sodium lights, a solitary figure watching from the tower. Once, years earlier, there had been a night like this when he had nearly convinced himself to leave—leave Harry Rose, Berlin, all of it. But at some point between composing a letter to explain himself and picking up the telephone he had thought . . . walk away from it now and you'll never see Harry Rose again. Go, and he'll just disappear behind you like a dream. Also, you'd be a damn cop-out. So in the end he went back to that Tiergarten house.

On his last years in Germany Wilde wrote only that he was conscious of being with an extraordinary man on the edge of a decline, at least in one area. It was hard to see it, though. As late as 1975 the networks continued to prosper with as many as twenty submissions a week. There were dozens of hidden resources, nameless people tucked away between the folds of bureaucracy, odd figures with special talents, Poles who owed favors from 1945, Hungarians with debts from 1956, Germans that Rose had delivered from the east . . . Harry came to them, one way or another, came to most all of them. On Saturday evenings he continued to dine on the Kurfürstendamm. Sundays were generally reserved for Anna, alternate Tuesdays for retired agents or the families of those who had died, disappeared.

As for the so-called decline, it began in the third week in October of 1976. At the heart of the matter was the creation of an outside committee to examine the annual Agency estimate of Soviet strengths and intentions. The committee had been formed on recommendation from the Foreign Intelligence Advisory Board. In response to this recommendation, then-Agency Director George Bush appointed a team of ten men, most of them from the private sphere, most proponents of the hard line . . . Richard Pipes, Polish immigrant and well-known advocate of the nuclear deterrent, some claimed solution; Paul Nitze and William van Vleave, long-time boosters of "containment." Critics called them Superhawks; the committee was more commonly known as Team B to distinguish it from Team A, the Agency regulars ordinarily responsible for the annual estimate preparation.

Wilde's first exposure to Team B came not in Berlin but in Langley, where he had been attending an extended briefing on the tactical end of the Backfire bomber. But it was not until his return to Berlin that Team B became a personal matter with overtones of conspiracy that had been at least vaguely with Rose for some twenty years. . . .

It was a Sunday, very cold. Wilde had left Langley on a midnight flight, landed in Templehoff in the late afternoon. Rose was waiting in a coffee bar near the Grunewaldsee. After an hour on the terrace they descended through a line of trees to a frozen stream among the ferns. Wilde felt as if he hadn't slept in days.

Harry said, "I assume you've heard about the Bush league."

"Yes. I don't like puns. A great critic of American literature . . . F. O. Matthiessen . . . said a pun was the cheapest form of humor."

Harry looked at him, smiled. "One for you and F. O. But if I can be forgiven, let's get serious. Whatever you call them, these people believe that the Reds are militarily superior, or at least aim to be so. They also believe that they've got a first-strike capability —Christ, what a godawful euphemism—and that unless we move fast they're going to use it to knock out the Minuteman and then hold our cities hostage. There even seems talk that a full exchange is *survivable,* that the dangers of nuclear chicken have been exaggerated. Would you say that's a fair assessment?"

"They also say that Bush will be out by the end of next year," Wilde said.

"So what? These people have been entrenching themselves for years. And you know where it's going to take us. Massive buildup, and then right to the brink of a full exchange . . . But there's a way to beat them—"

"I'm not listening, Harry. Not anymore—"

"It's really a question of getting to the truth of things. None of their stuff can stand up in the face of hard facts. I mean, look at it. Team B says the Russians are going for the big-strike potential while we fiddle around with SALT, that they've decided an all-out exchange is acceptable. So we better go and do and think likewise. Okay, but what if I were to get something that cuts away the speculation? Like a Kremlin Policy directive? One of the Red Army nuclear inventories? Facts."

"Harry, it's getting cold."

"You start telling people the Russians are ready and willing to blow us to hell and things start getting strange, particularly when it's not true. Yes, Russia is aggressive, duplicitous, stupid, scared, like us. But they know what happens when you lay down two thousand megatons. Charlie, you know that."

They'd come to a rutted track lined with pines and hollyhock. It was even colder here, but Wilde had given up pointing that out. His friend was on a roll.

"It's in the numbers, Charlie. Team B is trying to scare us into a war footing with stories of Russian monsters, windows of vulnerability. Windows, for Christ's sake. What would your famous critic say about *that?* I'm saying the argument falls down when you start feeding in real numbers. What are the Russians really worth? What's their real strength? . . . "

Wilde recalled another conversation with Rose in a restaurant

133

off the Havel wharf. It scared the hell out of him, with reason. The two had originally entered Wilmersdorf for a meeting with the British. When the meeting ended early Wilde suggested that they find a bar. It was a Friday.

Harry began deceptively by repeating much of what he'd said before about Team B's evaluation. Also that regardless of what was wrong with it, the evaluation would no doubt stand, and influence United States foreign policy for years to come.

Then he said that given the momentum of the Team B evaluation an attack on it would only harden the line. So the only effective rebuttal would be precise, undeniable evidence—the numbers, as he called it . . . "I'm talking about specifics," he told Charlie. "First-strike capability, preemptive counterforce, acceptable casualty rate. These are verifiable absolutes. If the Russians are really going for them, then the numbers will show it."

That was when Wilde began to see it coming, and when his stomach began to knot up. "You're talking about Kremlin access, aren't you?"

"That would be the most direct way, yes."

"Does that mean then you've actually got a line?"

"Maybe."

Afterward, they descended from the restaurant through an untended garden to the shore. A dirt path lay along the river banks, then a stretch of road to the west. There were fishermen among the reeds, sounds of waterfowl and the running lights of distant boats. Rose said it was understandable that members of the defense establishment would want to influence public opinion about the Soviet threat, but when that threat was seriously inflated, with conclusions drawn from it about national policy, it was the job of the intelligence community to get rid of the myth, present the facts.

How far, Wilde asked, did he intend to go?

"I need the numbers, Charlie. We can't stop them without hard numbers."

"We." The word echoed for Wilde long after they'd parted that afternoon.

In November and December Rose began to travel again. Hamburg, Zurich, London, Bonn. He would mostly leave on Fridays, return on Sundays or early Monday morning. Occasionally Anna went with him, more often he traveled alone. In addition to these brief trips abroad, he made internal journeys through selected field reports from the late 1950s, memos from the early 1960s, profiles of station personnel. He seemed involved with oddly unrelated matters . . . local real estate, courier routes, refugees from the Baltic states.

When toward the end of December Wilde returned from a week in Paris, he found Rose living with new locks on the windows, another array of electronic bafflers and mountains of files on aluminum trolleys.

"I guess you better tell me what's going on," Wilde said.

Rose's answer was: "I've found something here that might interest you," and handed his friend Charlie what appeared to be a rough draft of a strategic assessment on Soviet nuclear policy. It had been typewritten, possibly from an illicit photograph of the original.

"Who wrote this, Harry?"

"Clay . . . with maybe some help from Richard Pipes."

"Where did you get it?"

"I think you'd better just take a look at this. Third paragraph, second page. He admits he doesn't have proof . . . 'It seems that Soviet strategies reject the natural deterrence theory on technical grounds, although we have no solid evidence to this effect.' He admits it, actually admits it, which leaves him wide open . . . . "

Later Wilde found out that on two occasions Rose had purportedly traveled to Geneva but had actually slipped into Washington under the name of Donnelly, an identity he hadn't used in years.

All Wilde could learn about the trips was that Harry had seen no one on an official basis, which meant that he was once again dealing on the side.

Wilde further discovered that Rose had also made at least two clandestine entries into Yugoslavia, first to Dubrovnik, then to a Dalmatian resort along the Adriatic. On both occasions he traveled as Lester Greene, another untraceable identity from the past.

Eventually in mid-January, on a Saturday in Siemensstadt, after they'd met with two young women recently retired from the Potsdam network, Wilde and Rose went to a country tavern on the edge of the Havel estuary.

"We should talk," Rose began.

"I guess," Wilde said, without enthusiasm.

"It seems the fish are feasting on the bait."

"Very colorful, Harry."

"Fuck off, Charlie. You and your critic. The influential people have approved the evaluation. George Clay has called it the most significant strategic piece since the Cuban Missile Crisis, has made it required reading throughout the sphere."

"What's in the final summary?"

"Pretty much the same stuff. The new word is credible response, which means fifty million for the MX and another ten for the Pershing system."

"Where's Clay now?"

"Who knows?"

A waitress appeared, a plain girl in a short skirt. She took orders for whiskey neat, then turned to the other patrons, mostly pensioners and women from the factory.

"Charlie, I'd like to give the problem first, then what I think is the solution."

Wilde nodded. What else could he do?

"It goes like this. Given the drift of things in Washington, within four or five years we'll be very close to a shooting war with the Russians. It's an inevitable drift."

"And so you want to change the drift."

"So to speak. Look, the so-called spirit of confrontation is based on guesses. Wrong guesses. We don't need the MX. The Russians don't think they can survive a full exchange. They're not significantly ahead of us, and I can prove it. I can—"

"How?"

"Ivan Panov."

"Oh Jesus, Harry."

"His access may not be all it once was, but he can still get us what we need."

"Like what?"

"Well, how about one of the annual Kremlin policy briefs? Or a strategic-capability profile?"

"And how does he get the product?"

"Through Yuri Andropov's office. As one of the important undersecretaries, Panov has access to major briefs."

"How do you expect to maintain the link? And what happens to Panov if you do?"

"There won't be a sustained link. This is a one-shot deal. But when it's over Panov comes West. With his lady."

"Who carries the product back?" He knew the answer to that one.

"That's what I have to talk to you about—"

"Who, Harry? Who's it going to be?"

"He wants you, Charlie. I offered, but Ivan wants you. He feels like he knows you . . . can trust you."

"Where?"

"Over the border. South to the lowlands. Look, if you've got reservations I'll do it myself, never mind what he wants. I mean if—"

"When?"

"Six weeks, maybe eight."

"Someone to drive for me? Shoot for me?"

"No, you go in alone. You know the drill, less is more."

Wilde thought of saying stuff it. And knew he couldn't. Not after all this time. He returned to his home at half past ten, but did not sleep until three o'clock. He was surprised he slept at all.

There were four weeks of preparation. Wilde spent them consciously adhering to a normal routine. He and Rose tended to avoid one another in the daytime, while in the evenings Wilde made a point of excessive drinking in public. He spent hours lingering over coffee, chatting with the junior staff, discussing trivia with anyone who would care to listen. All as if to say . . . look at me, I'm an old man at the end of my career with nothing to do.

There were only two material conversations with Rose—both held in a deserted factory loft in Spandau. During the first Rose discussed the southern border installations and suitable crossing points. Wilde would travel as a Medieval historian on sabbatical from a foreign university. Apparently there had been a number of programs in recent years to catalogue and preserve the local artifacts. During the second meeting Rose discussed contact and retrival. The eastern courier would be a girl, a German. Wilde would meet her on the tourist route north of the Spree. There was a tavern on the water's edge—the Partridge, *Das Rebhun*. Wilde was to show up at noon. The girl would be sitting by the window. There would be a brown canvas satchel on the floor by her chair. After several minutes she would withdraw the book from the satchel and put it on the table. Wilde would glance at the book, then pretend to study it from a distance. He would approach the table, explaining that the book had been written by a colleague, a former instructor from Dresden. During the conversation Wilde would withdraw a pack of cigarettes from his pocket and put them on the table. Eventually the girl would do the same. And the film, Rose explained, the film would be inside the cigarette pack—two rolls, sixteen millimeter.

As for reentry, Rose said only that there were two safe routes to the south, where Panov had cleared the sentries on the pretext of passing an agent into the West. As for the girl, Rose said that she was young but capable. Apparently Panov had used her before.

Finally there were photographs, a dozen of them that Rose had spread across a card table. There were several long shots of the landscape, the border, even an interior view of the tavern. When Wilde finished looking at them Rose lit a fire in a wastebasket and burned them. By this time it was nearly half past three in the morning.

After this meeting Wilde spent a week of nights memorizing the details of the lowland historical sites, folk art, the early Huguenot settlements. He also studied maps, listed the names of river villages and the railway terminals. Generally he tried to be detached, indifferent, although now and then he found himself unreasonably cold and hungry, and knew that it was fear.

On Thursday, the last day, he arrived at the station early, spent an hour conspicuously wandering through the corridors, examining notices on the bulletin board, staring out of windows. Toward noon he met with one of the senior clerks, a dour figure named Singer. After a few minutes of small talk, Wilde suddenly confessed that he had a slight problem with a young woman in Reinickendorf. It seemed that he needed a little time to find her a reasonable clinic. Would Singer be willing to cover for him until Monday? "And keep it under your hat," Wilde added, which meant that by Friday the entire station would know.

Wilde spent the rest of that day sorting through meaningless outstation summaries, chatting on the telephone, sipping bad coffee in the third-floor lounge. Toward nightfall he descended to the second floor, removed his name from the duty roster, con-

139

tinued out to the motor court. A fog had been mounting since the late afternoon. Good.

Rose was waiting by a roadside bar eight miles west of the station. He was leaning on the fender of a Volkswagen that Wilde had never seen before. Wilde got into the Volkswagen without speaking.

They drove for twenty minutes, following a holiday route past youth camps and river retreats. It was now dark and the fog had settled in the valleys. Beyond a particularly dark stretch lay a pitted track along a river bank where the fog hung in thin shreds among the bracken, and at the end of a narrow dingle stood a timbered lodge half-hidden in the pines.

"What is this place?" Wilde asked.

"Just a place."

"Who owns it?"

"Nobody."

The door had spring cartridge locks. The furniture was a badly jointed table, four block chairs, cots. Rose lit a tiled oven, but the walls seemed to absorb the heat. Wandering into the kitchen, Wilde found two bottles of gin, a bottle of whiskey, eggs, a few potatoes, a dozen tins of meat. Also stacks of magazines, most of them years out of date.

"It's not on the books, is it?"

"What's that, Charlie?"

"This house, it's not on any of the books."

"No."

"Then who authorized it?"

"I did."

Rose prepared a meal of eggs, corned beef hash and sour coffee. They ate huddled by the oven, plates on their knees. Afterward they drank whiskey and smoked. Wilde had picked up an old issue

140

of National Geographic, leafed through it quickly, then tossed it into the fire.

"We're on the edge, aren't we?"

Rose looked at him. "What makes you say that?"

"This house, that car. You don't trust anyone, do you?"

Rose shrugged, took another sip of whiskey. "I trust you, Charlie. I always have."

There were sounds of mice in the attic, wind under the door. Wilde had begun leafing through another magazine. There were photographs of the north German countryside. Suddenly he said, "How much does Washington know?"

Rose poured another drink. "Only what they need to know."

"What happens when it's all over? I mean, who does the preliminary analysis?"

"I don't think there will be an analysis, Charlie, not with this stuff. People will read it, and that will end discussion right there."

"What about the border watch?"

"They'll be monitoring the radio traffic, that's all." And then after a brief silence: "Listen, Charlie. It's going to be an okay weekend. Believe me."

Wilde entered the East through Lichtenberg. It was a Friday, two o'clock in the afternoon. From Lichtenberg he moved south, mingling with tourists as far as the Spree. There he killed a couple of hours browsing through a shopping arcade, then found a room in a lakefront inn.

He ate a meal above a wharf—sausage, beer, stale bread. There were three Cuban boys at an adjoining table, probably athletes on a national tour. Ten minutes later two women came in with identical plastic handbags. One of them kept glancing at Wilde's shoes. The other whispered something to the waitress, a girl with acne scars.

When he finished eating he moved out to the streets again. By

141

now it was dark, with only the intermittent lights from streetlamps and the glow from shuttered windows. He ambled past a vacant movie house, an unused church. Along the main road there were loitering students by a dry fountain. At the edge of town he found a bar, one room off a littered courtyard. An old man sat in the darkness with a green guitar. Wilde took a table by the window, asked for beer. There were no other patrons.

"I'm looking for a place called the Partridge."

The old man turned, glared at him.

"The Partridge. It's a tavern."

"What about it?"

"I thought maybe you might have heard of it."

"Why should I have heard of it?"

"Well, they say it's a lively place."

"Oh, you want a little fun?"

"No, I just want to—"

"Forget it. There's no fun here."

He left without finishing his beer, the old man still sitting in the darkness, the green guitar across his knees. Beyond a footbridge three figures in overcoats stood on the steps of a gymnasium. Closer, Wilde thought he heard the static from a radio. Also, there were odors that he still remembered from those years right after the war. You never forgot them. Your nose wouldn't let you.

The inn turned out to be deserted except for a boy slouched in a chair by the window. The boy was half-asleep.

"Do you know where I can get something to drink?" Wilde asked.

The boy looked at him, but did not answer.

"Something to drink?" Wilde repeated.

"Water? You want water?"

"No, I wanted—"

"There's water in your room."

The room was narrow and bare with a marble basin in one corner, a cheap print of the harbor above the bed. The walls were gray plaster, in places crumbled, leaving patches of white mildew. The window looked out to a cobbled yard and a row of tenements. The door wouldn't lock.

Wilde slipped off his shoes and lay down on the bed. After a while he got up, found a cigarette but no match. He was thinking he shouldn't have talked to the old man.

He undressed, filled the basin with water, splashed some on his face, drank from cupped hands. I shouldn't have talked to that boy either, he thought. Some goddamn spook I turned out to be.

He slept, badly, continually waking to sounds in the corridor, passing trucks, a slamming door. Toward midnight there were voices from the neighboring room, a man and a woman. They seemed to be talking about the woman's husband, or lover. She yelled out, "What's wrong with these people anyway?" Then there was silence, which didn't help . . . .

He woke up at dawn but lay there for more than an hour. It was cold. There were footsteps on the staircase, then a dry cough. He got up and moved to the window. A yellowish fog had risen from the river. There were huddled figures moving in and out of doorways. Some wore pieces of uniform—greatcoats and forage caps.

They gave him coffee downstairs. Closer to the center of town he found another cafe where he got a boiled egg and some sort of fried potato. While he ate he was very conscious of two women obviously looking at him from the corner. He thought there may have been someone in the street staring at him from beneath a fire escape. Mr. Cool . . . .

He reached the lowlands by midmorning, then wandered through the ruins of some gutted monastery. Half a mile past a line of black hills lay another river village with a cinema, a granary, a few shops and a youth hostel. The Partridge stood on the waterfront above a gray wharf. There were schoolchildren along the path from the river, a few couples dining on the terrace. The outlying roads were deserted.

He approached the town from the north, across an abandoned

143

field. Twice he stopped to photograph what looked like significant rubble, then moved on as if thoroughly intrigued by this wasteland. Closer to the Partridge he stopped again to photograph a passing boat, then to browse in front of a carpenter's shop and a dusty display of wooden birds. There were two ravens, an owl and a fourth item he couldn't make out.

A woman smiled. "They're lovely, aren't they?"

"Excuse me?"

"The birds. Don't you think they're lovely?"

He first saw her reflected in the glass, absently brushing her hair from her eyes. She was slender, pretty, with a belted raincoat and a blue plastic handbag.

"Are you a collector?" stepping beside him, shifting her bag on her shoulder. "My uncle is a collector, although he prefers flowers to birds. You should see his flowers. Some of them are so real you can almost smell them. Can you imagine that?"

"Yes . . . I'm sure they're very nice."

"Can you guess what his favorite is?"

"Well I—"

"It's a Rose," and she looked directly at him.

They stepped into a vacant arcade that might have once been an amusement park. There were the remains of a carousel, the drive shaft of a Ferris wheel. Wilde lit a cigarette, one of the cheap Eastern brands that he'd bought the night before. The first puff made him dizzy.

She said, "Ivan Panov has been arrested."

He leaned against the wall, shut his eyes, then looked up at the sky. "How? How did it happen?"

"I don't know."

"Where did they take him?"

She shrugged. "Moscow."

"What about the film?"

"I have it."

"Where?"

144

"Hidden."

"How do I get it?"

"Come with me."

Beyond the wall was a partial view of a few choked trees and the path to the water.

"They're all around here," she said. "If we don't go soon then they'll arrest us too."

"How do you know Ivan?"

"From Berlin . . . *Listen* to me, they're looking for us right now."

"How did he give you the film?"

"Courier from Prague—please, we don't have much time."

She had left a truck along a side street. Dull green with a cracked window. She told him to kneel beneath the dashboard. If they were stopped he was to pretend that he was sick. *Pretend, hell,* he thought.

She drove slowly until they had passed through the village. There were no signposts, no sense of permanent life. Twice he found himself staring at her profile . . . her eyes, dark lashes.

"What do I call you?" he said.

"Lise."

"And you said that you knew Ivan from Berlin?"

"I was a friend of a friend."

"What friend?"

"Does it matter now?"

They had entered an unbroken stretch of marsh. Beyond lay patches of red forest. He guessed she was about thirty, maybe younger. They skirted another village. It was quieter than the open road. He smelled dung and gasoline. After twenty minutes he put his head back on the cracked leather seat. When he looked again they had left the highway for a pitted track between clusters of pine. There was a lake, then the shadow of low hills. Among the shadows stood an old farmhouse.

"Who lives here?"

145

She shook her head. "No one."

"Did Panov come here?"

"No one comes here."

They entered through a rear door. The main room was empty, the walls were bare. Someone had torn the legs off a table, the stuffing from a rotting sofa. Wilde sat down on a packing crate.

"There's food if you want," she said. "Ham, a little bread."

"How long do we stay here?"

"A night. There's also vodka."

"Then where do we go? Berlin?"

"Not Berlin. Berlin is not safe."

"Then where?"

"North, northwest. They say there's a safe route from Rostock to the border."

"*Who* says?"

"Friends."

"What friends? Friends of Ivan Panov?"

She had been standing at the window, peering through the torn curtain. Finally she turned, lit a cigarette. "I knew Astrid Jurgen."

She made a bed on the legless table, lay another blanket on the sofa for herself. There were candles, but she said that they could not take a chance that someone would see the light. So they just sat with the vodka, bread and a few slices of black ham.

"Did you love him?" he asked.

"Who?"

"Panov."

"Of course not."

"Then why are you doing this?"

She shrugged. "The Russians."

"But Ivan Panov is Russian."

"He's different."

"Then what Russians?"

She tore off another piece of bread. "Boris Tatlin."

"You knew him?"

"My sister did. Also her husband. Both of them are dead."

He shut up then and even slept for a while . . . three, maybe four hours. Waking, he saw that she had been watching him, with a cigarette in hand and another glass of vodka.

"These photographs, they are important?"

"Pretty important."

"Important enough to die for?"

He smiled. "Is anything that important?"

"Yes, I think so."

Just before dawn he heard the sound of a quietly shutting door. He got up, lit a cigarette and drew back the curtains. She was kneeling by a patch of moss beneath a shriveled walnut tree. There was a garden shovel on the slope, a mound of fresh soil beside it.

"A little something to die for." She smiled and dropped a cylindrical wad of adhesive tape on the blanket.

He picked it up, curled his fingers around it. *Two rolls, sixteen millimeter—subminiature.* "You didn't open it, did you?"

"Of course not."

They left at daybreak with the blankets, two cans of gasoline and food. The grassland was light, but the forest stayed dark until mid-morning. Occasionally in the distance he saw untended cattle, a tractor. Toward nightfall they stopped beside a lake at the foot of the hills. They cut rushes from the shoreline, laid them in the bed of the truck. Earlier it had been cold, but at dusk the wind died.

"Tell me," she said. "What is he like?"

"Who?"

"Your famous Harry Rose."

He reached for a cigarette, one of the last. "I don't know. I guess he's like anyone else."

"Like you?"

"No, not like me. And I'm not like him."

"They say he's the most dangerous man in Germany, in Europe. They say he's more dangerous than Boris Tatlin."

147

"Who says that?"

"Lots of people."

"Ivan? Does Ivan Panov say it?"

She pushed the bottle away. "No, not Ivan."

It took four days before Wilde managed to establish physical contact with one of the north German escape systems. In the end he had to settle for an unfamiliar route that had been organized by members of the Hamburg station. His operative link was a little man named Spengler. Wilde met him first in an abandoned granary south of Schewern. Their conversation was awkward, tense. Spengler kept asking about the film, insisting that Wilde give it to him immediately so that it could be passed to the West through the diplomatic route. When Wilde refused, Spengler told him, "It would be wise if you trusted us. Your Harry Rose can't help you now."

Eighteen hours later there was a second meeting near a village to the west. Again Wilde was questioned about the film. Again he refused to discuss a separate delivery. By now he began to grasp the seriousness of his position. Apparently not only had the Hamburg station been alerted, but so had George Clay.

Between meetings with Spengler, Wilde stayed with Lise in a boathouse beside some lake twenty miles east of the border. Here the weather was predictable with alternating periods of wind and stillness. Generally their hours together were subdued. She tended to talk a lot about the future and a subsidized resettlement in California.

As for himself, Wilde supposed that he had long since lost control of his future, and like any agent on the run he knew that there was nothing to do but wait. Although he had been told that Rose had been advised of the situation, he remained pretty well convinced that this was a goddamn lie. He also suspected he may not have been told the whole truth about the ultimate supervision of his escape. There seemed to be several forces at work, each competing with the other.

On Friday, the last day, he once again met briefly with Spengler, this time in a hawthorn grove on the edge of an onion field. Spengler seemed frightened, or upset, or both. He kept insisting that Wilde had endangered the entire network by refusing to give over the film. Wilde said nothing.

When Wilde returned to the boathouse he found Lise waiting for him in the doorway. She wore a gray sweater and a black skirt. Her shoes were dangling from her fingers. Without speaking they walked to the end of the wharf. Once again the wind had died with the approach of dusk.

"It's tomorrow," he said. "We go tomorrow night."

She put her head on his shoulder, closed her eyes. "Is it safe?"

He ran his fingers through her hair. "I don't know."

"What do they tell you about the sentries?"

"Supposedly they've been bribed."

"With American hundred-dollar bills, no?" And she laughed. Then quietly, "And what did they tell you about the wire?"

"Cut . . . maybe."

She began to toy with a button on his sleeve, and he guessed that she was either very tired or else had been drinking.

"I want to make love to you."

He kissed her, very lightly. "Tomorrow."

"No, tonight."

They undressed quickly because of the cold. She took his face in her hands, pressed her lips against him, breathing deep. "You're afraid, aren't you?" He looked at her, didn't answer. She put his hand to her breast, encircled her arms around him. "I'm afraid too . . . . "

Afterward they lay in silence, smoking, finishing off the vodka. At some point she had taken the canister out of his pocket and

149

began to examine it. He took it away from her when she started picking at the adhesive tape.

"I want to see," she told him.

"They haven't been developed yet."

"What are they? What are they pictures of? I suppose they are papers. What are they good for?"

"Peace, I guess. They're good for peace, or supposed to be."

She laughed. "Peace? What a bad joke."

When she finally fell asleep he wandered back out to the lake. The water was dead still. He supposed it was late, two, three in the morning, but since his watch had stopped he had lost all track of time.

They approached the border at dusk. There was nothing here as substantial as the wall which divided Berlin. There was only a shaven gully, a few rows of wire, towers along the rim of a hill. To the west lay billboards broken by the wind, shredded slogans across an empty valley, a field of bracken, scattered pines.

They followed an unmade road until they could see the first tower, then left the truck beside the barn of a vacated farmhouse. Beyond lay an acre of empty grass, then another mile of pines. It was quiet on the forest floor.

They spent the last hours on the spur of a hill two hundred yards from the final strip. Below, the ground descended sharply to bracken and a field of vines. There were telegraph wires to the west and a hawthorn grove on a grassy knoll where the reception team was supposed to be waiting.

They had told him to walk to the trees, directly to the trees. There were concrete bunkers flanking the highway to Ludwigslust, but here there were only inconsequential rows of dragon's teeth, a length of wire across slats of rotting timber. No one had been shot along this stretch for fifteen years, they had told him. Even the main roads were no longer patrolled.

But there were sentries on the towers. Wilde had seen them twice on the railing, peering out above the pines. Earlier the wind had even brought fragments of their voices; one shouting for coffee, another calling, *"Haben sie zigaretten?"* The girl had hardly moved except to pull her raincoat tighter to her throat.

"Will he be waiting for us?" she asked.

"Who?"

"Your Harry Rose?"

"I don't think so."

"How do we know when it's time?" she asked.

"They'll shine a light from those trees."

"What if the sentries see it?"

"It's not supposed to matter."

There were long shadows across the last field, clotted darkness along the forest edge. He thought that if they started shooting he and Lise wouldn't have a chance. He touched the film inside his pocket.

"Where will we go when it's over?"

"Hamburg."

"But you live in Berlin. You said you own a house in Berlin."

"Yes—"

"Then why can't we—" and stopped, suddenly pointing to the far trees on the western ridge. "The light, there . . . there it is again . . . "

He stood up, took her hand. He had never seen the night come so quickly. He stumbled twice in the vines, falling against her. "I'm too old for you," he had told her. Her answer was to kiss him hard on the mouth.

They began moving faster. When they reached the level ground he could see the wire and wooden staves. When they slowed to cross a shallow gully he looked back and saw the outline of the tower. A motionless figure stood at the railing, a second seemed to be watching with binoculars.

The wind had risen again, sounding through the wire. Ahead

lay the last fifty yards of sodden grass. She took his hand, said his name. Then twenty feet from the wire, she stopped, arms out, reaching for him, hair blown across her eyes. *"You see? It was easy—"*

Then the shot, and for one moment nothing moved.

Until he saw her stiffen, arching back as the smile faded, shaking her head in disbelief. He called out her name. She did not hear him. Then staggering forward, he caught her as she fell.

He lifted her slowly, took a step forward, then another. She was lighter than he had imagined, much lighter. Or else he had suddenly grown very strong. There was blood, a lot of it in her hair, but he kept his eyes on the wire ahead. Once he thought he heard a man's voice calling his name from the ridge, a woman also calling from the trees.

Then the second shot, not nearly as surprising as the first.

The impact threw him back, but he would not let her go, and glaring blindly at the trees around him, he struggled to his feet.

Until a third shot dropped him again and he lay there, one arm across her shoulder, the other twisted beneath him.

He was only vaguely aware of the pain, receding with a deeper cold. There were odors of leaf mold and damp earth. What he thought had been voices must have been the wind.

But later there were definitely voices, Russian mixing with German. And he was conscious of them taking him away from her, lifting him up, but leaving her there.

They brought him to a house beside a river where the modulated voices now mingled with an occasional ringing telephone and a solitary typewriter.

There were also faint bells in the evening and once or twice the sound of rain. Beyond these sounds were the disjointed impressions of a concerned young man, presumably the doctor, and a few nurses.

152

For the most part he spent the time trying to work out what he would tell them once the interrogation began. He knew that there were areas he had to protect—the northern networks, the radio links—but he also knew that silence would be impossible. There had to be dialogue and when it was over they had to think he had told them everything. So it was simply a question of constructing a matrix of interlocking lies and truths. He would give them a little something, resist, then give them a little more, all the while trying to lead them away from vulnerable agents in the field.

As for Lise, he hardly knew what to think. There were moments when he was certain that she was still alive, then moments when he was just as certain that she was not. Once, half-asleep after an injection, he actually thought he saw her standing there over him. It was only a nurse, feeling for his pulse.

On what must have been the second or third night a man entered the room. It was dark, and he could only make out the vague outline of a rather slender figure in a uniform. The man did not approach the bed but remained sitting on a chair in the corner. After nearly twenty minutes of silence he lit a cigarette, and in the brief flare of a match Wilde saw—like the sudden recognition of a photograph that falls from between the pages of a book—Boris Tatlin.

"How are you feeling? Better? You are better?"

Wilde turned away.

"It appears that you were very lucky. There was no internal damage to organs, nor broken bones. Very lucky."

A woman appeared in the doorway. Tatlin spoke to her in Russian and she left. But now with the light from the passage through the half-open door, Wilde could see the man closely. His hair was still full and swept back, his skin still smooth.

He said, "Now you must tell me, how is the legendary Harry Rose? He is well, yes?"

Wilde shut his eyes for a moment. "He's fine so far as I know."

"Ah, good. And he still talks about me?"

153

"No."

"Not even a little?"

"No."

Tatlin lit another cigarette but did not offer one to Wilde. Those bells had begun to toll again.

"Do you know what they told me in Moscow," Tatlin said. "They told me that I should not personally involve myself with this case, because if I were to harm you, then the terrible Harry Rose would not rest until he made the last full measure of revenge. Those were the very words used—'last full measure of revenge.' "

Tatlin had gotten up from his chair and moved to the doorway. Wilde could no longer see him, but there was the shadow of his profile on the wall and the rising cigarette smoke.

"Now you can imagine my surprise at hearing all this—in Moscow, no less. 'Harry Rose has long arms,' they told me. 'You should be careful, Boris.' Later of course I thought of a number of things I could have said in reply, but at the time I was speechless."

When the bells had stopped tolling there were only those intermittent sounds of people below . . . a voice from the garden, a typewriter.

"Now I don't know why I'm telling you all this, except perhaps to impress upon you that I am not frightened of Harry Rose, Mr. Charles Wilde. I am not frightened of him at all. So you should understand that if necessary I am prepared to use whatever is necessary to obtain what I want. Pain, drugs, deprivation of food and sleep. Okay?"

Wilde shut his eyes. "I want to know what happened to the girl."

Tatlin nodded. "I thought you would ask about her. In fact, as I was drinking my coffee this morning I thought that this girl could be your weak point."

"Is she alive?"

"What a question."

154

"I want to see her."

"You want to see her? I suppose that can be arranged."

"When?"

"As soon as you're strong enough."

For a long time after Tatlin left, Wilde laid awake listening to the random sounds of the night staff below. Toward dawn he fell asleep, but only for an hour.

They came for him in the morning. There were two guards in uniforms Wilde had never seen before, and a severe-looking woman in a white coat. Wilde had asked where Tatlin was. The guards shook him off. Although he felt capable of walking, the woman insisted he ride in a wheelchair. There was a faintly ridiculous moment when the guards could not decide which one of them would actually push the chair.

They wheeled him down a corridor, then into a service elevator. The elevator descended to a basement. Here was another corridor, concrete and damp. At the end of the corridor was an iron door. The guard had difficulty with the lock, and when he made a joke of it the woman told him to shut up. He did.

They pushed him inside and shut the door. It was very dark and at first he saw nothing. He said her name but there was no response. As his eyes grew accustomed to the blackness he saw her on a ledge cut into the wall, quiet. There was also a bucket and a drain in the center of the floor.

He said her name again, but there was still no response. He wheeled the chair closer, reached out and pulled a coarse blanket off her shoulder. "Lise, it's me." He bent down to kiss her before realizing what he should have known from the start . . . the eyes fixed and wide, dried blood still matted in her hair.

He wasn't sure how long they kept him in there with her. There was a light bulb enclosed by wire mesh. It seemed to burn for hours, then only for a few minutes. In the beginning he had moved

155

her from the ledge to the corner of the room, covered her in the blanket so that he would not have to see.

After what must have been a day there was food pushed under the door, thin soup. They left the light on while he ate. In the hours of absolute blackness he passed the time either lying on the mattress or else rocking back and forth. After a while he supposed that he even came to accept that she was really dead. At least he stopped talking to her.

They came for him again in the morning—two guards and the woman. Again there was an argument about the wheelchair. Along the concrete passage the two guards talked about a local soccer tournament. The woman said nothing.

Boris Tatlin was waiting in an oval room. There was coffee, biscuits and cigarettes. Tatlin's uniform had recently been pressed, his shoes shined. He also smelled faintly of foreign cologne. Through the window lay a view of pines against a near-white sky. Beyond a firebreak was a radio tower and a nest of antennae.

"I suppose I should apologize for what happened," Tatlin said.

Wilde took a sip of coffee, said nothing.

"Anyway, the girl was already dead when we found her at the border. She wasn't murdered or abused, in case you were wondering."

Wilde broke off a piece of biscuit. It was dry, tasted of cellar rot.

"I suppose I should also apologize for not being altogether candid with you the other day. That was crude, I'm sorry."

Suddenly voices from the hallway, Russian mixing with German again.

"As a consolation, however, I've asked the staff to prepare a rather special meal for you. Duck. You like duck, don't you?"

Wilde had lit a cigarette, one of the unfiltered Eastern brands.

"What are you talking about?"

"A last supper, so to speak. You see, Mr. Wilde, you're going home tomorrow."

156

Wilde looked at him. The cigarette had made him slightly nauseous.

"Yes, it's all arranged. In fact I've only just come from meeting with a representative from your service. A Mr. George Clay."

"Clay?"

"That's correct, and you really must make a point of thanking him. He went to a good deal of trouble to get you back."

Wilde shut his eyes, but when he looked again nothing had changed. It was no better.

"Now I really can't go into all the details, but I suppose I can tell you that there is going to be an exchange, like the old days. You for three of our people, which should give you some idea just how determined your Mr. Clay was to have you back."

Through the remainder of that day and night Wilde was kept in a white room with a view of the river. Toward dusk a doctor and nurse entered the room to change his bandages and examine the stitches. Later there was dinner, but not duck, just some sort of boiled fish. Boris just couldn't help having his little jokes.

There was much made of Wilde's return to the West. At the center of the affair stood George Clay, the man of the moment, a hero.

According to every account Clay had been on his way from Geneva to London when word came through that Wilde had been wounded and apprehended at the border. Following this first report there had been three or four hours of confusion while dozens of contradictory reports filtered in from the outstations. Some claimed that Clay had immediately flown to Berlin; others that he had begun the preliminary stage of negotiation from London.

Records were also vague concerning the intermediate stages of the affair. Code named *Shuttle,* the first efforts to contact Boris Tatlin probably occurred some four hours into the second day. It was said that at first Tatlin had been smug, obnoxious. Yes, he would consider discussing the prisoner's release but not before he had bled the man dry. When Clay had sent a plea for moderation, Tatlin had responded with a multipage condemnation of Western aggression. Following a second plea, Tatlin said Wilde was the tool of American duplicity, and so forth.

Toward the end of the ninth hour there was a dramatic change. Apparently Clay had just finished contacting a Dresden intermediary when suddenly Tatlin sent word that he would be willing to talk in Berlin.

There were three eyewitnesses of that meeting between Clay and Tatlin, all very complimentary about Clay. The two men met at about midnight in an auditorium not far from the Leninplatz. At first Tatlin again appeared snide, irritable. During Clay's opening remarks he had been toying with a keychain. Clay had gotten up from his chair and slammed his fist on the table. Although he had made no direct threat, the implications were clear: Release Charlie Wilde or else Soviet missions in the Western sphere would find conditions extremely uncomfortable, with their networks stripped to the bone, couriers harrassed, auxiliary staff deported. After this, there had been a noticeable silence, then an equally noticeable change in Tatlin's behavior. Clay had asked what would be required to secure Wilde's release, and without hesitation Tatlin wrote down the names of three Soviet citizens in Western prisons.

As a kind of footnote to the incident the record contained an unusually fulsome letter from then-Agency Director George Bush, and a formal commendation from the chairman of the Foreign Intelligence Advisory Board. There was, of course, no mention of Rose through any of these proceedings, but there were mutterings that Rose, having nearly succeeded in getting his best friend killed, had spent the nine or ten hours drinking alone in his room.

As for the exchange, Wilde was escorted to the Berlin border north of Wedding. Two or three hours were wasted in a bunker beneath a steel bridge. The sentries played cards, and at one point even asked Wilde to join them. Just after eight o'clock in the evening Wilde accompanied four guards up an iron staircase to the last gates. There were all the usual elements: snipers along the embankment, soldiers beneath the arc lights, rising exhaust from waiting cars—everything in place, except Harry Rose.

After his return Wilde spent six idle days in Hamburg, in a house on the outskirts of the city. He spent the mornings with members of George Clay's regional team, while a more formal debriefing was held in the afternoons. In the evenings he played cards or read. There was a lot of whiskey, and no one seemed to care how much he drank.

On the third day Clay appeared, looking very chipper in a charcoal-gray pinstripe and red tie. After a drink on the patio they wandered out among the crabgrass behind an ornamental pond. From the first Wilde had had difficulty sleeping. He felt tired all the time.

"I guess I should thank you," he said, thinking of that last chat with Tatlin.

"Just doing my job, Charlie boy."

"I'm sure of that." Everyone had been reminding him for days . . . *George saved your life, you know* . . .

"Besides, it gave me a chance to actually meet that son of a bitch, not that I'd want to do it again."

"Yes, I can understand that."

But Clay had smiled at this. "Well, I think it was worth the trouble . . . so long as you remember who your friends are . . . . "

Through the course of those days Wilde asked about Rose twice, and both times was given noncommittal answers. Still, it was made obvious . . . if Rose had still been a force to be reckoned with, then his buddy Charlie Wilde would not have ended up in Hamburg.

But finally Harry Rose did show. It was a Tuesday, the first

159

warm day in weeks. They met in the garden by a drained swimming pool. A rain had left leaves on the flagstones, standing water in the drive. Rose wore an old herringbone jacket that Wilde hadn't seen in years.

"How are you, Charlie?"

Wilde shrugged, asked for a cigarette. It was nearly three o'clock and he still hadn't had a drink.

"I suppose they told you that you can go home now."

"Yeah. They told me."

"So I was wondering if you'd like to stay with me for a while."

"Sure. That would be fine."

"Unless of course you wanted—"

"Harry, I don't have the film. Tatlin took it."

Rose nodded, bit his lips. "I know."

"And the girl is dead, probably Panov too."

"I know."

"They're saying that it was all your fault, that you pushed too hard and when you finally screwed it up George Clay had to come in and bail us out."

Rose sat down on a rusting lawn chair.

"It's true," he finally said. "At least the part about Panov being dead. Tatlin arrested him in Belgrade. Then they put him against the wall."

"And the rest of it?"

Rose shrugged. "Clay got you out of there."

A silence. "Harry, I'm leaving."

"What?"

"I'm leaving. I'm getting out."

"What do you mean?"

"I mean I'm leaving the station."

They sat for a while, both facing the unused ends of this safehouse garden, Wilde smoking another cigarette, Rose toying with a pebble.

Until he finally said, "So where are you thinking of going?"

"Someplace warm."

"When?"

"Pretty soon, I guess."

"How soon?"

"I don't know."

"What are you going to do about the house?"

A van had entered the lane beyond the hedgerow. Two men in white overalls from George Clay's Hamburg team were apparently waiting on the lawn.

"Charlie, listen to me. They stabbed us in the back. They knew we were onto something and they hit us. I mean, how the hell do you think Tatlin was able to bust Panov in the first place?"

Not accusingly, Charlie gave him the accusation. "They say radio links were blown because you didn't take the time to secure them."

"Come on, Charlie. You don't really believe that . . . "

"I guess I don't . . . I don't know what to believe anymore, Harry. I just don't know."

"Well, then think about it. We were close, very close. We were about to pull the rug out from under that whole Team B. And then what happened? You get blown right out of the water. Clay comes out smelling like a hero. It was fixed, Charlie. An inside job."

"Harry, please. What's the point? We made a play and we lost. So let's forget it, huh?"

"Can't, Charlie. Can't forget it."

"Then you're going to be alone, Harry. You're going to be all alone."

A little farther along the path, the lane was deserted again.

"It's that girl, isn't it?" Rose said. "You got close to her, didn't you?"

"I suppose."

"Do you want to talk about it?"

"Not really. Why should I?"

"Well, then, I guess I'll see you around."

"Sure."

Three days later Wilde returned to Berlin. It was bitter cold. One of Harry's people met him at the airport, drove him home to that Tiergarten house, stayed for a drink and then left. Toward midnight Wilde reopened a wound reaching for a bottle of gin. He managed to stop the bleeding, however, with some sort of ointment they had given him in Hamburg. He didn't see a doctor.

Berlin stayed cold until the middle of April. Mostly Wilde found himself wasting evenings in movie houses or outlying bars. On the odd nights at home he did not answer the telephone.

As for Harry Rose's actual fall, Wilde said it was pretty bad. Among those finally charged with reviewing Harry's case were two young officers from the Frankfurt clerical staff and a twenty-five-year-old attorney temporarily attached to internal affairs.

In their findings it was noted that Rose had been guilty of repeatedly violating agency regulations, of years of gradual disassociation from the overall Langley effort, of a reckless history of operational excess and gross financial irregularities. Also noted was the drinking.

Conclusion included a firm recommendation that Rose be removed altogether from the clandestine sphere and placed in one of the auxiliary departments (where he could *quietly* put in the remaining years necessary to qualify for his pension). For answers to the larger question of the station's operative status, one had only to turn to George Clay's piece on the "Soviet aggrandizement strategic capability," in which he observed that "the time has come to project a less compromising image of American determination." Which translated meant, implied, among other things, deployment of the Pershing II's in Europe and final development of the neutron bomb.

Also from these days were memories that Wilde had never quite been able to accept, memories of an incongruously fragile Harry, almost visibly aging, purchasing small gifts for Anna and then leaving them in coffee shops, staring at passing strangers so that they stared back before looking away. Although the drinking was said to have stopped, he often seemed as vague and disconnected as any habitual drunk . . . halting, diffident, losing track of conversations, misplacing things like his keys.

And there was the business about his job. Given the findings of the review board, no one actually expected Rose to remain with the station, not in any auxiliary capacity, not Harry Rose. But less than a week after the findings had been published, there he was, waiting for an interview with a twenty-two-year-old personnel director named Kluge. Later that same afternoon Rose was seen dining among the junior staff in the station canteen.

Initially they put him in Treasury, but he constantly bungled the minor accounts. From Treasury they moved him to the Central Registry, where a clerical error was less likely to prove critical. He could not seem to master the filing system. Eventually, on his own request, he was transferred to archives, where at least his experience counted for something, which was to say that in dealing with the records he was essentially dealing with a history, much of which he had shaped himself. He seemed remarkably content.

And finally, there was one last conversation on a Friday afternoon, the first week in May. Wilde had gotten up early, booked a reservation on an evening flight to Washington. Harry Rose had spent the morning cataloguing letters from 1956. After meeting on the staircase adjacent to a boiler room, they wandered past the motor court to a little garden by a drainage ditch. An out-of-season frost had turned spring cold.

"I just wanted to say good-bye."

"Sure."

There were coffee stains on Harry's raincoat, a button missing on the sleeve.

"When are you leaving?"

"Tonight. I'm leaving tonight."

"Direct flight?"

"No. I . . . I think it stops in London."

"Well, London should be nice this time of year . . . unless of course it rains." Harry tried to smile.

"So how do you like the archives?" Charlie said, scratching for conversation.

"Restful."

"Not too tedious?"

"Not at all."

"Oh, well, that's good," and then into the trailing silence . . . "Harry, what are you doing?"

"I don't know what you're talking about, Charlie."

"Yes, you do. You damn well do . . . "

Then, after shaking hands at the station gates, Wilde backed off slowly, fumbling for his car keys, while Rose just stood there, as always with a cheap cigar.

From London Wilde caught an evening flight that brought him to Langley on a Monday afternoon. Lyle Severson met him in a highway bar, six miles south of the Fairfax County line. Of course they talked about Harry Rose.

During the last week at Langley, Wilde tended to see himself as suspended between two lives. On Tuesday he bought an overcoat, a sweater and a pair of shoes. On Wednesday he dined with a casual friend in Georgetown, saw a movie at a local theater, spent an hour browsing in a bookstore.

And when he was done with the polygraphs, done with debriefing, done with a pointless conversation with some woman from Personnel . . . then he hardly knew what to do. There had been an offer from a firm in Pennsylvania: director of industrial security, twenty-seven thousand a year. Also from a Michigan surveillance agency: nineteen plus five, plus commissions. As for the eventual house on the Florida coast, he later told others that he had always thought about living by the ocean. Then, too, the price had been right.

So he went to Florida, what was left of him. In the beginning he passed the time remodeling a room overlooking the bay. Then he tried painting until the basement filled up with unfinished canvases. July and August were almost unbearable with nights that brought no relief from the heat. But by mid-October he was determined to stay. While in his heart still living with Harry in Berlin, and suspicious about what he was up to in the archives, he was determined to stay in Florida.

PART TWO
THE SEARCH

CHAPTER
SEVEN

ALTHOUGH IT HAD been more than a week since Charlie Wilde and Alex Petty had entered Berlin, it was not until the first Tuesday in November that a disciplined search began. Petty had gotten up early after another exhausting night. Charlie Wilde had not slept at all. The newspapers carried photographs of civil unrest near the north Rhineland missile cities.

Petty had gotten to the station at eleven o'clock. The corridors were deserted. By noon he had drawn the last notes: Rose to Frankfurt concerning the sale of property in Charlottenburg; a dozen letters of condolence on the death of his wife. There was a station memo attesting to the fact that "the woman's death was natural." After eight months of illness she had apparently succumbed to cancer. Also fragments of an unfinished letter—the signature and addressee were torn off—describing Harry as a solitary figure with a sort of hesitant charm . . . one could, it said, find him submerged among the files, where he seemed content so long as people left him alone.

Wilde spent a morning leafing through peripheral entries, finding two passing references to Harry Rose. Apparently he'd taken three weeks' vacation in March of 1980, then lost another week in May with the flu. Big deal. Harry, where the *hell* are you? From the third floor Wilde descended to the officer's lounge, where the consequence of another security probe had still not been cleared—doors off hinges, electrical tape on the windowsills, rows of dismantled telephones.

Toward noon Wilde caught a glimpse of Petty, obviously waiting for him by a chain link fence. Ten minutes later they had moved past the motor court and into those trees that Rose had planted years ago.

They faced each other, after eight more or less fruitless days. Wilde was in a jacket with a torn lapel, Petty in a dark Italian blend that needed pressing badly.

"I think it's time we talked," Petty said.

Wilde nodded.

"About Rose . . . I was wrong."

"So?"

"So I think we should work together now."

"Under what arrangement?"

Petty shook his head. "It doesn't matter to me."

"What about Clay?"

"Clay isn't here, is he?"

The two men found a tavern north of Wilmersdorf—essentially neutral ground. Wilde ordered white sausage and diced cucumber. Petty mostly just drank. But as if in recognition of this new beginning, they split the bill down the middle.

What had finally become Harry's office was hardly more than an alcove off the main passage. The walls were high, arched like a brick oven. The desk was cheap laminate riddled with cigarette burns. Thirty feet past the boiler room lay the actual archive

170

shelves: plywood, reinforced with black steel joints.

Station files were arranged chronologically with a cross-index for main subject titles. Once, years ago, there had been an effort to introduce a retrieval system based upon a color scheme—"active" operations in red, "pending" in yellow, "extinct" in blue. It never happened.

The archive director was a thin, sallow man named Robert Joyce. He wore rimless spectacles and rough tweeds, giving him a desired faintly academic look. His eyes were very blue, hair entirely white. Petty had found him on the second floor, but when it had become clear that they were going to discuss Harry Rose they immediately went to the basement.

"You were his nominal senior, is that right?" Petty said.

Joyce shrugged. "Nominal, yes. Definitely nominal."

"What's that supposed to mean?"

"Well let me put it like this . . . Harry always kept to himself."

"What did he do?"

"Oh, it varied. For a while we had him on one of the pilot programs, then he did a lot of general research for the Special Branch—"

"What was his attitude like?"

"How do you mean?"

"Well, was he happy?"

Joyce smiled. "I like to think so, yes. Naturally at first he may have had a little adjustment problem, but I think that in time he was bitten by the bug."

"What bug?"

"The files. They're seductive, you know. Extraordinarily seductive. Suck you right in if you're not careful."

They had left the alcove, moving slowly past reading tables that no one used because the light was so poor. There were musty odors . . . and possibly the lingering smell of cigar smoke.

"It's all here," Joyce said. "Early occupation, industrial disar-

171

mament, Russian trouble and the Allied counter-punch—all Harry's world."

"Must have been a real help, huh?"

"Oh, definitely. You see, Harry knew it cold. He actually lived it, after all."

"And didn't get tired of living it again?"

"I don't think so."

They had come to a particularly dark recess beneath another burnt-out light bulb. Petty had taken out a cigarette, but Joyce had told him not to smoke.

"I suppose in one sense you could say that they're alive. They think."

Petty looked at him. "Huh?"

"The files. In a sense they can talk to you, tell you things about this city that you never knew."

"And they talked to Rose, is that it?"

"Yes."

"About what?"

Joyce smiled. "You've got to understand something. In many ways Harry Rose *was* the Cold War. I mean, his life—that *was* the Cold War. Most of us lived a part of it, a little here, a little there. Harry lived it all. So these files must have been very special to him. I mean, imagine it, his whole life right here in this room. Who knows what went through his mind."

"But you never talked to him about it, did you?"

"No."

There were rows of unvarnished sorting shelves along a far wall, trays of requisition slips, a black ledger suspended by a chain.

"What's the procedure?" Petty asked.

"Mmm?"

"Withdrawing files for an extended project."

"Oh. Well, first you record the date and registry number of withdrawal in the master ledger, then pull the call slip and log it with the duty officer."

172

"And what if you wanted to take something *out* of the area?"

"Same procedure, but only third-floor personnel can take material beyond those doors."

"And Rose, of course, wasn't exactly third floor, right?"

"No."

"But there was no limitation to his access so long as he kept the stuff here, right?"

"Yes, that's right."

"So he had the run of the place. Kept his own hours, read anything he wanted to read, answered to no one . . . "

There were footsteps in the corridor above, a hammer tapping on a water pipe. Years ago there had even been rats, but Harry had put an end to them too.

"You never actually met him, did you?" Joyce said.

"No, never met him."

"Then you'll have to believe me when I tell you that no one ever told him what to do. Not me, not even George Clay. No one."

"Which means what? He was looking for something down here?"

"Maybe, but you've got to understand that these files don't just yell it out. They sort of whisper it."

"And just what the fuck were they whispering to Rose?"

Joyce shook his head. "I don't know. Little things, maybe. Little secrets about the lies, the half lies, the conversations that no one knows about."

"And you let him do it, huh? You let him come down here night after night. Anything he wanted, anything at all."

Joyce's voice rose. "Well, it's his story, isn't it? These files, what do you think they talk about? They're about Harry Rose." Then more softly, "Besides, it wasn't as if he was exceeding his jurisdiction. He was part of Research. He had the right to look."

Back along the first-floor corridor, Petty finally found a telephone in another vacant office. Here too there were signs of prowling security teams . . . dangling light fixtures, a pockmarked wall

173

where someone had been probing for microphones.

Petty left the station at a quarter to six in the evening. Wilde was waiting in an empty cafe off the Brandenburger Tor.

Petty said, "As far as I can tell he was doing *something* down there, I'm not sure what."

"You mean in addition to his authorized assignments?"

"In addition."

"Did you ask about the withdrawal procedure?"

Petty nodded. "If Rose pulled a file for more than a day at a time then there should be a record of it—with the registry number."

"In the duty officer's log?"

"No, that's changed since your day. Now they mark it in the master ledger."

A waiter appeared. Petty asked for beer. Wilde said that he only wanted coffee, then changed his mind.

"Well, I suppose we should begin where *he* began," Wilde said. "We can pull material on a chronological basis and then see if we can't reconstruct that last period . . . "

As they were leaving, counting out change for the table, Wilde said, "I suppose I should tell you that Harry was always good at covering himself, making things appear different than what they were."

"So?"

"So, bear it in mind."

They began methodically, both very conscious of a second beginning, also of each other. At the end of every hour they walked out of the archives to the stairwell and smoked. Then too there was coffee in the lounge. Toward midnight of the first night they were briefly interrupted by a roving sentry, and again there were voices from the ventilation shaft. They rarely spoke.

As predicted, at first the files talked only of Rose. In early

174

October he'd been helping to eliminate duplicate material from Frankfurt. He usually did not appear before ten o'clock in the morning and he was slow, painfully slow. There had been files pulled on a Tuesday, then pulled again on Friday, as if a subsequent check had revealed that his work had been less than acceptable. Further, there were suggestions that Harry had not been able to grasp the clerical procedure. First-floor supervisors, however, remained patient, perhaps even patronizing, as if consciously humoring a great man at the end of his career.

In November and December there had been a reprimand from a second-floor cipher clerk who found Harry's work poor, plus complaints about Harry's handwriting. Still, no one had the heart to fire him—not Harry Rose.

So he continued to more or less plod along. By March of 1978 he had become one of three research analysts in a study of local escape routes—surely Harry's province. But if he'd actually experienced those years in question, he still did not seem quite able to cope with the routine of retrospective study. Again and again the ledger showed that files he'd drawn in the morning had been passed to other capable hands in the later afternoon.

Then, gradually, almost imperceptibly, the pattern began to change . . . It had been late May, and Rose had ostensibly worked on a secondary project to index a backlog of outstation material. Even a superficial index would have required a certain amount of research, but according to the ledger Rose had drawn no less than three full volumes of material on unrelated subjects. Also he no longer appeared to be the fumbling incompetent of the previous months. Individual files were drawn every three or four hours, an entire sequence in less than a day.

A larger pattern seemed obvious, but another meaning remained obscure. And Wilde remembered his parting words to Harry about what was he up to in those files . . . By two A.M. Wilde found himself once more leafing through requisition slips and project notes, while Petty continued to scan miscellaneous

175

volumes from 1979. After another hour they wandered back out to the stairwell, then past a fire door to a landing near the motor court.

"We should get some sleep," Wilde said. "I'm beat."

Petty agreed.

"Listen," Wilde said, "you have to understand . . . we're starting where *he* started, so naturally things are going to appear a little confusing—"

"Why did you leave?"

"Huh?"

"I want to know why you left him?"

The question concluded the first night. It got no real answer from Wilde. How could it?

When Petty got to the station the next day he found Wilde by the radiator amid a litter of files. There were sandwiches on a reading table, potato chips and coffee. And gin in a paper bag. Old habits died hard for an old soldier like Charlie Wilde.

Again they worked independently—Wilde from the broader view of the project notes, Petty submerging into the files. Toward three P.M. Guy Campbell appeared briefly on the staircase above. This time, it seemed he had nothing to say. Good.

From August 1978 through November, Rose appeared to have been wholly content with another strictly legitimate effort to catalogue extinct operational summaries. Then suddenly from a week in early December there were twenty-nine pages on George Clay. The material had been drawn quietly, discreetly, all under cover of a mindless project involving East German electrical output.

It was nearly six o'clock when Petty turned to the first volume; six o'clock, the restless hour with sounds of departing vans in the motor court, junior clerks descending from above. George Clay, all over again.

The first documents Rose had drawn concerned Clay's steady

growth as a figure of consequence among those who believed in the "military solution." Next Rose had drawn letters: Clay to the Frankfurt Command concerning Soviet malfeasance in Poland; Clay to all outstation staff warning of Soviet penetration in Bonn. Rose had even spent an afternoon with a security officer's nine-page clearance report regarding George Clay's latest girl—Kristian Haas.

"Maybe you should take a look at this," Petty said. There was also a photograph tucked into the manila folder . . . Kristian Haas smiling from a doorway.

"I don't see the significance," Wilde said, and laid the pages aside, including the photograph.

"Well, don't you think it's interesting that Rose was looking at this stuff?"

Wilde shrugged. "Interesting maybe, important no."

"Why not?"

"Because there were a *lot* of things he was looking at, and if we start focusing on one we'll be lost. Harry had lots of moves, all going on at the same time."

"Well I think it's important," Petty said, and tossed the folder on a sorting shelf while slipping the photograph into his coat pocket.

Parting on the staircase half an hour later, Petty said that he wouldn't be back until the next day. Wilde was about to ask why when Guy Campbell began shouting from the coding room, asking what fool had left the door unlocked.

Petty reached the Kurfürstendamm a few minutes before midnight. The side streets were filled with wandering youths. Earlier he had found a jewelry shop, but nothing worth anything for less than two hundred marks. He had settled for perfume, a brand that the clerk recommended.

The Last Exit: tonight the crowd seemed less subdued. The

doorman kept searching for weapons. Along a backstage corridor two women in leotards were passing a joint and a bottle of beer. A third leaned against the dressing room door. Her hair had been streaked faint orange, a coiled snake was tattooed on her waist.

"I'm looking for Kristian Haas," he told her. *Wo ist Kristian Haas?"*

She frowned, ran her fingers along the doorframe. "You are a friend?" Then smiling, "Or admirer?"

"A friend of a friend."

He looked menacing. "Ah, in that case Kristian Haas is here," and she moved off.

The dressing room walls were red, fixtures black. There were two teenage boys on a ruined couch in the corner, a girl in black dozing on the floor. But through a half-open door, by her mirror —Kristian Haas again.

Tonight she wore blue with a lavender scarf and a single strand of pearls. There was a cigarette burning on a porcelain dish, champagne in a bucket of melting ice, an electric guitar. When he entered she slowly turned to him. Her eyes were gray, or gray-green, very clear.

"You have come to see me?" As if men never came to see her.

"I've been sent," he said, fumbling for the perfume. "That is, I'm supposed to give you this." If the scent was bad, at least the box had been attractively wrapped. "It's from George."

"Ah, how nice," and immediately laid it aside.

"I . . . work for him."

Her smile was wry. "An employee?"

"Sort of . . . I'm here on business so—"

"So he has asked you to spy on me?"

He laughed. "No, not exactly."

"Well, you may sit here with me anyway," and she reached for a plastic cup. "See, I even have champagne—for you with blessings from George."

178

He lit a cigarette. Yes, she was definitely a beautiful girl . . . and knew it, while pretending not to.

"So how is George?"

"Fine, he's just fine."

"He is still working hard fighting the Communists?"

"Oh, yeah."

"Then you must give him my love when you see him again," and she turned back to her mirror and the glass of champagne.

There was music from the corridor, a saxophone, a boy's voice . . .

Oh, baby, what's that sound in the street?
Doesn't this city ever sleep?

"For how long are you in Berlin?" she asked.

"A few more weeks maybe."

"Are you intending to see me perform?"

"Yes, sure, I'd like that."

Hold me baby,
Hold me close tonight.

"Then you must come Saturday. Saturday is the best show."

"Well, then I'll definitely try to make it."

"And perhaps you may even take me to dinner."

Very casually, almost threw the line away. It was up to him to grab it or not.

She took his hand when he got up to leave, possibly holding on an extra beat, watching him with those extraordinary eyes.

Then suddenly, "Tell me something. Are you also a spy?" The music had died, leaving him with nothing but silence, until she added, "Because I don't think you look like a spy."

"No? Then what do I look like?"

She thought a moment, one finger brushing her lips. "I think

179

maybe you are just a young man, a modern young man . . . oh, I don't know . . . cool . . . okay?"

"Sure, okay . . . " and he slid out the door. Bull's-eye.

There were still restless crowds on the street, a line of tourists waiting for a show, a few unescorted women apparently not interested in a modern young man. He moved quickly for the first block, then slowed, trying to recall something she had said. Along another street he found a quiet bar but didn't like the clientele . . . not modern enough?

Still farther there were soldiers milling on the doorstep of a brothel. Years ago George Clay had offered to buy Petty a woman in Detroit but he'd declined. He was exhausted, he'd said. Truth was, he had never wanted one of George's whores. So instead they spent the evening in a bar called the Rat Hole discussing Petty's career. After two or three drinks Clay began promising things he had no intention of delivering, while Petty just listened, not caring much one way or another . . . he'd slipped into the secret world mostly by accident and had lost sight of any particular future beyond the immediate.

He just kept walking along, first in Asia, now Berlin. Half a mile past the Grosse Stern he paused to browse in front of a window display, then paused again to light a cigarette . . . with the impression of someone moving behind.

There were two of them . . . a boy in a surplus military coat and blue jeans, a girl on his arm in black pants and sweater.

He hesitated, this time pretending to admire a passing Mercedes but actually waiting for an approaching bus that would screen him, at least for a moment. Then he moved, slipping between a row of parked cars. He heard the whine of brakes and a trailing horn as he sprinted through the oncoming traffic and into a crowd emerging from a theater. In the darkness of an alley there was nothing, no one.

He waited, pressed against the bricks, listening. There were vegetable husks by the entrance of a warehouse, garbage strewn across a loading ramp. A woman's voice broke from a window above, either laughing or crying. A light appeared on a fire escape.

The night had its own madness after that, with possibilities of people trailing him everywhere. Back along the Grosse Stern he counted seven potential watchers, three complete teams with a roving van. Farther west there may have been another team . . . two boys passing a cigarette on the balcony of an apartment block, a woman with a dog calling from a phone booth. There were also less obvious suggestions . . . shadows against the brickwork, a lingering gaze of a hotel clerk.

It was nearly three in the morning before he finally slept. And he dreamt of Harry Rose, George Clay and George Clay's girl, all mixed up in a weird composite.

Wilde also spent a restless night, with suggestions of things just a little out of his sight. He had returned to the archives at a quarter to nine, withdrawn another sixty-five pages by ten. There were only passing references to Rose: an October brief acknowledging his contribution to a report on internal security, a memo nothing his involvement with a certain Project Glass, but beneath the seemingly innocent routine of subordinate research there remained Harry's building, holding interest in Clay.

There were two images of George Clay in the records. First, the quintessential Cold Warrior, priding himself on technical expertise and an understanding of "hard reality"—the nuclear option. Playing this role to the hilt he successively became one of the leading advocates of the Minuteman system, the B-1 bomber and the Pershing II. He was not, however, particularly happy about Vietnam, but only because he felt that the confrontation was too indirect . . . presumably meaning that if one wanted to fight the Russians, then why not fight them in Europe?

Next there was a free-wheeling George Clay, an aggressive bachelor, hard drinker. Wilde remembered him best this way from the summer of '67. They had met by chance in California, where Wilde had spent four days helping to resettle a founding member of the Alternate Network. No one quite knew what George had been doing there, but on the afternoon before departure they had had a drink together at some house in the Hollywood hills.

The entire affair had been typically Clay with whiskey sours on a terrace, a silver Corvette in the drive, a mostly naked girl by the swimming pool.

"What's her name?" Wilde had asked for lack of anything better to say.

Clay had grinned. "Kim. Or is it Jan?"

"This is her house?"

Still grinning. "Who knows?"

Between them on the bricks lay an open briefcase filled with papers: a threat analysis on Soviet sea-launched weapons and a trade-off study on the Minuteman III.

"Went to this party last night," Clay began. "Big Hollywood bash. All the beautiful people. Chuck Heston, Bob Hope, Ann-Margret—and there I was, a nobody, right? Except that sitting here in this briefcase was more power than all those big shots ever imagined. Now, do you want to stay for dinner, or not?"

Eight months later an even more aggressive Clay actually met with the president to discuss what he called "visible power projection." As things turned out, it was not so much the visible power that Clay should have been concerned with, but the invisible power, the sort that Rose had mastered years ago . . . .

It was ten minutes to midnight when Wilde first caught sight of what he supposed he had been looking for from the start. He had just withdrawn another volume of material from 1977. At that time Harry had apparently been dividing his days between a number of meaningless assignments when suddenly out of nowhere came something called "Metropolis." Project Metropolis.

The early references were vague. Supposedly the project had begun when Frankfurt had asked Berlin to conduct a casual examination of Soviet influence among the East German services. At the end of two or three weeks a number of otherwise idle personnel had been enlisted to help with the preliminary steps, among them Harry Rose. But what immediately caught Wilde's attention was Harry's *standing* in the project. Not only had he served as research coordinator, he'd also been given license to move beyond the gates. Which was to say that whether out of stupidity or negligence, they had left Harry loose on the field again . . .

Fifteen minutes to one and Wilde had left the archives for a second-floor office adjacent to Operations. The night clerk was an obedient boy named Roger Crowe. Wilde had never met him before but he knew the type.

"It's about something called Metropolis," Wilde said. "Ring a bell? The operational code would have been ten-sixty. Project Metropolis."

The boy had brought coffee, weak, tasting of an unwashed pot. There were reams of blank paper in the wastebasket, telephone directories on the desk. Beyond the glass partition lay rows of vacant desks and a solitary woman staring at the keyboard of her typewriter.

"Apparently the project went operational about three years ago," Wilde continued. "There's an original charter, but the extended record seems to be missing, so if you don't mind I'd like you to pull the proposal."

"The proposal, sir?"

"If you'd be so kind."

The boy left, then returned with a single folder, green and very slim. He put it on the desk, but beyond Wilde's reach. "Uh, sir, this is labeled 'top secret' so—"

"So you can read it to me, but I can't actually handle it."

"I know it sounds silly."

He told the boy, "Take a look and see if you can't find some sort of staff roster."

183

Crowe began leafing through the folder. A moment later he said, "Well, sir, there is a kind of flow chart."

"Tell me, is there a spot for Harry Rose?"

"Yes, sir. Mr. Rose seems to have been in charge of research."

"Who else was in that department?"

"Mr. Rose is the only one listed."

"What about the overall director?"

"No, sir. I'm afraid that's not listed."

"Internal coordination?"

"The post is mentioned, but there don't seem to be any names."

"What about field director?"

"Uh, that would have been Stanley Kline."

"Kline?"

"Yes, sir."

"He's still around?"

"Yes, sir. Mr. Kline runs the watch teams."

Wilde had moved to the glass partition. At the end of an adjoining room a young man in seersucker now stood by the solitary typist.

"Are there any specific instructions about how the incoming product was to have been handled?"

"Specific instructions? No, sir. I don't see anything."

"Who would have been responsible for directing the field research?"

"Well, sir, it's kind of hard to tell from this, but it looks like it would have been Mr. Rose."

"Rose? Isn't that a little unusual?"

"I wouldn't know, sir."

Before returning to archives Wilde spent another twenty minutes drifting along one of the far northern corridors—once Harry's private preserve, now also under renovation. Up a narrow flight of steps lay an anteroom where Rose had occasionally spent evenings alone. Then too there was that balcony where Rose had

184

often been seen brooding toward the end. The end of his stay, before he disappeared.

In the morning, after wasting half an hour over coffee and an egg, Petty caught a crosstown bus to a tavern not far from the botanical gardens. There he found Wilde with brandy and a magazine. Apparently the proprietor had been a friend from the early days.

"It's called Metropolis," Wilde began. "Project Metropolis. Supposedly the preliminary budget came from Frankfurt, but the record is very thin. Some of the material seems to have been lost."

Petty smiled, chewing on the end of a matchstick. "Do you mean lost as in misplaced, or lost as in—"

"I mean shredded. Intentionally shredded."

"And Rose?"

"According to the original proposal he was in charge of research, but as far as I can tell he was doing a lot more than research."

"What was the actual target?"

"I'm not sure."

"Was Clay an issue?"

"Maybe."

"How about Boris Tatlin?"

"I don't know."

"I suppose I could give you the theory," Wilde said. "It goes like this . . . Having exhausted his immediate resources Harry decided that he had to move out into the field, only he had no real authority to do this. So he invented one—Metropolis."

Petty tossed away the matchstick, picked up another. "Actually invented it?"

"Or took it over. Point is, never mind the original proposal, there was a secrecy clause that said that Metropolis staff was to be given access to all so-called relevant resources. These resources were to be used to certify, corroborate, but since the product was

185

classified no one outside the Metropolis team was in a position to question whether or not the access clause was being abused. Which is to say that once the third floor bought the original lie they weren't in a position to stop the ones that followed."

Petty said, "What about the money?"

"Oh, he got that through the same tactic. Funding requests were filed when Treasury was swamped with paperwork, and the higher authority was gagged by the secrecy clause."

"How far was he able to take it?"

Wilde shook his head. "Hard to say, but you've got to understand that Harry was always very good at this sort of thing. Bureaucratic manipulation, running operations between the seams of the larger structure. Sometimes he was even able to turn the lines back on themselves so that he had one department spying on another."

"How many agents were involved?"

"Maybe a dozen."

"All working for him?"

"Not necessarily, but again, Harry was very good at getting people to do things for him while they thought they were doing something else."

"Did you get any names we can start with?"

"Maybe. Kline. Stanley Kline. Harry taught him everything he knows."

They left the tavern through a service entrance off the kitchen. "Tell me something," Petty said. "Is it possible that Rose still has a functioning organization? I don't mean Metropolis. I mean . . . a whole separate network."

Wilde was suddenly cautious . . . protective. "I don't know. Why?"

"Little things. A few people last night. Maybe something this morning."

Wilde glanced up at the rooftops around them, the blank windows of apartments. "Well, we mustn't jump to conclusions."

186

"Sure, but is it possible? Is it possible that Rose still has people working for him in this city?"

"I suppose it's possible . . . "

"How many people?"

"How the hell should I know?"

"Well, take a guess. Ten? Twenty? A hundred?"

Charlie Wilde looked at him. "Listen, Petty, that's all just a myth, okay? Like a ghost story. You hear that kind of stuff in Kreuzberg . . . 'Harry Rose still holds the power,' they'll say. 'He never really fell . . . ' Well, I saw him fall. Do you understand? I saw him fall, and there aren't any people left."

Did he really believe that?

Like others from the fringe of Harry's world, Stanley Kline had never known Charlie Wilde very well. They had met in the winter of 1965 when Kline had entered Berlin from Belgrade after four miserable years under the cover of a trading concern. After another five years of servicing Harry's Ratify Network, Kline had been put in charge of the watch teams from Kreuzberg to Neukolln. Then briefly in spring 1977, he had even spent a month in Langley, but failed to make the administrative grade so they sent him back to run the watch teams out of Templehoff.

He was a dark, intense man, one of those wary figures one so often found among outstation people. After an afternoon telephone call Wilde met him in the early evening two hundred yards from the Wall. Here lay blocks of used-clothing stores, gray tenements and cramped cafes. From a distance Wilde saw the man as he remembered him best . . . barely more than a shadow in the doorway of a cheap hotel. At the top of a staircase was a furnished room with no view.

It was cold. Wilde did not take his coat off. Kline sat in a chair by the window. He wore a blue, faintly iridescent suit, suede boots and a gold bracelet. His hair was long, swept back. He had obvi-

187

ously taken a lot of trouble to coordinate the color of his tie with his shirt. A sore sight.

Their first moments were awkward. There was vodka, but neither had touched it, cigarettes but no ashtray. Before entering the room they had not even spoken, and then Kline had said only, "So you're back, huh?"

"It's about Harry," Wilde replied.

"Yeah? I thought you came here for the sights."

"They're not out to hang him, Stanley. Not my people. They want to find him—"

"They? Who is this they, Charlie? Tell me who is this they."

"Lyle Severson's group."

"So now Lyle Severson is worried about Harry, huh?"

"Stanley, it's not a hanging party—"

"No? Then explain to me please who is this other character you've been seen with. Good-looking boy? Slender? A wolf? Who is he, please?"

"His name is Petty."

"And George Clay sent him, correct?"

"Yes."

"Then this is in very bad taste, Charlie, very bad taste. I say shame on you. Shame on you for hunting with that pack. And Harry of all people. Shame on you."

Wilde had moved to the window. Kline had poured the first drink. There were Turkish children in the street below, factory smoke above the rooftops.

"When did you last see him, Stanley?"

Kline shrugged. "Months ago."

"How many months?"

"I don't know."

"Three?"

"Maybe. Look, Charlie, I call on him once or twice. You know, for old times' sake."

"Where?"

188

"I don't know. A club."

"What club?"

"Just some club. A kid's club with rock singers."

"The Last Exit?"

"Yeah, maybe the Last Exit."

"And what did you talk about?"

Kline poured a second glass and laid it on the window sill next to Wilde's hand. Wilde still didn't touch it. "What did you talk about, Stanley?"

"Old times. We talked about old times."

"Nothing else? Nothing about something called Project Metropolis?"

Kline had returned to the table and the vodka. Wilde stayed at the window.

"Metropolis," Wilde repeated. "Supposedly you were the field director. Harry was the research coordinator. There may have been a few others involved, I'm not sure who they are."

"So that's why you came here, Charlie? You want me to give you names?"

"No, Stan, I don't want names. Not yet."

"Then what do you want? You want to talk about Metropolis? Okay, I talk about Metropolis. One of fifty projects for the year. No big deal. I get some orders to help run some spies, okay? That's my business, so I do it. No big deal."

"And what did the project deal with?"

"Russians. What else?"

"What Russians specifically?"

Kline smiled. "Hoods. First Directorate hoods."

"Like Boris Tatlin?"

"Sure, like Boris Tatlin."

"And as field director what were your duties?"

"You know, Charlie, this is starting to get crude, okay? It's all getting crude."

"What were your duties, Stan?"

189

"I helped maintain the radio links, supplied the couriers, maybe a little underhand support. Usual stuff."

"So then you never actually saw the product?"

"Of course not."

"Never were told the targets?"

"Hey, Charlie, what do you think? I'm an errand boy, okay? Just an errand boy. You know that."

Wilde had drifted to the far wall, and a crude portrait of John Kennedy. "Who gave you your orders, Stan?"

"Huh?"

"You were told to help service some networks. Well, who gave you the order?"

Kline smiled again, shook his head. "Christ, is that all you want? It was Clay. It was George Clay."

Watching him closely . . . "No, Stan. I don't think it was Clay. He may have signed the order, but I don't think he had anything to do with Metropolis once it became operational."

"Okay, so maybe it was Campbell. Yeah, it was Guy Campbell."

"No, Stan, it wasn't Campbell either."

A wail from a distant ambulance. Kline had moved to a blackened fireplace, Wilde still watching him.

"Shall I tell you my theory?" Wilde said. "I think you got your orders from the bottom, not from the top."

"What are you talking about, Charlie? What is this?"

"In fact I think the whole project was run from the bottom . . . from archives."

Kline turned to face the mantle, pressed his hands against the wall. "Okay, Charlie. So maybe Harry bends a few rules. This is a crime? After all the years he puts in, this is a big crime?"

"How did he run it, Stan? How did Harry run Metropolis?"

Kline shook his head. "Charlie . . . please. What are you doing here? This is Harry Rose we are talking about. Harry Rose."

190

Wilde kept looking at him. "How, Stan? How did Harry run Metropolis?"

Kline poured another drink. "Look, Charlie, I don't know very much. I only know that it was pretty big, okay? Lots of people involved, lots of little details—lots of shadows too, okay?"

"Where were the final records kept?"

"Third-floor vaults. Where else?"

"How did Harry get hold of them?"

"How should I know?"

"Were there others involved?"

"Maybe."

"Any idea who they might be?"

"Charlie, this is still Harry we're talking about, remember?"

He knew that. But he also knew he had to dig, because sure as hell Petty would, or some other agent of George Clay. And they hadn't been Harry's old friend . . . He had better be there at the end . . .

Kline went with Wilde as far as the staircase. "You shouldn't have come back," Kline said. "You should have stayed in Florida."

"Did he leave a trail, Stan? Is there a trail in the records?"

Kline peered out past a crumbling wall. "Listen to me, Charlie. Metropolis is gone. You'll never find it. Give it up. Go home. Go home to Florida and forget these crazy things. You understand? Go home . . . "

Half a mile farther west Wilde found Petty in a student cafe with a newspaper, beer and a tuna fish sandwich. It was nearly six o'clock, which meant that they still had an hour to kill if they hoped to avoid the evening crowds.

They moved into archives for five unbroken hours. They began with the lists of retired personnel, the Book of the Dead. Wilde

191

withdrew another thirteen loose-leaf folders from the spring of 1980.

There were two contradictory portraits of Rose etched in those files. By late 1979 he was still officially little more than a clerk. He continued to keep to himself. Again notes that his health had not been good, which may have accounted for another absent week in October. Then too he was said to have been afraid that an arbitrary third-floor decision would leave him jobless and so in an effort to prove his worth, he tended to work very long hours.

From a different angle a different protrait: Rose once more as the spider at the center of his web. Although Metropolis had never been granted an operational budget somehow Harry had managed to siphon funds from the main Treasury accounts. Apparently the money had been routed by courier on night flights out of Hamburg, while Technical Services reported the theft of three voice-activated recorders.

And there were some things that even Wilde could not decipher. While probing through the expenditures from late January suddenly there was Metropolis again, stalking through the station corridors, testing the locks on the third-floor vaults . . . "We are concerned about the safety of our Eastern networks," Rose had written, except there hadn't been a danger to the Eastern networks, only to those undisclosed Western networks that had been quietly aimed at the heart of Langley Center . . .

First Petty had asked questions about the distribution of Metropolis' product, then toward midnight after Wilde had finished with the last correspondence they wandered out to one of the radio shacks where conversation was supposed to have been more secure. It was cold, but only Wilde seemed to feel it. Florida had thinned his blood. Petty did not turn on the light, and there was a view from the door of another blackened passage.

"I've found a name," Petty said.

Wilde looked at him.

"Milosz, Adam Milosz. Seems he was in charge of the branch

192

lines. Maybe he was one of Rose's people, from the old days."

A sentry appeared on the landing, a flashlight playing briefly on the walls.

"Do you know him?"

Wilde nodded. "Yes, I know him."

"Will you talk to him?"

Wilde shrugged. "I guess . . . tomorrow."

"Do you want me to watch your back?"

"No, I don't think that will be necessary."

"Well, maybe I'll watch it anyway."

As a kind of epilogue to the night, Wilde spent still another hour trying to reconstruct Harry's movements from the autumn of 1980 through the early winter of 1981. Trying . . .

Milosz. One evening in the spring of 1966 Wilde had returned from a week abroad to find Harry Rose in his library with a grubby little man in a sailor's coat.

"Charlie, I'd like you to welcome a new member of the team. Adam Milosz."

Later that evening after Milosz had left, Wilde cornered Rose on the staircase from the cellar.

"So who is he?" Wilde had said.

"He's damn good with numbers, Charlie."

"Fine, but who *is* he?"

"A Pole . . . well, half a Pole."

"Great. Where did you get him?"

"Oh, he just sort of turned up. The British used him for a while in Cracow, then he did a little spot work with ciphers."

"So why do we want him?"

"I don't know"—Rose had shrugged—"I kind of like his style, don't you?"

"Not particularly."

Four days later Milosz appeared again, this time as the

hunched, myopic figure that Wilde would always remember. Eventually he was even given a room in one of the cramped tower cells above the vaults. No one knew exactly what he did, and although station rosters listed him as a program evaluator, Wilde soon suspected that his talents were considerably more varied. In late 1968, for example, the man was said to have spent two weeks in Bern drawing money out of a Soviet operational account. The following year he surfaced in Dresden lending technical assistance to a blackmailer. Like others from Harry's personal staff, Milosz had never formed a connection with the larger Langley effort. Consequently when Harry fell, Milosz went down with him.

Milosz lived in a ramshackle cottage on the southern edge of the Spandau Forest. It was three o'clock in the afternoon when Wilde appeared at the gate. His arrival had set a dog barking, but there were no other signs of life. Then from behind a row of empty kennels at the end of the gravel path—Milosz in a soiled yellow sweater and corduroy trousers.

"Hello, Adam."

"Go away, Charlie. I got nothing to say, nothing at all."

"It's about Harry."

"Harry doesn't exist anymore. Go away."

There were newspapers stacked in every corner, magazines littered across an unvarnished table. The clapboard walls were bare except for two landscapes and a child's drawing of an elephant, rather carefully framed above the fireplace.

"This was gift," Milosz explained. "From a neighbor's kid."

He spoke English with an accent that no one had ever been able to identify . . . Polish, Hungarian, no one really knew for sure.

"It's nice," Wilde said.

"Yes, very nice. But you never had any either, did you?"

"Excuse me, Adam?"

"Kids. None of us ever had any. Not me, not Harry, not George Clay. This must mean *something,* no? Here we all have lots of money, power, never any kids."

194

There was tea. Wilde sat in a crumbling wicker chair, Milosz faced him from a decrepit sofa. There were unpaid bills on a rolltop desk.

"You know I haven't seen him, Charlie, not for long time now."

"Of course, Adam, but maybe there are a few questions you might be able to answer, areas you might be able to clear up for us—"

"*Us,* Charlie? Now I must ask you who this *us,* Charlie?"

"Severson and myself. Lyle Severson."

"Lyle Severson. Well in that case I must tell you go to hell, Charlie Wilde. You think I don't already know about George Clay's boy? You think I don't know this? Sharp eyes. Fast hands. A very technical boy with maybe a little pistol in jacket. You think I don't know this already? Go to hell."

"Well, he's not with us now, is he, Adam?"

"Maybe, maybe not."

"It's about Metropolis."

"So we are on the trail, huh?"

"According to the roster you were one of the clerical aides attached to the steering committee."

"Sure, I helped some on this Metropolis. My scientific expertise is in great demand."

"You did a lot of work between divisions, in the gray area. There were some tricky withdrawals from an operations account in Hamburg, a little surveillance in Brussels, a catch-and-carry job in London. What I need are the specifics."

Milosz had picked up a porcelain bird from the mantle. "I think perhaps you should not have come. You should not have come back to Berlin."

There were photographs on a window ledge . . . including Milosz with Rose by a lake.

"Adam, specifics."

"Well, here's a specific story, Charlie. Once upon time there was magic land. With castle and forest, like in fairy tale. Ruler of this

195

magic land was magic prince. Magic land wasn't real, but no one who lived there knew it, and so were happy people. One day a knight leaves magic land for world outside. Prince tells him, don't go, don't leave, but young knight determined and leaves. But moment he leaves magic land he suddenly old and tired, then realizes his mistake, because once in outside world knight now knows that magic land was never real. Now it's too late. He can't come back to dream."

"Very colorful, Adam, you should have been a writer. Anyway, I just want to find him, I just want to—"

"Oh, please don't kid me, Charlie, okay? You want to stab Harry Rose in back, to get him back, then at least use clean knife."

Goddamn him, Charlie thought. *Is he right?* . . . "There were two primary targets," Wilde said aloud. "A lot of smoke but so far as I can tell there were only two primary targets."

" . . . Clay and Tatlin," Milosz said. "Different ends of same problem. Look, you want drink now or what?"

"How did Harry run the lines into Clay?"

Milosz grinned. "Who knows? Not me."

"Did Harry have a man in Clay's office?"

Milosz shrugged.

"Who ran the Western surveillance teams?"

"I haven't any idea."

"What about the East?"

"Stanley Kline, but I suppose you know that already."

"What was Harry looking for in the vaults?"

"Secrets. Okay?" Milosz had moved from the mantle to the window, then finally slumped down on a folding chair. "Metropolis . . . you know, Charlie, I think this Harry's best. Metropolis. Like some beautiful structure. You would not have believed how beautiful. All linked together like by some architect. No one part left hanging out there. One time Harry was drawing from nine different stations. This you can probably not even imagine, but it is true. Nine stations, right in palm of Harry's hand."

"But, Adam . . . I've got to know what Harry was after." And once he'd thought he didn't give a damn anymore. That's what he'd said to Harry. But even Florida couldn't bake sense into an old spook's head . . .

"Charlie, leave him alone. For sake of past, your old friendship, leave him alone."

"Adam . . . "

Silence. Then . . . "Damn you, Charlie . . . he wanted to find out what happened that night they shoot you, okay? He wanted to prove something. Look, this now history, okay? This old story we both know. You went over border to get something from that Russian, Ivan Panov. This is old history. You went over border to get something hard, something to pull rug out from under Team B estimate, pull rug out from escalation of atomic weapon. So what? So maybe George Clay had lot invested in escalation. Maybe he had lot of friends in Pentagon, in industry, lot of support all the way . . . Okay? Big secret, huh? Big surprise."

"Harry was trying to prove that Clay blew the operation, right? He was trying to prove that Clay told Tatlin that I was coming over to meet Panov . . . he said we were set up . . . Where did it take him, Adam?"

"How should I know?"

"Well, you were coordinating the internal lines, so where did they go?"

"They go everywhere. Look, I don't know any more, okay? I'm dried up."

"Adam—?"

"Hey, you go *away* now, Charlie. Just go away and leave me alone."

They parted without saying good-bye. Back along the route to Wilmersdorf, Wilde passed the granary where he had once spent an evening waiting for an agent who never appeared. Closer to the Grunewald was the tavern where he and Harry had met on that Friday before the fall. By nine o'clock the night had grown out of

197

focus, but with specific memories he had been trying to avoid for years.

Before leaving the station shortly after dusk Petty met with Guy Campbell in a windowless room next to the Treasury.

"They told me downstairs I'm supposed to see you about my expense money," Petty said.

Campbell smiled. On the desk were balance sheets from Accounting, two theater tickets and a telegram from George Clay.

"What about my money?"

"See Operations."

"They're not operating."

"Then come back tomorrow."

And then while moving back to the door . . . "Hey, Petty. I got a message for you. You're supposed to call Kristian Haas. That's right, Kristian Haas. You going to tell me what this is all about?"

Petty just looked at him, then turned away.

Toward ten o'clock he found himself in a tavern filled with tourists. An hour later he left. It was nearly one o'clock when he finally returned to his hotel. The night porter was drinking underneath the stairs again. There were two homosexuals in the foyer. Along the hallway to his room another wedge of plaster had fallen from the ceiling. There was a breeze through an open window.

He inserted the key. The lock was jammed. Then he saw the faint yellow glow beneath the door. Did he leave the light on? He heard the footsteps and moved back.

The door was yanked open from the inside.

At first he saw only a pale round face, hair cropped short. Then a second face—lean, full lips. And then he saw the leather stitching of a gloved fist, his stomach folding. It was no ordinary fist. The second blow fell behind his ear. His kidneys seemed to explode. He knew that if they hit him again he would go down and never get up. They all knew. But in the momentary pause he

198

struck out, thrusting from his hips for speed, converting the momentum into a back-knuckle. As the arms slid around him, he stomped hard, raking down the shin. Then again until those arms fell away. It was over before he could finish, first one slipping free, then another. He was pretty sure they'd only come to search the room. The evidence lay everywhere . . . his clothes on the floor, the bent hinges of his suitcase, open drawers . . .

For a long while he just sat, back jammed against the wall, waiting for the pain and the night to end.

CHAPTER
EIGHT

THERE WAS A story about that night before the fall. It concerned Harry's movements on the evening that Charlie Wilde was shot, and a brief conversation with a night clerk named Matson . . .

Rose had first entered the Station in the early afternoon. No one could recall having spoken to him at this point, although apparently he had left instructions with someone about the radio traffic. Not long after four o'clock a telephone call had been routed to this office, and he was seen staring from a third-floor window. Then at five he was seen again, this time peering from a balcony with that famous raincoat on his shoulders.

There were about six hours between the first rumors of an incident and confirmation of a shooting. When the last reports had been confirmed, four night clerks drew straws to determine which one of them would break the news to Rose. As it happened the youngest chose the shortest straw—Matson. He was a doe-eyed kid with curly red hair and an occasional stutter. He had entered the service the previous March, but had never formally met Harry Rose.

At that time there had been a narrow flight of concrete steps from the second floor to the executive suites on the third. From the staircase one continued along a corridor that Rose had had painted dark blue. Then along another passage with storage closets and fire extinguishers until one reached the double doors of Harry's room.

Matson said he'd not even had time to knock before Rose, sensing his presence, told him to enter. There had been the light, steel-blue through those enormous french windows, while the lamplight on his desk had been green. Rose was wearing some sort of wrinkled smoking jacket, gray trousers and a silk shirt, also badly wrinkled. Of course there was the smell of those cigars.

"Sir? It's about Mr. Wilde."

Rose had looked at him, watching but not speaking.

"It appears he's been hurt, sir. Shot."

Then Harry's voice, barely above a whisper. "Sit down."

The chair a Biedermeier, nineteenth-century with the face of a cat in the back. Along the far wall hung two lithographs of nymphs exchanging glances with a fawn.

"You've something in writing?" Rose asked, and Matson passed him the uncoded transcription of a Hamburg telex. A long silence while Rose read the message again and again, or maybe was just staring at the page.

"Sir, there's also a query from Langley. They're asking about someone named Ivan Panov and a young lady. Apparently they've been shot too and Langley requests—"

"No more requests."

"Sir?"

"Tell them I'm . . . tell them I'll answer their questions in the morning." And then—"Just a moment. Shut the door. What's your name?"

"Matson."

"Your Christian name."

202

"Julian."

"Julian, I want you to do something for me . . . I want you to find George Clay."

"Yes, sir—"

"I want you to find him and then tell me where he is. Don't contact him, just tell me where he is."

"Yes, sir. I will."

"And, Julian . . . try to do it *quiet.*"

There were other stories from that night, mostly implausible. There also remained the record, more than three hundred pages sealed in the third-floor vaults.

It was a Saturday when Wilde began withdrawing these documents. He had entered the station at eight o'clock in the morning, passed through the foyer without speaking to anyone. He began with the broad-issue summaries, working in a cubicle adjacent to the vaults. There were six statements of the period, all concerned with that controversial Team B estimate of Soviet strengths and intentions. To dispel internal criticism of the estimate, Langley published two circulars in defense of the hard line and a biography of Team B members Richard Pipes and Daniel O. Graham. Next there was a lengthy chronology listing notable events from the formation of Team B to the Congressional debates on the MX system. And there were those two dozen pages that Rose himself had written in response to the Team B charges that Soviet tactical capability had been dangerously underestimated. Also two memos by Clay in fulsome praise of the Team B movement for a stronger America . . . "After years of ignoring an intolerable threat we are at last embarking on the road to peace and freedom."

Toward noon Wilde left his cubicle and wandered out to a fire escape for a cigarette and a view of something besides papers and linoleum. Years ago, just before Harry's fall, he'd wandered out here with Rose. At that time there had been pines along the path, black pines and ivy to the outer gates. Beyond a wall had stood a line of receiving sheds and a nest of rusting antennae. It may have also been raining that day, because Wilde distinctly recalled Harry's black umbrella . . .

"I suppose you know that he called today," Rose had said.

"You mean George?" That had been obvious from the tone of Harry's voice.

"He wanted to inform me that the Reds are going to attack a week from Tuesday, assuming that the weather clears. And Boris Tatlin has been telling his people that we're going to attack next Sunday, assuming the president is feeling better. God . . . " Then closer to a rank of interrogation huts: "You know what really intrigues me, though, Charlie? I'm beginning to think those two idiots actually hate me more than they hate each other."

Considering the final record, that may have been true: December, 1975, and a defector from one of the Soviet missions in Prague openly admits that Tatlin keeps a photograph of Harry in his office, a study of Rose on a bridge with his raincoat and cigar. Not to be outdone, there is George Clay in October explaining that if Harry continues to oppose the Team B estimate "his house will be torn down around him."

It was Harry who appeared to have had the last word . . . if not as the prince of Berlin then at least as the master of the Archives. Once more tracing requisition slips, Charlie Wilde found that Rose had withdrawn literally hundreds of pages on Boris Tatlin's halcyon days between the spring and summer of 1979. As for Clay, if Harry's feeling about him had been quieter, it was certainly no less intense. You were like an astronomer, Wilde thought, watching from a remote observatory. You stayed late every night, explaining to others that you found the work restful, but in fact you believed that time was running out . . . .

It was two o'clock when Wilde emerged from the vaults again, two o'clock in the afternoon with the undertones of an early winter's evening. He and Petty found a tavern on the edge of a holiday camp.

"What happened?" Wilde asked.

Petty shrugged. His ribs hurt when he lifted his arms. The cut behind his ear was only visible from certain angles. "Ran into a search party."

"Did you report it?"

"Burglars? Supposedly they were only burglars."

"Who told you that?"

"Campbell—after a so-called discreet inquiry."

"You mean he spoke to the hotel detective?"

"Something like that."

"Look, there are a lot of possibilities. I mean, they could have been burglars."

"Sure, and Harry Rose just took off on a holiday."

"Then what do you think?"

Petty shrugged. "I think this is Berlin."

"Meaning?"

"Meaning what I told you before . . . I think Harry Rose still has some friends around."

"Well . . . look, I'm getting close to something. I'm not yet there but I'm getting close . . . Harry was all wrapped up in a specific event. I'm sure of it—and there's something else. Kristian Haas. I think you were right. I think she may be involved."

"How?"

"I'm not sure yet, but Harry was definitely watching her."

"In order to move against Clay?"

"Maybe. Do you think you could get to know her? Sort of casually, of course."

"Yeah, I guess I could . . . . "

Petty slept through the rest of that afternoon, woke in the darkness. He finished dressing by the window with that photograph of

205

her propped on the nightstand. He supposed he had known women like her before. He had never had much to offer them, not money, not security, not a future. But he'd thought about them now and again, trying to imagine what it would be like slipping into their lives for more than just a night.

He reached the Kurfürstendamm at eight o'clock, ate in a restaurant filled with Turks, then wasted another hour moving in and out of the loitering crowds. When he finally reached the Last Exit it was nearly eleven o'clock. Kristian Haas had already performed, and the audience had grown restless and drunk.

This time he found her at the bar with friends. She wore a black leather skirt, blue stockings and a sweater. When she saw him standing in the doorway she raised her glass, then slipped away from the bar.

"So you've come back to me." She smiled.

He nodded, glanced at her wrist. She was wearing a bracelet studded with diamond chips. "Did George give you that?"

She looked at it. "Buy me a drink, okay?"

They found a table in one of the darker corners, beside a plastic palm and a blown jukebox.

"I understand that you tried to call me," he said.

"I think so, yes."

"Why?"

"Buy me a drink."

"Have you talked to him lately?"

"Who?"

"George."

She slipped off her bracelet and began to spin it around on the table. "He always calls on Mondays."

"What do you talk about?"

"This and that. Listen, you ask too many questions, okay?"

A boy in a green jacket appeared in the doorway. When Petty turned to watch him, she noticed the cut behind his ear. "Hey, what happened to you?"

He turned back to her. "An accident."

206

"You don't look like the sort of man who has accidents."

"Sometimes I do."

"Maybe I should take you home and nurse you to health?"

He watched her eyes, her hands, half-smile.

"Wouldn't you like to come home with me? . . . You're frightened of what George would say?"

"Let's go."

They left through a fire door along a concrete passage to a flight of iron steps. Past an unlit arcade lay a parking lot and a blue Porsche. Neither spoke as they got into the car.

She lived near the Hansa Viertel in a loft with a skylight. The walls were rough brick, painted deep blue. The floorboards had been covered with imitation Oriental rugs. There was little furniture, a few steel-and-canvas chairs, a bed, a Chinese chest, a low steel table. There was a painting of an enormous moon in a black sky, another of an empty street in the rain. And photographs, a number of them mounted on a shelf.

Petty picked up a black-and-white study of a bottle on a table. "Did you take these?"

She let her coat slip to the floor. "Those? Yes, I shot those."

"They're nice."

"Thank you," although it sounded as if she couldn't have cared less.

"What sort of camera did you use?"

"A little one."

There was another photograph of loose papers on a desk, then another of an open book propped against a reading lamp—both black-and-white.

"Don't you ever take pictures of people?"

"No, no people. Just things."

She left him for a moment, then returned with a bottle of iodine and a bag of cotton balls.

"Sit there," she told him, pointing to the end of the bed. "Now, let me see," and lifted the shade of a chrome lamp so that the light fell behind his ear. "This isn't so bad . . . not so good, but also not so bad. Does that hurt?"

He winced. "Damn right."

Cleaning away the clotted blood, she said, "Now tell me the truth. How did this happen?"

He felt a quick stab of pain. "Ran into a door."

"No, I don't think so. I think someone hit you."

When she had finished she moved to an embroidered cushion on the floor. He remained on the edge of the bed.

"So how do you like working for my Georgie?" she asked.

"It's great, real great."

"Does he pay you a lot of money?"

"Probably not as much as he pays you."

She laughed. "Maybe you won't believe me, but actually George is a very attractive man."

"I'm sure."

"Not like you're attractive, but he has strength, don't you think?"

"Yeah."

She had poured him a glass of wine, kicked off her shoes, lay back. "I think you're a strange person, Petty." She pronounced it *Peteee*.

He put his glass on the floor. "Mostly I'm a little undernourished right now."

She reached out her hand and placed it on his shoulder. "Yes, maybe undernourished. But also I think you are dangerous."

"What? To you, you mean? George will—"

"Be quiet." And then they were lying on the bed, facing one another. She loosened his tie, opened a bottle of mint sherry. There was also music now, a slow piano.

"When did you first meet him?" he asked.

"Who?" She had shut her eyes for a moment.

"Clay."

208

"A long time ago."

"How long?"

"Months."

"Where?"

She sighed. "I don't know."

"But you must know where you met him."

"Oh, a club maybe."

"What were you doing there?"

"Singing . . . Listen, shut up about George now. Shut up about him and kiss me."

He leaned closer, brushed his lips against her cheek.

"No, not like that, stupid. Like this," and she reached for him like a child, linking her arms around his neck.

She undressed him, almost casually. Then her own clothes fell away. *So you're George Clay's girl* . . . and every bit as beautiful as they'd said.

She kneeled, drawing him up to her small breasts, holding him. From certain angles in the darkness, she looked very young, slender, almost boyish. Then tossing back her hair, she was suddenly all woman again, and not likely to let you forget it.

"Don't be afraid," she told him. "George isn't here . . . . "

Afterward he lay very still beside her, smoking, staring at that painting of the street in the rain.

"I should go," he said.

She reached for a cigarette, brushing her fingers across his lips. "Why? Are you feeling guilty?"

"No."

"Then scared?"

"No."

"Then why? Why do you want to go?"

He leaned over and kissed her. "Tell me something. What the hell are you doing with George Clay?"

She glanced away. "I don't know. The money? The power? Who knows?"

Later, as he was leaving, he tried to ask her again, and the answer was still evasive. Who knew? Who cared?

Wilde also spent a somewhat bewildering night, with questions that seemed to have no answers. He had begun at six P.M. in the relative stillness beside the third-floor vaults. He had drawn the political estimates from those critical weeks just before the fall. He read them as Rose must have read them, skimming through the index for indications of a sequence. He again withdrew those notes on the Panov affair: "The most disastrous excess of a man out of control," Clay would call it. And he drew the last summaries with several pages on Panov's death and a photograph of that girl . . .

Lise. He had never even known her last name. According to a later evolution she was listed only as a courier, and before that from Harry's Entropy Network. When Tatlin had finally returned her body there had been a problem about the burial date and no one had been able to attend the services.

Harry obviously remembered her, drawing out many pages to establish that she could not have been working for Tatlin. He had focused on Ivan Panov through outstation reports concerning his arrest and execution. Then it seemed he had turned back to Clay, but this time looking for something, as Wilde had told Petty, very specific, an event, a place—a something.

As for Wilde's own sense of something specific, he recalled a conversation with Harry, early June, out among the crabgrass behind the annex. Two days before another Langley assessment had appeared with an unusually complimentary note about Clay's performance in the Panov affair. Whether or not Harry read the note seemed irrelevant. Everyone had been talking about how George had saved Charlie Wilde with his wit, his strength and obvious grasp of the Soviet mind . . .

"I assume you've picked up on the irony," Harry had said. "I

210

drop you in Tatlin's lap, and George pulls you out again, with flair."

He had been looking pretty shabby that day with nicotine stains on his fingers, dark circles under his eyes. "And you know what the word is in Langley. If I'd only shown one half the intelligence of George, Boris Tatlin would have never been a problem in the first place, and—"

"Harry, let's just drop it, okay?" Wilde had said.

"No . . . it's so perfect . . . after years of trouble with us, old George still has the compassion, the decency to bail us out from our—"

"Harry, please . . . "

"I'm telling you, Charlie, it *stinks.*"

Before that he'd said they'd been set up. Especially Harry Rose had . . .

By nine P.M. Wilde had found numerous indications that Rose had been trying for nothing less than a full reconstruction of those last seven days before the fall. By ten he realized Harry had even drawn travel vouchers in an effort to trace Clay's movements between London and Berlin. Finally, after what must have been a week of indecision, Harry had apparently turned his attention back to the political assessments—but again looking for something very specific, a single event, a particular place.

And then he found it—between what had been written and what had been omitted, between the conclusive record and the suggestion of a record—Harry hadn't been looking for something. He had been looking for *someone.*

In all Wilde spent three more hours sifting through cables from Frankfurt and Langley, watch-team reports from Wedding and Pankow, selected letters that Rose had apparently studied not long before his disappearance. Returning to his hotel room, he spent another hour reviewing those random notes he had compiled the previous days. A sequence that had once seemed complex now seemed simple, while certain issues that had once appeared simple now appeared complex. Even up.

As for Petty, he also found himself with a shifting sense of the odds. Waking in the morning he recalled just one vivid image of the girl, eyes fixed above the rim of a glass. When the telephone rang at nine-fifteen he half expected to hear her voice. It was only Charlie Wilde.

They met in the lobby of the Sylter Hof Hotel, found a table in the rear of the dining room. There were half a dozen restless tourists still lingering over breakfast, a few soldiers in uniform.

"I suppose I could give you another theory," Wilde began.

"Sure," Petty said. "Let's have another theory."

The music had switched to Bach. "I think we can assume that Harry didn't like the record, didn't believe it. I mean the official record about what happened to Panov."

"And you?"

Wilde shrugged. "I went over the border on Saturday. But from the records Harry wasn't interested in Saturday. He was interested in the Thursday or Friday *before.* Now, I don't understand it all, but maybe I'm starting to. Harry's case may well have depended on one person, maybe not the most stable sort of fellow but still—"

"Who is he?"

"They call him Johnny Tull. Apparently George used to keep him as a sort of bodyguard, but that ended a few years ago."

"Still around?"

"They've got him on the book as an occasional, which probably means that he does a little street work. I'd guess he's also into a few deals on the side—narcotics, intimidation. Most of them are."

"I thought Harry Rose didn't allow that kind of shit."

"But Johnny was never one of Harry's people."

"When do you see him?"

"I thought we might try tonight."

212

"We?"

"If you're not busy."

Wilde had only met Johnny Tull once, but he remembered the boy well enough . . . tall, wiry, nasty. Tull had come to Berlin as a George Clay protege, slotted to head the Special Operations unit. Yet after only a week or two even Clay had realized that Tull was not third-floor material. Back in the streets Tull quickly earned the reputation as a tough survivor, mostly existing from day to day. Others in his sector were afraid of him. He was also known to have been rough with women. A consistent fellow.

Tull lived in the Kreuzberg district between factory yards and tenements. Half a mile west of the apartment block stood a Turkish cafe where Wilde and Petty met. There were rows of cheap jewelry shops, second-hand clothing stores and a railroad line. Wilde and Petty walked quickly because of the cold, because everyone walked quickly here. They passed a service garage and paused to scan the street behind. No one, nothing.

The entrance was concrete and smelled of liquid soap. There were four flights of rubberized steps, graffiti on the walls. Islamic music mixed with the sounds of a television set. The last passage was cramped. There were no lights on the landing. The door was green and half-glazed. Petty had stepped aside, pressed himself against the wall. Wilde knocked softly, then louder. There was an echo like a child's cry or a scared cat, then silence. Wilde knocked again. There were footsteps, then the sound of a turning lock.

The door abruptly slid open, and Wilde saw a nasty grin, black hair. He tried to spin away but someone grabbed his shoulder, wrenched him inside the room. He tried to call out, but a massive arm had locked around his throat. Sagging to the yellow linoleum, he realized even Petty would never be able to match this kind of strength.

Petty did not try to match it. He just slipped in beside it. His

213

first blow was a rising knee, very fast. Then he struck again with a circling elbow. When Wilde turned, he saw only the aftershock of a swinging palm, then the very pained face of Johnny Tull.

Tull was able to sit, but only if he leaned forward, lacing his arms across his ribs. He was thinner than Wilde had remembered. His hair was long, nearly past his shoulders. He wore a dirty undershirt and blue jeans. His feet were bare.

"You do know me, don't you?" Wilde said.

Tull shrugged. "Yeah. I know you."

"And I suppose you also know what we've come here to talk about."

"Up yours."

"Now, you understand how these things can go," Wilde added mildly. "Either tough or easy. It's up to you. You know that."

"Look, I don't know where Rose is."

There were photographs of naked women on the wall, most of them torn from magazines. Also on the table was an unloaded Colt revolver.

"You last saw Harry Rose eighteen months ago," Wilde said. "Is that correct?"

"Maybe."

"Do you remember what you talked about?"

"I don't even remember what I had for breakfast, okay?"

"Did you talk about George Clay?"

"Look, I don't have to put up with this shit."

"Actually, Johnny, you do," Wilde told him.

Tull wanted whiskey. Petty poured him half a glass. They watched while he drank in silence—Wilde on the edge of the unmade bed, Petty smoking in the corner.

"I was never one of Harry's boys," Tull said. "He never even liked me."

"But he came to see you, didn't he?" Wilde said.

Tull smirked, took another sip of whiskey. "He didn't come to see me. He had a couple of guys bring me to him."

"Who were those guys, Johnny?"

"Kline and some Hungarian."

"Where did they take you?"

"A house."

"Where?"

"They put a blanket over my head. I couldn't see."

"But you spoke to Rose, right?"

"Yeah, I spoke to him."

"About George Clay?"

"Okay."

"What else did Harry ask about?" Silence. "Johnny?"

"He asked about the Panov thing, okay? He wanted to know about the Panov thing."

"And what did you tell him?"

"Oh come on, Wilde. Do I have to spell it out? I'm the jerk that covered Clay's ass when he met with Boris Tatlin."

Jesus. Just like that. Hands across the curtain.

"And Harry wanted to hear that story? He wanted to hear how you helped Clay arrange a meeting with Tatlin?"

Tull glanced at Petty. "Sort of."

"What do you mean?"

"I mean that Rose wanted to hear the truth, okay? He wanted the truth."

"So what *is* the truth, Johnny? We're waiting. Johnny?"

"Okay, there were two meetings. There was the one that everybody knows about, when Clay got you out of the cooler, and there was the one before that when he put you there in the first place."

A moment of stillness while everyone gazed at the litter around them—clothing over the backs of chairs, empty bottles, magazines.

"So you told Harry Rose that Clay was responsible for the failure of that last run. Is that correct?"

Tull nodded.

"And when was this first meeting between Clay and Tatlin supposed to have taken place?"

"Wednesday . . . Look, if Clay finds out that I've even *seen* you—"

"He won't find out, Johnny."

"And the same goes for Rose."

"Sure."

"And when it's over you've got to get me out of this city—fast."

"I'm sure we can arrange something."

"Paris. I want to go to Paris," Tull said, and asked for more whiskey . . . .

Tull began the story like Wilde had always imagined it would be told . . . flat, passionless, with no sympathy. By introduction he described the London station in late February of 1976. He had been serving as one of George Clay's liaison officers—twelve hundred a month plus expenses. His duties varied. There were weeks when he found himself shuttling alone between the outstations, and there were weeks when he worked very closely with Clay. The primary concern of that period had been tactical. Clay had been trying to rally support for a massive Cruise missile program while Tull ran four dirty networks into the heart of the opposition.

Tull said he had been treated fairly well, although Clay demanded absolute obedience and secrecy. Things were generally informal and sometimes Tull and Clay had even spent nights drinking together. Once Clay had bought him a girl, English and very young.

As for the Panov affair, Tull began by describing a conversation with Clay. It had taken place on a Sunday evening, three days after Tull had reached London. Earlier Tull had received a telephone call instructing him to meet Clay at a house not far from the station off Grosvenor Square. Two empty rooms and a bar. It was cold, the windows opened onto brick walls.

Tull had arrived at a quarter to eight. Clay arrived about thirty minutes later. Before speaking Clay turned on a radio and drew the curtains shut. He had also opened a bottle of Scotch. As another odd detail, Tull recalled that Clay had been wearing black cashmere. Fancy. Rich.

There had been an extraordinary sense of, well, intimacy to the briefing: the room washed in shadows, music to drown their voices. Although Clay's briefings were generally succinct and to the point, that night it seemed he had prepared a sort of introductory speech. He began by describing the Cold War as a different kind of war with unusual problems and even more unusual solutions. He went on to say that such an unusual situation had recently arisen in Berlin where certain individuals within the Berlin apparatus had mounted an unauthorized operation that was about to endanger the entire American tactical position. After careful consideration it had been determined that the only way to stop these individuals was to ensure that their operation failed. To this end a Soviet officer had to be contacted. This officer was to be met in Berlin and given the details of the renegade operation so that his people could abort it.

At this point Tull had asked if the Soviet officer wouldn't suspect that by acting on information supplied by a Western representative, he would in fact be helping the Western cause. Clay had said it was conceivable but in this particular case there were personal considerations that would take precedence. Which was to say that this officer was expected to ignore, at least temporarily, the broader implications of his actions in order to settle a personal score.

Everything had made sense to Tull. He learned the names of those involved . . . Harry Rose, Ivan Panov, Boris Tatlin and Charlie Wilde.

As for the practical details, Clay had said only that he would be meeting the Soviet officer in a house along the Reinickendorf border. Tull's job would be to watch the roads and operate the sound system. The latter would be especially important because a taped record of the proceedings might constitute the only guarantee of the Soviet officer's full cooperation. Also there was Clay's personal position to consider—he would be conspiring with a Russian officer against an American operative, so a precise transcription of exactly what had been said might one day prove critical.

Beyond this, Tull said only that he and Clay had spent another fifteen or twenty minutes discussing women, but by this time it had been nearly one o'clock in the morning and the night was dead.

Two days had followed. Tull said he had divided his time between the London station and a Chelsea flat with a girl he had met the month before. This had been a fairly tumultuous period with a lot of internal disagreement over that Team B estimate. There were those who believed that a renewed sense of a Soviet threat would probably prove healthy, particularly in the economic sphere. And there were those who were deeply concerned, frightened. As for himself, Tull said, he drank a lot in the evenings, slept late in the mornings.

If Tull had had any illusions about the nature of this job with Clay they were shattered on entering Berlin. He had traveled under deep cover before, but never like this. Clay had even insisted that they wear disguises, and brought some ridiculous wig for himself, a coat and a knit cap for Tull. They had taken a military transport from London, landed in Templehof just after dawn. Although neither had mentioned Harry Rose at this point, Tull said that they had probably both been thinking about him. He said that everyone who entered the zone thought about him. Even the junior staff from the London station knew that Berlin belonged to Harry.

From Templehof they had spent six hours in a warehouse beside the canals. Tull said that he had slept a little. Clay didn't seem to do much of anything. Toward noon they left in a gray Opel sedan. It was raining and travel was slow . . . there had been rumors of roadblocks in the north, housing riots in the east.

Tull said that the house where they were supposed to meet the Russian was pretty much what he had expected. It was old, shuttered, a long way from anything. There were pines along the surrounding hills, a pebble track to the highway. The furniture consisted of a crapped-out sofa, a table and a few chairs. But the sound system was new and very good. There were two voice-activated tape recorders in a room above the parlor, half a dozen microphones embedded in the walls.

Tull had said that he was familiar with the equipment, but Clay had insisted that they test it. In all Clay had spent more than an hour reading from a Bible he had found in the kitchen while Tull monitored the machines upstairs. After that there had been an awkward moment when Clay had given Tull a weapon, a nine-millimeter German automatic and fifteen rounds of ammunition. Clay hadn't really said anything. He had just appeared with the thing and then put it down on a table.

Waiting had been the hardest point. Tull remained upstairs watching the roads. Clay sat below in a chair by the window. Toward eight o'clock a black Volkswagen van emerged from the trees along the highway. Although there had been no moon, Tull had been able to see fairly well by the light of a porch lamp. The van stopped on a strip of gravel in front of the house, and two men stepped out. There was a driver in a yellow raincoat, and Boris Tatlin. Tull said he recognized the man from photographs that had passed through the London station from time to time.

Because the microphones fed directly into the recorders, at first Tull had only been able to hear fragments of what was said. Later, after he had opened a door, he heard more. But at first there had only been fragments . . . "Would you care for a drink? Did you have any difficulty at the border? What time did you . . . ?" Through all this Tull had kept very still watching the revolving spools of tape, toying with the nine-millimeter.

Tull said it was that sense of stillness he remembered best—the stillness against the voices below, against four slowly turning reels of tape, against the awful face of a half-glimpsed truth. Later there were sleepless nights and whiskey in the afternoon, but mainly he recalled the stillness . . . By nine o'clock Clay and Tatlin had been speaking fairly casually. Apparently there had been a disagreement about what was to be done with Charlie Wilde, but eventually that question too had been settled.

As for the aftermath, Tull recalled only that Clay's primary concern had been the tapes. He had insisted on rewinding them immediately and locking them away in an aluminum case which he would not let out of his sight. Even later, on the road back, that case had stayed on his knees. As for their last words together, Tull remembered only long stretches of silence in the rain west of Tegel, and that twice Clay had told him, *"Look, I had to do it."*

Three days after that night in Berlin Tull left Europe for a month in Los Angeles. Ostensibly he had been sent to help deal with the Soviet penetration of the software industries, but in reality it seemed that Clay had just wanted him out of the way.

He ended up living on the edge of the city in a rented condominium above a boating marina. There were plenty of women, but they did not seem to want him. There was a lot of spare time, but he did not know how to spend it. For a while they had him drafting damage reports on the theft of high-tech material from an optical research plant in Riverside. There were problems, however, when the actual numbers didn't tally with what Pentagon evaluators wanted them to say. Then too it had been about this time that the MX system began to figure in the public mind and issues had to be presented very simply in order to justify the money. But if there had been moments when Tull told himself that the time had come to take a stand, he only had to remember what they had done to Harry Rose.

By the time Tull finally returned to Berlin the Panov affair had presumably ended. Harry Rose was out of operations. Charlie Wilde had formally resigned. The emphasis of that period had still been Soviet tactical strength, but the basic methodology had changed. There were really only three active networks left over from the Rose era, and their productivity was not particularly good. As for Tull's view of his life and career, he said that from the start he had known that someone would eventually ask him about Tatlin and Clay, whether in Langley or Frankfurt, London or Berlin—eventually, he knew, someone would ask . . . .

It was half past one in the morning when Tull finally finished his story. The whiskey was gone, the glass filled with cigarette butts. Wilde still sat on the unmade bed, Petty had not moved from the corner. He had found himself watching the street, the door, the roofs of adjoining buildings. Earlier there may have been something below, but now he wasn't sure.

"I'd like to talk about motives," Wilde said. "Clay's motives."

Tull looked at him, wiped his sleeve across his mouth. He felt beyond exhaustion, in a kind of stupor. "What motives?"

"You said that Clay told you that he had to do it."

"So?"

"So what do you think he meant by that?"

"I don't know. I guess he was referring to the numbers."

"What numbers?"

"You know, the Reds got ten, so we need twenty—the numbers. I mean you don't spend a billion dollars on a system and then let some guy like Harry Rose come along with stuff that the system wasn't needed in the first place. You just don't let that happen."

"And so Clay believed that the Panov material would invalidate the—"

"Look, guys like Clay are telling everyone that we need to catch up with the Reds, but that's not the game. They don't want to catch up, they want to move ahead. They want leverage. You take a guy like George. It doesn't matter that the Team B estimate may be crap. The average voter on the street doesn't *appreciate* the Red threat. So you've got to jack up the scare—especially if you want to sell a twenty-billion-dollar system that just sits in some fucking hole in the ground."

221

"Did Clay ever give you any indication that there were others involved in the arrangement with Tatlin?"

Tull glanced at Petty. "Let me put it like this . . . You talk about the MX system or the Pershing system, you're talking about big money, big money. Now a guy like Rose comes along and starts in about how the emperor doesn't have any goddamn clothes on . . . well, there's going to be trouble all up and down the line."

"You mean trouble with the Pentagon?"

"Sure."

"And the private sector?"

"Sure . . . the private sector. You think Lockheed or General Dynamics wants to hear about how maybe we've maybe overestimated the Russian clout? Man . . . they don't want to know about that, about Harry Rose. I mean, *he's* the fucking enemy. The Russians they can deal with. Shit, they're buddies, they drink fucking vodka at the trade meetings. The Russians keep them in business. But a guy like Harry Rose . . . well, they just don't want to hear about it."

"Did Clay ever talk to you about the Panov material? I mean the actual product."

"He didn't have to talk to me about it. I'm not so dumb. I knew the score."

"What do you mean by that?"

"I mean Rose was bringing in hard stuff, stuff that was supposed to have blown the roof right off the Pentagon, blown the whole game apart. Obviously something had to be done. I mean in Clay's mind something definitely had to be done."

"Do you remember what Boris Tatlin's reaction had been when Clay began to talk about Rose?"

"For Tatlin it was probably personal. For Clay I guess it was personal too, but Tatlin sounded like he was really out for blood. Look, I need another drink."

There was Scotch in a cabinet above the sink. Petty poured half a glass, left it on the table and moved back to his corner.

"I'd like to ask you about Harry," Wilde said. "What was he like when you saw him?"

Tull shook his head. "I couldn't see his face. He was sitting in the dark."

"Did he get angry at any point?"

"He was cool, very cool."

"What did he say to you after you had told him about Clay and Tatlin?"

"He told me to keep my mouth shut."

"Anything else?"

"You mean like what the fuck he's trying to accomplish? No, Wilde, he didn't tell me any of that."

"Have you seen Stanley Kline at all?"

"Hell, no."

"How about Adam Milosz?"

"No."

Tull had finished the Scotch and wanted another, but from his eyes, the way he moved his hands, it was obvious that he'd had enough.

"I'd like to talk about the house where you actually met Rose," Wilde said.

Tull frowned, still staring at the bottle on the table. "I already told you that I don't know where it is. They took me there in the back of a van with a blanket over my head."

"Yes, but once you reached the house didn't they remove the blanket?"

"Yeah."

"So what did you see?"

Tull shrugged. "An empty room. They sat me in this chair in an empty room."

"How big was the room?"

"I don't know."

"Were there windows?"

"I can't remember."

"Rugs? Carpets?"

223

"Maybe a rug. I'm not sure."

"Was there one level or two?"

"Huh?"

"Was there a staircase?"

"Yeah, I think so."

"What about smells?"

Tull signaled Petty for another cigarette. "Yeah, there was the smell of cigars."

"You mean Harry's cigars?"

"That's right. Place fucking reeked of them."

"What about the background noises? Traffic?"

"It was dead quiet."

"Birds?"

"Huh?"

"Do you recall hearing birds?"

"I don't *know.*"

"From where exactly were you abducted?" Wilde asked.

"What?"

"Where did Kline pick you up?"

"Here."

"And then you were brought downstairs to a waiting van?"

"That's right."

"Then how long did it take to reach the house where you met Rose?"

Tull glanced up at the ceiling and a patch of disintegrating plaster. "I don't know, maybe thirty minutes."

"Do you recall anything distinctive about the roads? Were there potholes, for example. Sharp turns?"

"Dirt. There was a dirt road, a long dirt road." Then suddenly turning to Petty . . . "Look, I've got to have another drink."

It was raining again, softly against the windowpanes. Wilde had gotten up from the edge of the bed. Petty had drawn the curtains back. Sensing that the night had finally ended, Tull grew restless, irritable. After a drink he wanted cigarettes, after cigarettes, something to eat.

224

"I suggest you find a safe place to stay for a few days," Wilde told him.

"I thought you were going to get me out of here. Paris. I want to go to Paris."

"Yes, but until arrangements are made I suggest—"

"Forget the suggestions, Wilde, and just get me out of here."

Petty had moved to the door, Wilde had begun to button his coat.

"And I want some money," Tull said suddenly. "You've got to get me some money."

But Petty had already slipped out of the door, and Wilde did not bother to answer.

From Kreuzberg Wilde and Petty wandered west until they found an open bar filled with soldiers and exhausted women.

"You realize that the house is vital," Wilde said.

Petty had ordered gin, but the waiter must have forgotten. It was very dark with only tiny blue bulbs along the ceiling.

"I guess I could ask you about Clay," Petty said suddenly.

Wilde stiffened. "I don't know what you mean."

"Well, now that you know the truth, what are you going to do about it?"

"I'm afraid I still don't—"

"Oh come on, Wilde. Don't tell me you can't even—"

"Look . . . it's not my province. It's Severson's. Anyway, the testimony of Johnny Tull doesn't constitute a real proof. Or is it that you can't really *act* . . . ?"

Wilde stayed awake until well after three, with more brandy and cigarettes in a chair by the window. He was very near to understanding what had happened, but still could not understand why he *felt* almost nothing; not anger, not disgust, not even regret. He thought of Petty and supposed that regardless of appearances the boy was very dangerous and close to a breaking point. He thought of Clay and wondered why he could not hate the man. He thought of Harry and a particular vision from 1954 . . . Harry

225

grinning like the Cheshire cat from the platform of a railway station.

Harry. As always, he managed to get himself in the way . . . even of a man's deepest emotions.

Among the charges finally leveled against Rose was that he had continually used agency resources for what amounted to personal gain. To support these charges more than fifty pages had been amassed detailing nine specific instances wherein Rose had actually drawn from operational accounts in order to take advantage of local investment opportunities. Also scattered among the two hundred pages of testimony from that board of review were dozens of references to dwellings that Rose had ostensibly purchased as agency facilities (but in fact had simply given rent-free to prematurely retired agents and their families).

It had been noon when Wilde had first begun to review this material, about two when he had started to focus his attention on a particular house northwest of Zehlendorf near the banks of the Grosser Wannsee. Earlier he had passed Guy Campbell along a second-floor corridor, but Campbell had had nothing to say.

At first Wilde found only one brief notation concerning the house. Apparently it had been purchased two years before as a training facility under the auspices of a certain Operation Lullaby. When Lullaby had been terminated there had been a dispute between Treasury and the Programs staff over what was to be done with the property. Ordinarily disputes of this kind were settled by the station director or the Frankfurt Command, but in this case it seemed that a solution had been found with the intervention of a higher authority. The house had simply been absorbed into another existing project—Metropolis.

It was nearly four when Wilde finally met Petty on the edge of an amusement park.

"Naturally I could be wrong," Wilde said. "It was definitely a Metropolis acquisition, but I can't be certain that it's still operative."

Petty had picked up a stick, snapped it in two. "If Rose wanted a house why did he use the station lines?"

"Because he wanted a place that would conform with a broad cover. After all, why would security look into one of their own establishments?"

Petty shrugged, tossed the stick away. "Okay, makes sense. He was smart."

"More than smart. He was the last of his kind, and I wouldn't forget that if I were you."

The house was shuttered, dark, lost in surrounding trees. To the south lay hills overgrown with bracken. There were pines along the edge of the water. Beyond the hills stood a radio tower but no other sign of habitation. From the highway one saw only a glimpse of shingles and a fallen gate. Closer stood a green house and the remains of a garden. A few blossoms grew between the hedgerows.

Wilde approached the house from the rear across a field of weeds beside a crumbling wall. Petty watched from the rim of a hill. It was cold and the sun had dropped below the pines. Once Wilde had looked back and saw Petty nod with a cigarette between his lips, collar up against the wind.

There were birds in the surrounding pines, sparrows in the grass beneath the wall. Earlier there had also been crows and the echo of more barking dogs. Closer to the garden gates Wilde saw a shovel propped against a shed, a rake half-buried in dead leaves. Not that Harry had ever been much of a gardener. He tended to plant things with a momentary fervor, then let them live or die on their own. There was a pond filled with rainwater, and years ago Harry had kept goldfish in a pond for his wife.

Wilde paused at the gates. There were no lights, no sounds

227

except the wind. He lifted the latch and slipped in between the hedgerows.

Years ago there had been a house like this where Rose had brought a boy who had been shot in the groin after Tatlin had rolled up the Catalyst Network. A doctor had spent an entire afternoon trying to remove the bullet, but it came to nothing. Then in the evening there had been Rose, staring at his hands in an upstairs room. Which was how Wilde imagined him now . . . past that door, up a wooden staircase, staring at nothing in an empty room.

He entered through a door to the kitchen. There were tins of food along a pantry shelf, a stack of unwashed dishes in the sink. A pair of rubber boots had been tossed in the corner. Mice had gotten to a loaf of bread. On a dining table past the kitchen two burnt candles and a newspaper. On the arm of a chair, *The Kabbalah Unveiled.* Just a little farther along the corridor, one of those damned cigar butts on a dish.

"Harry?" Without any sense of conviction. "Harry?" Still tentative. "Dammit, Harry!" When even in the worst of times he had always thought that Rose would come to him just as he had come to all the others.

There were undeniable traces of the man everywhere: a wine glass on the rim of the bath, paperback edition of *Divine Emanations,* another cigar in a coffee cup. But if Rose had actually *lived* in this house, he had obviously *lived* in an oblong room at the end of the hall.

Wilde had to sit. There was a chair by the window and he had to sit down. Beside the chair was a rolltop desk and a reading lamp that had been clamped to the wall. Beneath the lamp hung a map of Berlin. Pankow and Reinickendorf had been circled in red. Rose had used vegetable crates as filing cabinets, the contents arranged alphabetically. There were eight crates in pairs against the far wall, another six stacked to the ceiling in the corner. There were also stray papers on a card table, newspaper clippings in a shoe box, a dozen canisters of undeveloped film and a lot more that had been developed.

He lit a cigarette with a box of matches that Rose must have used. He switched on the lamp and held a strip of film to the light: one page from a Langley circular on civil defense—one frame of film, one page from a George Clay letter to the Frankfurt Command—one frame of film. There was a drab green blanket on the sill and he thought: You even remembered to black out the windows. There was a tiny porcelain dancer for luck, an early portrait of Anna for love.

He heard footsteps below but knew that it was only Petty. An alarm clock on the table said quarter to three; when he looked again, still a quarter to three. When Petty appeared in the doorway Wilde told him: "Go away. Will you please just go away!" He dragged a chair over the first row of crates, pulled twenty or thirty pages at random and began to read.

There was a bottle of sherry on the floor, but only enough for one glass. He pulled another ten or fifteen pages from the crates in the corner, laid out the newspaper clippings on the table. There were also three folders bound in canvas for mail dispatched and mail received.

He supposed that he began where Rose had begun, with that map on the wall and a notebook filled with dates. He told himself: this room was the heart. It must have all started here. Then he lit another cigarette with those matches that Harry had used.

Some of the files were old, half in German, half in English. Slips of black cardboard had been used to divide the main subjects. There was also some sort of color scheme: green for what had happened before the fall, black for what had happened after. Eight months of George Clay's life had been diagramed on a sheet of yellow posterboard. A year of Tatlin's life had been plotted against a strange chronology to chart the interplay of East and West. There were pages of observations on the nuclear threat.

There were notes from what must have been an extraordinary

night when Rose backtracked to the early years, as if searching for some reason, some deeper meaning to thirty-five years of an undeclared war. There were case notes from Metropolis, and pages that had been cut from archive records with a razor blade. I've been sleepwalking, Wilde told himself, sleepwalking while Harry has been piecing it all together again—his whole life back together again.

He left when there seemed to be no point in going on, no point in reliving what had been too much the first time. Descending the stairs, he found Petty on the sofa with a glass of gin.

Wilde poured himself a drink. He was tired, exhausted.

"That newspaper on the table is two days old," Petty said.

Wilde slumped down in a chair. "Yes, he hasn't been gone too long."

"And there's a darkroom in the basement."

"He was photographing a lot of material from the vaults. I suppose that's why he worked nights, he needed the solitude."

"So why didn't he burn the notes?"

"Maybe he hadn't time, or he knew that it wouldn't matter at this point."

Petty had gotten up from the chair to pour another drink. There was a lopsided portrait of a woman on the wall, an absurd brass eagle on the mantle.

"We're down to a specific event, a single night," Wilde said. "An element in the community conspired with a Soviet officer to suppress information that would make invalid the popular justification for a new weapons system. Harry wanted to document that event."

"And did he?"

Wilde shook his head. "Not entirely, but he came damn close, too close for some people's comfort. Eventually he'll pop some embarrassing questions."

"So you think he'll go public with it?"

"It's possible, yes."

"And where does that leave us when it's over?"

"Oh, I imagine that there will be comparisons made between Harry's material and the Pentagon Papers. I mean, having failed to document all the way the last Panov affair, he focused on the broader story. He seems to have gathered an awful lot on the so-called missile gap thing, an awful lot on deception by contract."

"Where do you think he'll place it?"

"Don't know. New York, Washington, Bonn . . . "

In another corner of the room there were porcelain birds and a collection of gnomes. Wilde had picked one up, held it to the light.

"There is, however, the possibility of a last card," Wilde said. "You see, what Harry really wanted were those tapes Panov was supposed to get. Clay and Tatlin—I think Harry would have killed for those tapes."

"But you think he got a copy?"

Wilde nodded. "Yes, I think he did."

"How?"

"Kristian Haas . . . it's classic. Harry burned George once before with a girl, and I imagine that he must have loved the idea of doing it again."

"But does she really know anything?"

"Hard to say until you talk to her."

They returned to the window again and a back view of the garden. Three days ago *he* might have been standing here too, Wilde thought.

"You realize that I'll have to pull in Lyle Severson now," Wilde said.

Petty shrugged. "Sure, pull in Severson."

"And I'll have to call someone from the station to collect all this. I mean the material upstairs—we can't just leave it."

"Sure."

"But I don't want you to contact Clay."

Petty smiled, "Now what makes you think I'd do that?"

231

They left through a rear door, then down the path between the hedgerows. At one point Petty had asked, "You think he's still in the city?" But either Wilde hadn't heard, or else had not wanted to answer.

Then above the field along the spine of the hill, they both suddenly stopped.

"They used to say that he had the ability to influence people from a distance—psychologically, I mean."

Petty was staring at him. "So?"

"Well, of course it was only a story, but still . . . "

"Still what?"

"One wonders."

There appeared to be something burning on the highway, and miles of backed-up traffic.

Petty turned. "Look, what are you getting at?"

"Only that you should be aware that it can affect you. Harry, this city . . . they really can affect you."

"I don't know what you're talking about." But he was beginning to think he did.

After returning to his hotel room at a quarter to ten, Petty tried to telephone Kristian twice. No reply. Then toward midnight he found himself in that chair by the window with her photograph propped against the sill.

As for Charlie Wilde, toward two in the morning he contemplated calling Lyle Severson, but in the end he decided to spend a few more private hours thinking about Harry Rose.

CHAPTER
NINE

BY THE FIRST hours of the fifteenth day a preliminary assessment from Wilde had been forwarded to Langley from Berlin. In response Lyle Severson alerted the outlying stations between Hamburg and Bonn; relevant documents were once again sealed. Closer to the heart of the search, Wilde would later describe a sense of imminent climax.

Petty remained restless, distant. He called Kristian Haas at a quarter to six in the evening. Kristian Haas—he would have known from the start that he would never be able to let her go, not after five years of working for Clay. On the telephone she had sounded indifferent. She said that she had tried to call, but he figured that was probably a lie.

When he met her, though, in the doorway, she kissed him on the mouth. There was a bottle of champage in a plastic bucket, two glasses on the table. Against the city lights from the window her dress was near-transparent. She had even remembered to wear

233

that perfume he had given her—on George Clay's behalf. Nice touch.

"So what have you been doing, Petty? Spying?"

"Sort of. More like working."

"Do you speak to George a lot?"

"No, not too much."

"Me neither. In fact, he hasn't called in days."

Her apartment was different, but he wasn't certain what had changed. There was still that painting of an empty street, still the full moon in a black sky. There were also still those claustrophobic photographs, but something had definitely changed.

"I met a friend of yours the other night," she said suddenly.

"A friend?"

"From where you work."

"Yeah? Who's that?"

"Don't remember his name."

"What did he look like?"

"Red hair."

Petty frowned. "Campbell."

"Yes, Campbell. His name was Campbell."

"What did he want?"

She smiled. "Nothing much. He just came by the club."

"Did you talk to him?"

"Of course."

"About what?"

"Different things. Are you jealous?"

He shrugged.

She had poured him more champagne, her hand on his wrist to steady the glass. She had also turned on the radio—hollow saxophone.

"Does this Campbell also work for George?"

"I don't know."

"But if he is a friend of yours—"

"He's not a friend."

She leaned closer, as though to kiss him, but she only lit a cigarette.

"Tell me about your work," she said.

"There's not much to tell."

"Why? Because it's secret?"

"Because I don't understand it myself."

"But you're good at what you do. I can see that in your eyes. So tell me what it's like to be a spy."

He turned to the window. The light was blue, steel-blue. Raining again. "You feel each day sort of go by."

"Then why do you do it? If you don't like it, then why do you do it?"

He just looked at her.

"Have you ever shot anybody?"

"No."

"Blown up a bus?"

"No."

"Do your parents know that you're a spy?"

I should have never come to this city, he thought.

"You think I'm playing with you, don't you?"

"Yeah. I think you're playing with me."

"Well, actually I'm not. Actually I simply want to understand you, get to know you."

"Like you know George Clay?"

"No, not like George Clay," and this time she did kiss him.

He didn't realize how tired he was until he shut his eyes, didn't realize how long he had been waiting until she told him to lie down on the bed.

She undressed in the darkness. Her skirt across the back of a chair threw a shadow on the wall that looked vaguely like a woman's face. When he touched her breast she glanced down at his hand. When he kissed her again she whispered something. He wanted to ask, but was afraid. Finally even the rain must have

235

stopped, and he forgot to remember what he had been trying to forget.

Afterward he lay unmoving for what must have been an hour. Then he got out of bed without speaking. He knew that she was watching as he dressed in the corner. The champagne had made him thirsty. There were only a handful of cigarettes left.

"You don't have to go," she said.

"I'm not going."

"Then why are you getting dressed?"

Because it's time, he thought, but said only, "I'm cold."

"Then come back to bed and I'll keep you warm."

He shook his head. "I have to ask you something first."

"Ask me something? What do you want to ask me?"

He moved to the window, leaned against the sill. "How long have you known Harry Rose?"

She may have smiled again, but he wasn't certain. He could only vaguely see her reflection in the glass.

"How long, Kristian?"

She drew the blanket around her shoulders. "You're right. It is cold."

"A year? Two years?"

She reached across the bed and pulled a silk robe from the closet. "Don't you know that you can get into trouble asking questions about Harry Rose?"

"How long?"

"Please. Don't do this."

"How long?"

She let her head fall to her knees. Maybe she was crying, he wasn't certain.

"If you don't tell me about it, Kristian, I'm going to have to make a telephone call."

"What are you *doing?*"

"Tell me how long you've known him."

"I don't know."

"Years?" Now he was certain she was crying.

"Yes."

"Did he put you together with George Clay?"

"Alex, why are you doing this?"

"Did he?"

"Yes! Yes, he put me together with George Clay!"

The last pack of cigarettes lay on the nightstand. He lit one and placed it between her lips. Although he didn't want to look, her eyes held him for a moment.

"I have to know about it," he told her. "One way or another I have to know."

"Alex, please listen to me. Harry Rose is a . . . well, he's a power. It's not good even to discuss him."

"I have to know, Kristian."

Then suddenly shouting: "How can you know? How can you possibly know? You don't know anything!"

He waited.

"It was because of my father," she said, quietly now. "I owed Harry Rose because of my father."

"You mean Rose helped your father?"

"He got my father out of the East."

"And in exchange you spent a little time with George? Is that it?"

"Yes."

There was a photograph on the dresser of an old man in a tweed coat and cloth cap. The man appeared to be smiling, but his eyes were fixed on something beyond the camera. Petty picked up the photograph and held it to the light.

"Is this your father?"

She nodded again, and he saw that her face was tracked with tears. But he still couldn't be sure if she was lying or not.

"Where does he live?"

"Hamburg."

"What does he do?"

"He makes glass, glass for cameras."

"When did you see him last?"

"I don't know. October."

"What's his name?"

"Peter."

"Does he live in an apartment or a house?"

"Apartment. Why are you asking me all this? What does it matter?"

Then for a moment he only saw her eyes again, staring at him from the darkness. She had drawn up her knees, locked her hands around her ankles. And he thought, *I should let it go. I should run away with her and let it go.*

But instead . . . "Look, I can keep you out of this, but you've got to tell me everything."

"I want a drink, please, I want a drink."

He found a bottle of brandy in the kitchen among the soup cans. He poured a glass and gave it to her. "Nothing you tell me will make any difference to Rose now. He's got what he wanted, but if you don't tell me, then others are going to ask and they're not very nice people."

"Does George know?" she asked. "Does he?"

"Not yet."

"Because if he finds out he'll kill me. Yes, he'll kill me."

Petty shook his head. "Not if you tell me everything now."

She told it in pieces. She said that she had been born in Pankow. Her childhood was like a walk in the dark. Her friends had been delinquents, everyone living on the fringe of a socialist state. Her mother had died in 1966.

She had entered the Western zone with a boyfriend, a Czech refugee named Josef. Her father was supposed to have joined them

238

the following month but by that time the Pankow routes had closed. She had tried to buy him an alternate route through Treptow, but after a shooting at the wall Treptow had also closed. Then too her father's health had not been good.

Her next boyfriend was a drummer named Max. On Saturday nights he played with a band called the Lock. When the lead singer died of an overdose, she began to fill in. After five or six weeks she was fairly well-known throughout the east-side cellar clubs. After a year she was more or less a local star.

Twice through the months that followed she had tried to arrange her father's passage out of the Eastern zone. First she worked with one of the northern escape teams, then with a group called the Black Express. Finally after fifteen thousand Swiss francs and almost a year of nothing, a Polish boy named Wholtat introduced her to Harry Rose.

Everyone had heard of Rose, she said. One way or another, good or bad, they had all heard of Harry Rose. As for herself, she was originally told only that he had been known to help those with relatives in the East. Later she was also warned that when dealing with Rose she should always tell the truth because he had a way of knowing when you told a lie.

There was a certain magic to that night she met Rose. First there had been a telephone call in the early evening, then a waiting car near the botanical gardens. Finally she found herself in a room above a nightclub called the Cat. It was late, at least three in the morning.

She saw him first from the doorway of an oblong room. He was half-hidden in the shadow of the curtains. A dark boy stood attentively at his shoulder, another watched from the corner. There were mirrors along the panels and the reflection of a porcelain goat. He appeared to be wearing a green corduroy coat, white sweater, green trousers.

She remained standing for more than a minute before he told her to sit. Then he lit a cigar and faced her from across the room.

239

The two boys had vanished through an alcove. There was music from below, the strains of an electric guitar and a singer named Jean Pfeffer, who was said to have been popular abroad.

"I understand that you're an entertainer," he told her.

She nodded but said nothing.

"Do you like Wagner?"

She shook her head. "No, not really."

"That's good. I don't like him either."

He asked about her father, and she responded with only the pertinent facts. While she spoke, he watched her hands, her eyes. Occasionally he would nod, occasionally ask a question on incidental points . . . Was her father well enough to travel? Did he live alone? Was he a member of the Party?

Then he asked that she talk about herself. He wanted to know who her friends were. Was there a special man in her life? Did she plan to continue living in Berlin or did she one day hope to live abroad? He was also, it seemed, interested in her career.

Concerning her father's passage to the West, Rose said only that these affairs were becoming more and more complex and she should not hope for too much. She was also warned not to discuss the matter with anyone. In response to her question about the cost, Rose told her that money was not a problem. Regardless of what she may have heard, money was not a factor.

Apart from these practical details she tended to remember the night only in terms of Rose as a man. She described him as someone with a special kind of power. He briefly took her hand and told her that she had very beautiful features. Then later, drinking alone in her room, lying in bed, she still had not been able to get him out of her mind.

Four weeks passed without word from Rose. Once she thought of trying to contact him but decided against it. Then on a Sunday afternoon she received a telephone call instructing her to meet Rose in the Wedding district beside a railroad line not far from a youth camp. There she found him sitting in the back of a

Volkswagen van with what appeared to be a short-wave radio. A little farther along the track two young men were waiting by an Opel sedan. Through the trees lay dark water and low hills.

"Write a note to your father," Rose told her. "Tell him that the people carrying this note are friends." When she had done this, Rose had her pose for a photograph with the two young men beside her. He used a Polaroid Land camera and encouraged her to smile. In all he took three photographs with the pines behind and her arms linked casually in the arms of the young men.

There were five hours waiting alone with Rose. He had brought a bottle of wine, sandwiches and chips. Mostly they talked about nothing that really mattered . . . music, life in the streets among the refugee quarters. Earlier when she had asked if her father would make it out of the East, he had told her only that everyone was hoping for the best.

What might have been complex was very simple in the end. Her father appeared about eight in the evening, and looked relaxed, dozing in the back seat of that Opel sedan. She ran out along the track to meet him. Rose and the two young men watched from the side of the road. Later she was given a few minutes alone with Rose, but hardly knew what to say.

Then there was a brief conversation with one of the younger men, a blond boy called Niki. "You understand that reuniting families is something of a hobby for Herr Rose. The satisfaction of helping others is all the compensation he requires. Occasionally, however, those who have been helped are called on to perform small favors in return."

"You mean there is something he would like from me?" she had asked.

"Oh no, no. But one day perhaps he might telephone you, or have someone telephone you on his behalf. Then perhaps you might be willing to . . . help him."

Throughout this conversation she had noticed only that Rose

241

was still watching, then later chatting with her father. It was a warm evening, and someone had opened a bottle of wine.

There were four years between that evening in Wedding and the final events concerning George Clay. Through these years Kristian saw Rose only twice, once in a restaurant, then again in a club called the Raging Bird. Occasionally she also heard his name mentioned along the Ku'damm, or closer to the Wall in Kreuzberg, but mostly she did not think about him very much.

It had been late August when the affair with Clay had begun. Through June and July she had toured the continent—Hamburg, Paris, London, Rome. Then in the spring she spent a month in Athens with the American singer, Moon Martin. In retrospect she tended to think of this period as her dog days, mainly living out of a suitcase from one air-conditioned room to another.

Then came Tuesday, her fourth night back in Berlin. She received a telephone call from a man who identified himself only as Alfred. Alfred explained that it was vital that he speak to her, and asked if they could not meet in a small cafe near the Europa Center.

Alfred turned out to be a Hungarian—lean, dark, about forty-five. He wore a gabardine suit, black shirt and white tie. Without asking what she wanted to drink he had the waiter bring her wine. He drank only brandy.

He began by saying that he was now speaking to her on behalf of Harry Rose. He went on to say that although she had not heard from Rose in many years, Rose had nonetheless not forgotten about her. And quite recently, in connection with a certain problem, Rose had been thinking of her quite a lot. He asked if she would be willing to meet with Rose. When she said yes, she was given the address of a residence in Wilmersdorf and told to meet Rose there in twenty-four hours.

Following the conversation, Alfred walked with her as far as the Kantstrasse, then vanished into a crowd . . .

A brief affair with George Clay. In the beginning it was only to have lasted a week. Rose had explained that a woman was

242

needed to involve herself with a man for a while. This was the word he had used—"involve." Although she was not told precisely how it was that he came to choose her, she later learned that files were kept on those he had helped.

Regarding how she was to meet this man in question, she was told that he would appear at a club where she had been singing since the previous spring. The man would be sitting at a table with a mutual friend. After her performance she was to join them for a drink.

As for the target, she was initially told only that he was a man who appreciated beautiful girls, a man who had never been able to resist them. She was not, however, asked to sleep with him. She was simply to spend a little time with him, which was really a small price to pay for all that Harry Rose had done.

So they met on a Saturday night in a club called the Red Shoes, *Rot Schuhe*. Clay had come for the last performance with that Hungarian Alfred. They had taken a table at the rear, and Alfred had sent a note to Kristian's dressing room.

Clay had started by saying, "You sing very well."

"Thank you."

"Ever made a record?"

"Only limited distribution."

"Yeah? Well, I got a few friends who might be able to help you."

"That would be wonderful," except that she was pretty sure he was lying.

"So maybe we should discuss all this over dinner sometime?"

"Yes," and she smiled. "I would like that," and jotted down her telephone number on a cocktail napkin.

After this first encounter with Clay, she and Rose met briefly on the banks of a canal. She remembered that, although the man had looked tired, he had obviously been pleased with her initial performance. "But now something else," he had said. "Ask him about his work. Tell him that you have always hated the Communists. He'll believe you if you remind him that you were born in the East . . . Also, flatter him a little, let him know that you're impressed with power types like him."

She met Clay next on a Monday for dinner, then again on Wednesday for a drink. He told her that he would sooner die than let the Russians take over her city. Later he suggested that she go with him back to his hotel but she managed to convince him that she was too tired.

Between evenings with Clay she continued to meet with Rose. "What you are doing is important," he had told her. "It is very important." He said that the issues, the politics, nuclear weapons —they weren't abstractions. They were real. Real as a chair, a door. Then too there was also a little money from time to time; money for clothes, a guitar, equipment for the band.

So she became George Clay's occasional woman. They met whenever he passed through Berlin. He sent her small gifts: jewelry, perfume, flowers. He called once a week. In early December she had no alternative but to spend four days with him in Zurich. Afterward, against all rules of the trade, she placed a telephone call to Rose because she desperately needed someone to talk to. And he told her, "What you are doing is important, very important. Thank you."

What she would later see as the finale to her relationship with Clay began on a relatively casual note. It was the first week in March. Rose had met her in the warehouse of a deserted fishery near the Grosser Wannsee and they talked for an hour in a loft above the waterfront. He told her that so far she had done very well, but there was a last detail, a last favor.

There was a certain item, Rose had said, a critical item that Clay probably kept in a personal safe in his home just outside of Langley. Because of an elaborate security system and the continual presence of a housekeeper and gardener, previous efforts to obtain the item had failed. But if Kristian could gain access to that house and a few hours alone, with a little instruction she would be able to open the safe and obtain a copy of the item.

As if anticipating her first question, Rose went on to explain

244

how she might gain access to the house. He said to tell Clay that a New York agent had recently expressed interest in representing an American tour for her. A few weeks later she would bring the subject up again, and tell him that there was a distinct possibility that she would be in New York sometime during the next spring. Then, during a period when Clay was certain to be in Langley, she would fly to New York, telephone him and explain that she had completed negotiations with her agent and would like nothing better than to spend a few days in Virginia before returning to Berlin. Assuming that Clay would invite her to his home, she would only have to wait until his duties at the Langley center called him away for an hour or so.

As for the contents of the safe, Rose said she would probably find one of two items . . . either there would be a typed transcription of a conversation or there would be the actual tape recording of that conversation. If she found the transcription she would merely need to photograph the pages. If she found the magnetic tape she would make a copy of that tape, which would require two machines, one to record and one to play. Since she was a musician nothing would be more natural than for her to travel with this type of equipment.

After this meeting in the warehouse Rose had walked with her along the waterfront. By this time it was very dark.

It happened almost exactly the way Rose had said it would happen, except that in the end it had taken over an hour just to open the safe, and another two hours to copy the tape.

In the months that followed she tended to see Clay only when she could not avoid it, and then only for an afternoon or evening. Occasionally he still sent small gifts: perfume, jewelry, a cloth doll that she kept in the closet.

And when she had finished with what amounted to her confession, she poured another drink and dragged out that doll. It was the sort of thing that tourists bought with an oil-painted face and real hair.

"When did you see Rose last?" Petty asked.

The doll lay on the bed between them. "About three months ago."

"What's the procedure for contacting him if you want to talk?"

She looked at the doll, picked it up, let it slip to the floor. "They gave me a telephone number. I call it and leave a message on an answering machine: 'Hilda for Kurt.' There's never anyone on the other end of the line, just the machine."

"What about the machine? Is there a recorded message?"

"Just, 'You have reached this number, please speak at the sound of the bell.'"

Petty stood up and moved to the far wall where she had propped the photographs against a bookshelf. "Did Rose tell you to take these?"

"Yes."

"For practice?"

"I never had to use the camera. It was a tape in the safe. I had to copy the tape."

"Did you listen to it?"

"No."

"Have you talked to Rose about me?"

She lit a cigarette, possibly the last.

"Kristian?"

"I talked to Stanley."

"Stanley? Stanley Kline?"

"I don't know his last name."

"What did he say?"

"Nothing. He said maybe I should get to know you, that's all."

"Like you got to know George, huh?"

She was crying again, but he did not want to look at her. When she whispered his name, he still didn't turn around.

Finally he told her, "I want you to give me the exact procedure of how you arrange those meetings."

"Alex, please. Don't do this anymore."

"You leave a message on an answering machine. You say, 'Hilda for Kurt.' Then what happens?"

"Alex, you don't know what you're doing."

"Then he meets you someplace, right?"

"Alex . . . "

"Where?"

She ran her fingers through her hair. "Alex, you can't win. He knows you. He knows—"

"Where do you meet him, Kristian?"

"A factory. An old factory. No one uses it anymore."

"Where?"

"Templehof."

"What's it called?"

"Alex!"

"What's it called?"

"Alder-Hof."

"Alder-Hof what?"

"Just Alder-Hof. The sign is down."

He moved away from the wall and back to the window. The fog had spread through the side streets but it looked as if the rain had stopped for good.

"I'm going out for a little while," he said. "If you contact anyone, I'll know."

"Alex, listen to me, please. Harry Rose . . . you can't beat him. He's everywhere."

He left her watching from the bed. In the corridor he thought he heard her call his name. Then in the street below, he definitely saw her shadow moving across the window.

He found a telephone booth by a service garage. Thirty minutes later Wilde was waiting for him in another basement cafe beside a movie house.

"I suppose you realize that you'll have to stay with her from here on out," Wilde said. "In fact, you really shouldn't have left her as it is."

Petty had ordered brandy, downed it and then ordered another. "She's all right," he said.

"For the moment maybe, but given a little time to think, she may start to panic. If that happens you'd better be there."

Past Wilde's shoulder stood a boy in a drab green jacket. He appeared to be reading a magazine but hadn't turned a page in over twenty minutes.

"I want you to have her make that call tomorrow morning, tomorrow afternoon at the latest. That should give us time to assemble a team."

Petty had been staring at the boy with the magazine. "What team?"

"Well we're going to need *some* help to cover that factory, aren't we?"

"But not Campbell's people?"

"No, of course not."

Then back on the streets again. "You understand that we're close, very close."

Petty nodded, didn't speak.

"That's why it's vital that you stay with her until this is over. When she makes that phone call we're on the edge."

They parted on the corner beneath a movie marquee: "Incidentally, you didn't actually get rough with her, did you?"

Petty looked at him. "What do you mean?"

"You didn't hurt her, did you?"

He thought of telling Wilde to fuck off, but instead said only, "No. I didn't hurt her."

And she was waiting for him when he returned to her apartment, sitting just as he had left her except that the brandy was gone. At one point she asked him, "What are you feeling? I want to know what you're feeling." But he did not know how to respond.

CHAPTER
TEN

WILDE WAS EXHAUSTED. He had entered the station at about nine o'clock, spent an hour on the telephone with Severson. Toward ten he had met with two reliable stringers, two of the few who had never known Harry Rose. Toward midnight he wandered back up to the third-floor vaults, where the last of Harry's papers had been stored. There was a letter that Rose appeared to have started but for some reason never finished:

> Dear Charlie,
>   I have always tried . . .

And among those papers from the Zehlendorf house were dozens of fairly cryptic notes . . . "It's not that I ever wanted to be a hero, it's only that I'm always *angry.*" On a sheet of yellow foolscap . . . "We're a cog in the wheel, but we're a wrench in the works too . . . "

It had been January or December. Wilde remembered the snow. And early '46 or '47. He remembered the rubble. Harry had just come back from a week in Frankfurt, where everyone had been talking about the bomb.

"They want another damn war," Harry had said.

"Who's they? Who wants a war, Harry?"

"Oh, stop playing games, Charlie."

He had been tired, nervy, also a little drunk. From an officers' club on the Friedrichstrasse they had wandered to what was left of the Postsdammer Platz. There had been children sleeping in gutted streetcars, women beneath a bridge.

"I suppose it's the attitude that irritates me the most," Harry had said. "You know, they see themselves as the ruling elite—"

"Harry, don't you think—"

"The question is, can we do something about it? You and I Charlie. Can we actually make a change here in no-man's-land?"

All around them had been the mud flats of what was then the Tiergarten, charred stumps of trees, more blasted concrete.

"Do you know why my people believe in me, Charlie? Because I believe in them. That's the secret. I mean, what's the point of fighting for freedom if you have to lie to your own people to keep them marching?"

Eighteen months later at the start of the so-called bomber gap, Harry had gotten even more irate. "What do you think, Charlie? You think I should tell them all the truth? I mean they've got a right to know it."

Not that it had been clear just what the truth had been, nor even who had had the right to know it. . . .

It was nearly two A.M. when Wilde came down from the vaults, half past three when he lay down in a second-floor room beside the elevator shaft. He'd found blankets in a utility closet.

Years ago there had been nights like this, waiting on a sofa or a cot for a crisis to break. During the airlift he and Harry had spent more than a week living off of sandwiches in a third-floor room, playing cards in the slack hours, drinking in the evenings on a balcony. "This city is the pits," he'd said, but after a month of bad days he had to admit that in a way those had been the best of times.

He lay down on the sofa, turned out the light. As always, Harry seemed to return to his memory in images . . . smiling from a doorway, waving from the back seat of a convertible Chevrolet, grinning with a, God help him, rose in his teeth. After the death of an agent in Pankow he'd written, "What have these people been told that makes them so willing to die for us?" And on the advent of the hydrogen bomb, "What have these people been told that makes them believe they can survive?"

There was a view through the window of radio antennae, but Wilde turned on his side to face the wall. *Well, we're alone now, Harry.* There were sentries moving through the corridors, the momentary sound of a shredder below. *I want to talk to you.* A wind had begun to stir the trees that lined the motor courts, another out-of-season wind. *Not that you ever really listened, did you?* He turned back to the window, and that nest of antennae. *Ah, Harry, you spent your life trying to keep your enemies from fighting each other, and when they finally stopped for a night it was only so they could get together to destroy you . . .*

There were footsteps in the corridor, closing from the staircase; Harry had always had a distinctive walk. There was a muffled voice in reply to an indistinct question; Harry had tended to whisper. The doorknob began to turn, light falling from the hall. *Harry?*

But George Clay said only, "Hello, Charlie. How the hell are you?"

Clay entered the room and sat down by the window. Guy Campbell remained standing behind him. When Wilde had reached for a cigarette, Clay had supplied the match. There was also whiskey, suddenly whiskey and two glasses on a drab green filing cabinet.

251

"I understand you've been having quite a time," Clay began.

Wilde looked at him briefly. "What are you doing here, George?"

Clay smiled, poured the first glass. "What's wrong? Not so happy to see me?"

Campbell moved closer to the window. He appeared to be watching for someone below.

"This is my operation," Wilde said, and realized it sounded hollow. "You've no right to be here. I suppose I can't ask you to leave this station but I can formally request that you—"

"Hey, Charlie"—no longer smiling—"I've already talked with Johnny Tull. That's why you're going to have to stay with me for a little while," Clay added quietly. "Until we get this matter sorted out."

"I want to call Severson."

Clay shook his head. "No, I'm afraid I can't let you do that, Charlie," and poured him another drink. "I'm afraid I'm also going to have to ask you where Petty is."

"I don't know."

"Oh come on, Charlie. The way I heard it you and Petty have gotten right friendly. So how about it? Where is he?"

"I told you, I don't know."

"He wouldn't be with a little German girl, would he? About twenty-five? Platinum blond?" Then finally raising his voice, "Come *on,* Charlie. He's with Kristian, isn't he? You're using her to contact Rose."

Clay dragged his trousers from a chair, tossed them on the cot. "Get dressed, Charlie. It's time to go."

There was a car on the edge of the motor court, a beige sedan. A driver sat smoking behind the wheel. A sentry may have been watching from the gatehouse. As Wilde got into the back seat Clay said, "You understand that I'm taking charge of this station again."

Wilde said nothing.

They drove west, then southwest to the marshland and canals. At one point Wilde laid his head back and shut his eyes. When he looked again there was a house on the edge of a mud flat. It was also very dark. Closer along a dirt track from the highway he saw two figures waiting by a van. *I've come back, all right . . . this is Berlin.*

The house was cold, the furniture crammed into a few rooms. Wilde found himself sitting in an armchair by an electric heater. Campbell had brought him another drink, then disappeared. There was food on a table—sandwiches, coffee, an apple. Someone was moving in a room above.

"I'd like to ask you a few questions," Clay said.

Wilde glanced at his wristwatch, a gift from Harry years ago. It was almost four-thirty A.M.

"Is Harry planning to go public, Charlie?"

"Come again?"

"And what's he got? A little on the MX, on the Pershing?"

"He's got your tape, George. He's got your tape."

Campbell turned, whispered something in Clay's ear, then moved back outside.

Clay turned to Wilde again. "When was the girl supposed to have made that call, Charlie?"

Wilde stared at him, at the cropped head that Harry had compared to a bullet. "You've been tapping my line to Severson, haven't you?"

Clay only said, "Come on, Charlie. You and Petty were going to have her activate the contact procedure, weren't you?"

"Go to hell, George."

"When, Charlie? Tomorrow?"

"Go to hell."

Another face appeared in a doorway, indistinct. Wilde remembered vaguely—Jerry Mace.

"Now why don't you check my arithmetic, Charlie? You and Petty were about to move in on Rose, correct? Meanwhile Rose had a little package for the press, correct again?"

"Is Boris Tatlin in on this one too? Is he, George? Not meeting him again tonight, are you?"

Clay turned, and for the first time actually looked into Wilde's eyes. "I'm sorry you got hurt, Charlie. I never wanted anybody hurt, but you got yourself in a dangerous game—"

"Go to *hell.*"

From the top of the stairs Wilde heard Clay's voice again. There was a subdued reference to Kristian Haas, then what presumably was a reference to Alex Petty . . . "You should remember that he's very fast . . . "

Or maybe it was to Harry Rose . . .

There was only one furnished room at the top of the stairs, with a writing table, chair, lamp and bed. The windows had been barred, the door locked from the outside. There was whiskey and magazines—Time, Newsweek, Playboy and a Pentagon publication called Watch Tower. There were also more sandwiches, but Wilde wasn't hungry.

Clay must have kept people in this room before. The hard interrogations were probably conducted in the basement, but those informally detained were kept here—with whiskey, sandwiches and magazines. He picked up the first magazine, Time. Someone had defaced the cover, used an eraser to white-out the eyes of an up-and-coming politician. He poured a glass of whiskey. Why not? Earlier, on the road from Zehlendorf, he'd calculated that given what Clay knew, Harry Rose would probably not last a week. Of course there was the possible impact of publicity, the chance that Harry might have already slipped out of the city. But still, as a force, on his own, Wilde figured Harry wouldn't last a week.

He sat on the edge of the bed to face the window. There were lights on the water. He lit a cigarette, remembering that years ago

254

Harry had said that whenever you looked at the landscape you ought to envision a mushroom cloud. If you wanted to play games with the Russians, then you had better remember where those games could end.

Past the far marsh lay Wilmersdorf and three lights along the rim of a lake where Harry had been known to spend Sunday afternoons. In a way I'm Berlin, he used to say. And this Cold War too . . . and in the end it was more than a little true. Clay . . . Tatlin . . . Team B . . .

He lay down on the bed when the whiskey was gone, turned out the light . . . Harry had always felt more comfortable talking in the dark. Toward dawn he supposed that he slept a little, or else dreamed without really sleeping at all.

Okay . . . if you want to talk, Harry, I'm listening now. Make it good . . .

Petty also sat in the darkness with cigarettes and an empty glass. The girl lay sleeping across the room, but he could not see her face. Earlier she had told him, "When you came to this city you were neutral, but you can't stay that way for long."

He had found photographs in a drawer, several shots of her posing with the band, even a shot of George, leaning on the fender of a black Rolls-Royce. There were no photographs of Harry Rose.

She said Rose would come back when the opposite forces canceled each other out. She said that he was like a puppet master. He knew where you were vulnerable, knew when you were alone . . . She'd said that Rose would kill him in the end, but by this time she'd probably had too much to drink.

He heard her stirring and turned to watch again. For the last hour she had been sleeping badly, breathing irregularly, occasionally murmuring in German. He looked at his watch—still more than two hours before dawn.

255

He picked up the photographs again, glanced quickly through them until he found the one of Clay. "George *believed* in the bomb," Rose had once written, and Petty supposed that was true. Not that you could blame the man—as a symbol of power nothing matched the hydrogen bomb. It was the only absolute. It was simple.

He put the photograph of Clay aside and picked up another of Kristian, framed in the doorway of a nightclub. "You investigate the lives of other people so that you don't have to live your own," she'd said. That was probably true. She'd even told him that given the chance they could have been friends, real friends. He put the photograph aside.

She seemed to be breathing more regularly now. *I'll let her sleep until the last minute.* He glanced at his wristwatch, still another hour. He heard a footstep on the staircase, assumed it was Wilde. He started to get up to open the door, but Campbell had already picked the lock.

Campbell entered now, slowly, one hand in the pocket of his overcoat. Jerry Mace stayed in the doorway. Petty backed off to the window. The girl woke up, staring at them.

"Let's go," Campbell said. "Mr. Clay is waiting for you."

Petty turned to Mace. "How's it going, Jerry?"

Mace shrugged, grinned. "The man wants to see you, Alex. Her too."

"When did you get into town, Jerry?"

"Little while ago."

"Charlie Wilde tell you where I was?"

But before Mace could answer, Campbell said again, "Come on, let's go."

They waited while Kristian dressed in the bathroom.

"She's not too bad-looking, is she?" Mace smiled.

Petty ground out a cigarette. "Shut up, Jerry."

"You been fucking her?"

"I said shut up."

256

Campbell moved closer to the window. He spoke without looking at Petty. "When she comes out I want you to take her down to the street. I'll be right behind you."

She came out of the bathroom in a raincoat, purple sweater and blue jeans. Petty looked at her but said nothing. When he looked again Mace had disappeared. Outside it was cold and still dark. A black Chrysler had been parked beneath a streetlamp. Mace was sitting behind the wheel. Petty, Kristian were put into the seat beside him. Campbell sat in the back.

They drove west along the side streets past unlit store fronts and apartment blocks. Beyond the Grosse Stern lay evidence of another disarmament rally—shredded posters, broken glass, the remains of bonfires.

There were low patches of fog in the suburbs, rising mist along the canals. Twice Petty had glanced at Kristian, but her eyes remained fixed on the road. There were military trucks at the edge of the marshland but no soldiers.

Like Wilde, Petty saw the house first from a distance outlined against the mud flat. There were lights in the lower windows, a van beneath the trees.

"Your pal Charlie is in there." Mace grinned. "He's waiting for you."

Dawn had begun to break along the far ridge. The radio towers were very distinct against the sky.

"Where's George?" Petty asked.

"Inside . . . waiting for *her.*"

They stopped on a patch of gravel beside a veranda. Campbell opened the rear door and told Mace to keep an eye on them, that he'd be right back.

When Campbell had gone, Petty, Kristian and Mace remained sitting very still together in the front seat.

"I guess you know you're in a lot of trouble," Mace finally said.

Now Petty smiled. "Is that so?"

"Not that I can't appreciate your problem here," glancing at the

257

girl, "but George is a little upset."

"Sure, he's a little upset."

"So if I were you I'd just play it cool for a while. I mean, George can be a forgiving kind of guy, providing . . . "

"So what happens to her?" Petty said, not looking at him.

Mace shook his head. "Now, Alex, that's exactly what I've been talking about. You have got to get your priorities straight. She's not your problem anymore." And looking at her, "Are you, baby?"

Petty had also turned to Kristian, watching as Mace's hand slid along her thigh. *No,* he thought, *she's not my problem . . . but maybe she's my solution.*

And he struck, reaching across with a blow to Mace's throat. Then grabbing Mace's hair, he slammed the man's head against the steering wheel—once, twice, then again.

He told her to lie on the floor beneath the dashboard while he pushed Mace out the door. He slid behind the steering wheel and started the engine. The tires slipped briefly on the gravel before catching. He thought he saw two figures running from the house as he drove off.

He drove for what must have been an hour. The fog had gathered in the valleys. There was a deeper mist on the water. When they finally got to a pitted road and a clearing among the trees he stopped the car. Kristian hadn't spoken.

He told her, "We're going to need some place to stay."

She shook her head. "This is Berlin. There's no place . . . You killed him, didn't you?"

He laid back his head, shut his eyes. "No. I didn't kill him."

"But he wasn't moving."

"He'll be all right."

There were spots of blood on the dashboard and the steering column. There was also blood on his trousers.

"What will they do to us if they catch us now?"

"I'm not sure."

258

"Would they kill us?"

"Maybe."

He looked at her, and half-smiled. It was no time for speeches.

For a moment he thought she would kiss him, and then she said, "I think I know a place we can go."

The boathouse lay at the end of a path that led from the pines to the water. It was hardly more than a weathered shack, but there was a bed, a table, a few other necessities. It was cold. Through a dusty window was a view of water reeds along the far shore. The fog had still not lifted.

"Who lives here?" Petty asked.

"A friend, but he doesn't come here very much."

"Do many people know about this place?"

"No, not many."

"What about the beach? Does anyone ever use the beach?"

"No."

She prepared a meal of canned meat and vegetables. There was also a little coffee heated on a kerosene stove. Afterward they shared a cigarette because there weren't many left. Then they lay down together on the narrow bed. For a long time he'd been trying to remember something he'd read last week, or the week before . . . and then it came back to him from an account of the Panov affair . . . Charlie Wilde had hidden in a boathouse too, and with a girl . . .

"Tell me about him," he said. "Tell me about Harry Rose."

"What can I tell you? He's different things to different people."

"Did he ever talk to you about George?"

"A little."

"What did he say?"

"That George is like most other men in power today . . . he survives on bad news and when there's no bad news he invents it."

259

"What about a Russian named Boris Tatlin? Did he ever tell you about him?"

"He said that Boris Tatlin is just like George. They're supposed to be enemies but they're almost just the same . . . "

He slept a while, then woke and found her sitting at a table, staring out across the lake.

"We've got to get out of this city. One way or another we've got to get out."

She looked at him with a kind of smile he had never seen before. "This is Berlin, Alex. I am not sure there is a way out."

He crossed from the bed to the window. "What about Rose? Rose could get us out, couldn't he?"

"It would be very dangerous, even to contact him."

"I don't think we've got much choice."

Later they made love, without speaking. Toward dawn they left the boathouse, moving on foot through the pines to the highway. After an hour they finally caught a ride with students from Hamburg. Toward noon they found themselves alone again in a cheap hotel near a railroad line.

Noon. Clipped German voices. Wilde did not even hear Clay enter the room.

"We've got to talk, Charlie."

Wilde almost smiled. "So you lost Petty?"

Clay poured himself a drink. "Charlie, I'm willing to deal with you."

Wilde allowed a grin. "You *are* scared, aren't you?"

"Charlie, there's a telephone in the next room. I want you to go in there and call Lyle Severson. I want you to tell him what's going on here and then ask him if *he* doesn't think you should help stop Rose . . . Let me put it like this, Charlie. If Rose goes public with what he's got there are going to be problems you can't even imagine. I'm talking about very serious problems. You think the

260

Russians don't read the goddamn newspapers?"

"I'm sure Harry wouldn't compromise any existing—"

"You're sure? Look, Charlie, Harry Rose has been out of the *real* game for a long time. He doesn't even know the stakes anymore. He doesn't know where we're vulnerable. I'm talking about agents in the field, your people and his too . . . people living on the edge. Now you tell me where it's going to end for *them* once this stuff hits the press."

Wilde had moved back from the doorway to the window. A few drops of rain had spattered on the glass, but it did not seem to be raining now.

"Charlie, you came here to find the man and keep him from hurting this agency, right? Just like Petty. So you came from a different direction, but—"

"Where's Campbell?"

"He's at the station."

"Jerry Mace?"

"He's with a doctor. Petty beat him up pretty bad . . . Charlie, I want you to know that it wasn't my idea to meet with Tatlin that night. I was ordered to do it, I swear to God—"

"Ordered by whom?"

"Come on, Charlie, you know how it is. The word just comes down from the top. You never really know—"

"Why?"

"Why do you think, Charlie? Harry Rose thought he knew it all. He was obstructing. The people in charge wanted the Cruise, wanted the Pershings. They wanted those systems, they had their reasons—"

"And Harry was going to spoil the party, is that it?"

"Look, Rose used to say it himself. In a democracy you've got to exaggerate the problem some if you want to get the money. I mean, everyone does it. That's what a lobby is all about. Our lobby is for the country—"

"George, we're talking about killing, people getting hurt."

261

"I know that. Don't you think I haven't thought about it every night since . . . look, nobody thought anyone would get hurt, least of all me . . . I told Tatlin not to play rough, I told that bastard . . . "

Wilde was hearing a confession and hardly cared. But it proved one thing . . . George and his people must really be desperate to come clean this far . . . *Harry, where the hell are you?*

"Charlie, please listen to me. I understand how you must feel, and if you want to nail me to the stake later, that's okay. But help me stop crazy Harry Rose before it's too late . . . If not for anyone else, then do it for *him.* Right now we can still keep it within the family, but if he goes public there will be nothing anyone can do for him. They'll lock him up for years. Ten, fifteen years. That would kill him, you know that . . . Listen, all I'm asking you to do is to help me find him. When I do I promise I'll let Severson step in."

Bullshit. "What about Petty? What happens to Petty?"

"I'll let Severson handle that end too."

Gorgeous George . . . "And the girl?"

"We can keep her out of it if you want. We think that Petty and the girl are going to try and contact Rose. If that happens we would like to be there to pick them up—"

"So you want the contact procedure, is that it?"

"Yes, Charlie."

"And the meeting place?"

"Yes. Hey, Charlie, you can talk to him first. No problem . . . "

Kristian put down the telephone, absently reached for a glass on the table. "Now we have to wait," she said.

There had been sounds of distant trains, and Turkish children playing by the tracks. Now, however, it was quiet.

Petty said, "Does Rose always come himself?"

262

"Yes."

"And we meet him in Templehof at that factory, the Alder-Hof?"

"Yes."

"What do I say when I meet him?"

"It doesn't matter."

"What will he say to you?"

She touched her cheek. "He always kisses me here, then he says, 'Hello. How are you?' It is very casual."

"And afterward?"

She shook her head. "I don't know, maybe he will send us to Switzerland. He has friends, I think, in Switzerland. Or maybe Paris, which is a very nice city."

"And what about us? You and me?"

She glanced at him and smiled. They dozed for an hour, once more together on the narrow bed. It was dark when they woke up and went down to the street. It took them a long time to find a taxi.

The factory lay between a gravel embankment and a wrecking yard. It was like something from the war with ranks of empty window sockets, scorched brick and rusting sheet metal. The sign in burnt-out light bulbs read "Alder-Hof."

They got to the factory from the south. There were odors of chemical waste and charred rubber. Past a loading dock lay a narrow strip of concrete where she said that Rose used to wait for her.

They entered through a steel door with a key that had been hidden at the foot of a staircase. There were no lights, only the rank of windows leaving shadows on the concrete. Ropes had been suspended from the rafters, discarded pipe heaped against the walls.

They sat on packing crates beneath a heating duct. There was a view through the slats of the ruined street, a warehouse and vacant lots. Rose always came from the east, she said, always with two boys to watch the road behind him.

Petty lit a cigarette. "What if he doesn't come?"

"He always comes."

"How did he find this place?"

"He has places like this all over the city. Some are very old."

"How many people are still loyal to him?"

"Who knows? They think he's, how you say, over the hill. In fact he is not."

"Why do they help him? Do they owe him too?"

"You sound like George. They help him because . . . they love him. That is the real secret of his power."

A beat, then: "Do you love him?" But before she could answer there were footsteps on the stairwell, light from the factory door.

"That's him," she whispered.

He tried to grab her arm, but she slipped away. He tried to call her but she ignored him. Then he could only watch . . . the sudden fading smile, the awkward attempt to turn back as Guy Campbell appeared on the landing with a shotgun.

Above the last warehouse lay a side street. The black van stood on the rise of the hill in the shadow of a wall. With the rear door slightly ajar, Wilde could see well beyond the rooftops to the wrecking yard and the highway. George Clay was in the driver's seat.

"Will he come alone?" Clay asked.

Wilde said nothing.

"But he'll bring a few snipers to watch his back, won't he?"

Silence.

"Well, my people won't touch him until he gets *inside.*"

Earlier a boy had appeared from nowhere, leaned into the window and whispered something to Clay. When the boy had vanished Clay had said, "Campbell just tagged Petty and the girl. He's holding them in the factory. He didn't hurt them."

Wilde noted a rifle, a German automatic with an infrared scope. It was wedged between the seats.

"What's this?"

"Standard issue, that's all."

There were trees along the road below, places where the roots had broken through the pavement, clumps of high grass. Clay said that only three men had been placed behind the wall above.

"You don't think he'll do something rash, do you?"

Wilde shut his eyes for a moment, said nothing.

"What about Petty? He nearly killed Jerry Mace, and he's even worse when he gets nervous."

There was a movement in the shadows by the wall, then the crackle of a radio.

"Of course it's my own damn fault. I should have never sent him here in the first place."

"It wouldn't have made any difference who you sent. In his way Harry would have gotten to them."

There were footsteps on the gravel.

"They may have spotted him," Clay said. "He's left a car just beyond those trees." Then a solitary figure between the line of trees.

"What do you think, Charlie? Is that him?"

There were hawthorns beside the road, weeds among the paving stones. Wilde had slid back the door of the van a little further but saw nothing except a fanged shadow on the brickwork, the remote possibility of a raincoat . . .

"Charlie, that's him, isn't it? That's Rose!"

But there were no lights along the road below so that all Wilde saw was an indistinct figure moving at a moderate pace. It seemed to pause once where the pavement had slipped away, then again to avoid a patch of sodden grass.

"He's coming, Charlie, he's coming."

But there was a path through the trees to a clearing above the factory. From where Wilde sat he could only imagine the view from the clearing, imagine himself standing there, calling to him.

He stepped out of the van.

Clay was fixed behind binoculars. There were pools of rainwater along the path, tangled vines and blown leaves. Wilde moved slowly at first . . . he'd never moved too well in the darkness, unlike Harry. At about twenty feet he vaguely heard Clay call his name.

"Charlie, what the hell do you think you're doing? Charlie . . . ?"

He glanced back but only for a moment. Two men were running toward him from the wall, but he did not think they could stop him now. He heard Clay calling again, but only very faintly above the wind.

From here the path descended sharply to the clearing. Ice, like a mirror, lay between the rocks. Past the trees he again heard the voices and thudding footsteps. But it was very still in the clearing.

At first Harry appeared only as another shadow, still moving slowly between the loading docks below. But there were lights along the last stretch of pavement, and suddenly Wilde saw him very clearly . . . a little thinner perhaps, but essentially the same. *Harry.*

Only this time he had to shout it out. *"Harry."* Then even louder. And over and over.

Behind him Clay was also shouting something as he sprinted from the ridge.

Wilde shouted again. "Harry, go back, go back—"

Clay struck from behind, using the rifle like a club. Wilde took a step before he fell, one step into the white light behind his eyes. Then even crumbling, he called out Harry's name again . . .

They brought Wilde back to the van, laid him on a rear seat with a blanket. For a long while he lay very still in the darkness, not sure he could even move his legs. Earlier there had been voices from the wall, fragments of a conversation ending with a slamming car door. Someone, perhaps on Clay's instruction, had given him an injection. It seemed to help the pain.

After what might have been an hour he was conscious of Petty's voice and the girl kneeling on the floor of the van. Their wrists had been bound with electrical wire. The girl's raincoat was torn at the shoulder. When he finally asked if Harry had escaped, Petty nodded. Did he smile?

CHAPTER
ELEVEN

IT WAS HALF past nine in the evening. Petty poured two glasses of Scotch. Wilde lay on the bed. Kristian sat on a chair beside him with bandages and disinfectant.

"This is bad," she said. "Maybe a fracture."

Wilde looked at her. "No, it's just a bump." Although for more than an hour he hadn't been able to sit up without throwing up . . . .

Twelve minutes past ten: Petty still drinking at the window, Kristian still sitting beside Wilde. There had been voices from below and the rattle of a departing truck. Now there were footsteps approaching, someone sliding back the bolt. Petty turned, put down his glass on the dresser. A young man's face appeared briefly in the doorway, then receded to make way for George Clay.

"How's it going, Alex?" But actually he was looking at Kristian.

269

"George, he needs a doctor," she said.

He ignored her, said to Petty, "Well, you really took the plunge this time, didn't you? Just couldn't leave it alone."

Petty took another sip of Scotch. *Go down a hero,* he said derisively to himself . . . "Go and fuck yourself, sir."

Clay also dropped his front. "You ignorant . . . you think I'm playing this alone? Everything comes down from the top." Then, glancing at the girl, "And incidently, she comes with me."

No one moved except Petty, who had taken a step into the center of the room. Behind him stood a German youth in blue jeans and a nylon jacket. He held a shotgun under his arm.

Petty looked at Clay, then at the shotgun. "If you want her, you're going to have to do it right now, right here." He pointed his finger to just below his rib cage. "Right here."

Eleven o'clock. Fog lay matted between the trees. Petty stood at the window again. He had still not finished the first glass of Scotch. Kristian had left Wilde's side and moved to the far end of the room. There were lights in the distance, suburban lights or the lights of a military installation.

Earlier she had said, "You should stop thinking like a spy, you are always thinking like a spy."

But if he wasn't to think like a spy, then what?

"Like a refugee," she had said. "From now on you should think like a refugee."

He poured her a drink, left it on the dresser and turned back to the window. Wilde had not moved for a long time.

"How is he?"

"Sleeping."

She picked up the glass and joined him at the window. There may have been someone moving below, Campbell or one of those German boys.

270

"What will they do to us?" she asked suddenly.

He ran his fingers through his hair.

"Will they shoot us?"

"I don't think so."

"Then what?"

"I suppose they'll take us to the station for a while, because George has things to take care of. After that they'll put us on a plane, a private plane. Then they'll take us to a place in the country, a long way from anywhere. They'll keep us in rooms without windows, and the food will make us feel a little strange so we won't always know what's real and what's not. After a few months or a year, no one will care anymore." *Us included,* he didn't add.

"But Harry will care. Harry will reveal everything to the newspapers and then the whole world will know. How can they hurt us if the whole world knows?"

He said nothing, but the answer was in his eyes, in the way he looked at her before turning away . . . .

Fifteen minutes past eleven and he told her, "Maybe you should try to get some sleep."

She shook her head, moved across the room to sit down. There had been voices from the corridor again, a question in German, the answer in English . . . *Because he's a tricky fucker, that's why* . . . Then returning to the window, Petty saw that the fog was definitely advancing.

Suddenly, as if completing an unfinished sentence, she said, "Anyway, Harry Rose won't let them hurt us."

He wanted to touch her, to hold her. What he did was to say, "Maybe."

"What do you mean by that?"

"It's just that people like Clay don't only make up the rules, they make up the game too. Once in a while you might be able to slow them down, but I don't think you can stop them."

"You only say all that because you've never met Harry Rose.

271

If you had you would never talk like that. He's not an ordinary person. Believe me."

He'd like to . . . .

Eleven-thirty and Campbell stepped into a room below the staircase. Clay was sitting in a chair by an electric heater. The German boy was drinking in the corner.

"There's a flight leaving for Hamburg in an hour," Campbell said. "Military transport."

Clay nodded, lit a cigarette. "I'm not leaving until I find him."

Campbell glanced at the German boy, who smiled but said nothing.

Clay added, "As long as we've got his buddy Wilde and the girl we still have an edge on him."

Campbell said, "Sir . . . I really don't think we can legally hold—"

"Guy, just bring the girl downstairs. Do it . . . . "

Eleven-forty and she entered the room slowly. Campbell remained in the doorway until Clay told him to leave. For more than a minute they just looked at one another—he still sitting in the chair, she standing in front of him with her arms at her sides.

"There's paper on that desk, a pen in the drawer," he told her. "I want you to write down the telephone number that you called to contact Harry Rose."

She hesitated a moment, moved to the desk. Afterward she stood facing a window and a black view of the trees in fog. "May I go now?"

He stood up and went to the window beside her. "I want to know why you did it."

"Leave me alone, George."

As she moved past him, he grabbed her arm and for a moment she thought he was going to hit her.

"I could have given you everything," he said, understanding nothing, but for the moment seeming almost human . . . .

Midnight, almost. Kristian had returned to the room at the top of the stairs. Wilde was still resting on the bed, Petty still watching from the window.

"He wanted the contact procedure, didn't he?" Petty said.

She nodded and sank down to the chair beside the bed. "But Harry will never surrender," she said. "He will never do that . . . Anyway, Harry will never bargain with George. He won't have to. He knows where we are, probably right now he is coming for us."

"Kristian, I think—"

"I feel it. Right now I feel it. He's out there, waiting . . . . " Ten minutes after midnight and Clay had returned to the chair by the electric heater. Campbell stood by the desk. There was a telephone on the table between them. From the kitchen came sounds of a radio and the German boy searching for food. Otherwise it was very quiet.

"You might as well give me the telephone," Clay said.

"Yes, sir." Campbell put it on the arm of the chair.

"You might as well get some sleep too," Clay added. "It could be a long night."

"Yes, sir," and he started backing out of the room as Clay lifted the receiver, listened a moment, then let it slip from his hand. They looked at one another.

"The phone is dead," Clay said.

"But I don't understand, I just—"

"The goddamn phone is *dead* . . . . "

Wilde had awakened. A moment earlier Petty heard what sounded like a distant truck, now there was nothing.

273

Suddenly Kristian reached out and touched his hand. "You feel it now, don't you?" she whispered.

He looked at her and saw that her eyes were very bright, cheeks flushed. "Well, I think—"

"I think he's very close now, very close."

There were voices from the corridor again. Clay, obviously furious, was shouting at Campbell. Campbell began to reply but stopped mid-sentence at the sound of something outside . . .

"He's toying with them." She even smiled. "He likes to do that."

"Kristian, don't . . . "

"Why do you think they call him the prince of Berlin . . . ?"

The last room along the upstairs corridor must have once been a child's nursery. There were remnants of painted stars on the ceiling, a chest with the faces of animals on the knobs. Clay had sunk down onto the edge of a narrow bed. Campbell had picked up another telephone, then let it drop again. "This one's dead too."

Clay nodded, ran his hand across his mouth. "Who's at the station right now?"

"Just the night staff."

"How many?"

"I don't know. Ten, fifteen."

"All right, then tell Niki to bring the van around. We're getting out of here."

Campbell leaned out the door and spoke softly to the German boy. When he looked again Clay had still not moved from the edge of the bed.

"You never really knew him, did you?"

"Sir?"

"Rose. You never knew him."

"No, I guess I didn't."

"Well, he's a clever bastard . . . it's easy to underestimate him, very easy. That's why you've always got to watch him—What the hell is that?"

"Sir?"

"That *sound. That.*"

It was like a melon falling on concrete.

Clay moved to the doorway, peering down the staircase into the darkness. He could not recall having turned off the lights. It was silent again, very still.

"You'd better go down and take a look," Clay said.

Campbell did not move.

"Guy?"

"I'm sorry, sir. This just isn't my fight anymore."

"I said get down there and take a *look.*"

Then again softly: "I'm sorry, sir . . . "

Clay withdrew a revolver and moved to the staircase. He paused at the landing, heard nothing and continued. He kept his left hand on the bannister, testing each step before he committed his weight. There was a breeze through a door that should have been bolted.

Rose . . .

The shadows of tossed curtains played on the woodwork. He had to pause again to wipe the perspiration from his hands.

He crouched at the bottom of the stairs. The corridor ahead was very dark. When he started moving again he had to guide himself with his fingers on the wall.

Among the shadows of billowing curtains lay another shadow, suggestive of someone waiting by a wall. Clay leveled the revolver, knees bent, weight on the balls of his feet . . .

Hey, Harry . . .

The shadow had shifted slightly. Clay could hardly keep from smiling now, drawing closer, cocking back the hammer.

Harry, son of a bitch . . .

Clay fired as the shadow tried to spin away, three rapid shots.

275

He fired again and the head snapped back, lifting part of the skull. The last two shots severed an artery, spraying blood across the plaster.

Clay lowered the revolver. The stricken shadow had stumbled into the corridor, the left leg still shuddering. He took a step forward, another.

Harry . . . ?

Not Harry, but the German boy with the eyes wide and staring.

For a moment Clay stood motionless, the spent cartridges at his feet. The revolver was empty and had to be reloaded. Further along the corridor someone had removed the light bulbs. The darkness was nearly total, so that Clay saw little more than a hint of him, waiting in an empty room.

"You . . . you . . . "

"Hello, George."

As Clay brought the revolver up something black and hard swung down from behind his shoulder. The blow caught him above the ear. As he sank into unconsciousness, he vaguely recognized the face of Stanley Kline. Beside Kline there may have been a Turkish boy occasionally seen around the station. But framed in the doorway with a raincoat on his shoulders, there was also, definitely, Harry Rose.

Rose now moved slowly up the staircase. He paused at the first landing, pulling at the sleeve of his raincoat, then paused again to relight a cigar. Finally at the last door he took another moment to compose himself. Entrances and exits had always been important.

Charlie Wilde was to write: *You told us that there is no absolute right and wrong, only degrees. You told us that both the East and West are inherently flawed, and now look at us—we're stranded in the middle ground . . .*

Later there were to be a number of stories from this last night, but again the truth was something less . . .

After regaining consciousness, George Clay was led to a waiting car, a black Chrysler. He moved unsteadily along the path, his arm slung over Guy Campbell's shoulder. Harry Rose watched from only a few feet away.

Rose and Petty met on the gravel beside the van. It was very cold.

"I expected you to be different somehow," Rose said. "Don't know why." Then, turning to Kristian, he said, "I'm sorry that I had to involve you. I never intended it to go so far. There's a plane leaving for Paris in an hour. It would probably be best if you were both on it."

Petty glanced at Kristian, nodded, said nothing.

Charlie Wilde and Harry, old friends, met at about four o'clock in the morning. Stanley Kline helped Wilde down the stairs.

"Hello, Charlie. How are you feeling?"

Wilde nodded. Earlier he had thought, *He hasn't changed at all.* Now he said, "It's good to see you, Harry."

Rose smiled. "It's good to see you too, Charlie. Very good."

What might have been extraordinary now seemed almost natural. "Where's George?" Wilde asked.

Rose poured a glass of brandy for each of them. "Halfway between here and the station, I'd imagine."

"Then he's all right?"

"Sure."

Suddenly Wilde said, "I don't suppose you want to talk about it?"

Rose shrugged, "Oh, I don't mind, Charlie, although there's not much to say at this point . . . I mean, the real question has never changed, Charlie. Just the details . . . the weapons, the rhetoric, the strategy. But the basic question has never changed. That's why we keep saying it over and over—how can we stop war? The one to end us all."

He stood up and moved to the window. "You know there's a

theory that man originally descended from some killer ape. We survived by beating rivals to a pulp with clubs. So the instinct for war is in our genes, uncontrollable. I don't believe it, Charlie."

"What about the documents?"

"A statement, that's all. A small attempt to try to put a little light on the subject. Of course originally I'd hoped to expose the whole Team B charade . . . yes, it's that . . . but it seems a lot of the material was shredded. Still, there are a few nice bits. There's also a pretty enlightening piece on the Pershing II. Nothing that will stop the nuclear dance overnight, but it's a start. A start."

"What if they don't print it?"

"Oh, I think they'll print it. No question, though, the timing might have been better. I'd originally hoped that publication would coincide with the spring disarmament rallys in Bonn . . . but just the same, I think they'll print it."

"So you gave it to the German press?"

"No, I didn't say that."

"What about George?"

Rose shook his head, but still faced the window. "George isn't so important, Charlie. You know, I don't even believe that he met with Tatlin on his own. I think he was ordered to do it—which is not to say, of course, that he still didn't enjoy it."

Wilde was conscious of the stillness, and Rose at the window, almost, it occurred to him, like an effigy of himself.

"I'm going to have to call Lyle Severson," he said.

"Oh, by all means call him, Charlie. After all, someone has to put the order back in things."

"You realize they won't forgive you for this one, Harry."

Rose allowed a smile. "No, I don't imagine that they will, but it's ironic when you think about the possibilities."

"What do you mean?"

"Well, suppose I had brought them a little statement from Boris Tatlin, something to fill in the blank spaces, end the speculation once and for all about those lost photographs. Obviously they couldn't crucify me then, could they?"

"Did you try?"

"Oh, lord, no. Boris wouldn't tell the truth to save his mother. But it's an interesting thought, just the same. I mean, Tatlin is the one person who really could clear me—in more ways than one."

It seemed that there was nothing more to say, or at least nothing that hadn't been said before. Rose remained standing at the window. Wilde had gotten up and moved to the door. What might have been complicated was finally very simple.

"Hey, Harry. We did have some good times though, didn't we?"

Harry Rose nodded. "Some times, all right. I'll say that, Charlie. Well, you have it easy . . . there's more where they came from . . . "

EPILOGUE

HARRY ROSE RETURNED on a Saturday, but only stayed a few hours. Those who claimed to have seen him said that he was pretty much the same, moving freely through the city. Toward dawn he vanished again, and a subsequent search revealed almost nothing.

There was snow in the morning, the first clean fall of the season. Wilde spent the early hours resting in his room. Shortly after ten o'clock George Clay appeared on the steps of the annex. Between Harry's departure and Severson's arrival, everyone's status remained uncertain.

Within an hour of Severson's arrival he and George Clay met in a third-floor room with a view of the northern perimeter. Although Clay had spent the morning complaining of a headache and nausea, a medical report noted that he had not been hurt badly at all.

"I suppose you realize that I would have had him if Wilde hadn't started yelling his head off," Clay said.

But Severson did not seem to want to discuss it. Since his arrival he had hardly left this half-renovated room with its rank of telephones, two chairs and a coffee machine.

"I'm afraid they want you back in Langley, George."

"Oh?"

"Today."

"Sure, I'm the one that's going to take the fall for all this. Well, that's nice, real nice."

"It's a technical matter as much as anything. I mean, you did, after all, allow the girl into your house, didn't you? Then too, there's the matter of that German boy . . . the one you shot. Not to mention Boris, and Wilde almost being killed."

Clay pressed his hands against an oval window. There were a number of vans below, a number of loitering young men in overcoats. For me, he thought.

"So I'm out, is that it?"

"Unofficially, yes."

"What about Petty?"

"Well, that depends on whether or not we ever find him."

"Which means no one cares, right?"

Severson started tapping his fingers on the desk. "Oh, cheer up, George. It could have been worse. After all, you might have had to deal with Harry Rose directly."

Later that afternoon Severson and Wilde were seen on a balcony watching as Clay stepped into a blue van. Still later Wilde was seen along the northern perimeter, walking. Just walking.

And Wilde wrote . . . *You told us that you depended entirely on our belief in you. You told us that we made you up from fantasies. You said that you were nothing without us. In fact, I'm afraid it's the reverse. What are we without you?*

In all Wilde spend a month of listless days helping to draft the damage reports. It was cold by now, firmly winter. The nights, however, were clear. When the first newspaper articles appeared, drawn from those stolen documents, Wilde noticed that the younger staff tended to avoid him. So he generally dined with Severson, or else ate alone in restaurants he remembered from before. Once he even found himself in Kreuzberg again, two hundred feet from the Wall.

There was, however, one more incident. It occurred eight days following publication of the final notes. In response to the final verdict against Harry, Wilde had written some forty pages in defense of him, but of course it was not enough. So on a Tuesday afternoon, without any firm expectation, he managed to slip across the border for a last conversation with Boris Tatlin.

Initially he contacted Tatlin through an intermediary in Dresden, then entered the East with an ephemeral cover and a diplomatic passport. About Boris Tatlin, Wilde only noted that the man hadn't really changed all that much. Although rumor had it that his power had been waning since the previous July, he still managed to dress fairly well.

They met in a one-room apartment in Pankow. Out of habit, Tatlin had laid a table with cold cuts, smoked herring and vodka. It was half past seven in the evening.

"You are surprised that I came?" Tatlin said.

"No, not really."

"Then perhaps I am surprised that you came. There is not so much to say."

Although there were chairs and a sofa, neither man seemed to want to sit. While Tatlin drank slowly by an extinct fireplace, Wilde looked down through a window to an empty courtyard.

"It's about Harry Rose," he said.

Tatlin nodded. "Of course. I have read your newspapers. Harry Rose has become a man of conscience. Also a traitor, perhaps, in some eyes."

"But the newspapers didn't tell the whole story, did they?" Charlie said.

"I don't know. What is the whole story? Harry Rose was bitter, frustrated. He attempted to prove that the Western military estab-

283

lishment had deluded people into thinking very expensive dangerous nuclear systems were necessary for national security when, in
fact, they were not. When Harry Rose failed to provide accurate,
undeniable proof, he went dirty, as they say. He passed embarrassing documents to foreign journalists, documents stolen from
Western intelligence files. Now, is not that the whole story?"

"He had the proof, Tatlin, and you know it. Only it cut both
ways. You didn't like that."

Tatlin had drifted back to the table and poured a glass of vodka.
"Tell me, Charlie Wilde, what are you doing here?"

"I want a statement from you. I want a statement about what
happened that night with George Clay, and I want a description
of the photographs you took from me that night at the border."

Tatlin poured a second glass and laid it on the table for Wilde.
"I envy Rose, you know. I envy him because I do not believe that
I have ever had a friend that would do for me what you have tried
to do for him. George Clay naturally is the same, I think. He also
does not have any real friends. I think that is the price we pay for
survival in this so-called secret world."

"I'm not asking you to compromise anything, to jeopardize
your career. I'm just asking—"

"I know what you are asking, Charlie. This time Harry Rose
has truly entered the middle ground. He cannot go home. He can
only keep running. Perhaps one day when the world gets rid of
all weapons, then maybe Harry can return a big hero. Right now
he is in the middle ground, and you want to get him out. But I
do not think that I will help you."

"Why?"

"Because it is not my nature. Also, to hell with Harry Rose."
He did not add that he preferred the likes of George Clay. He
didn't need to.

The details concerning Wilde's last three days in Berlin were
scarce. It was assumed, though, that he spent them alone, wander-

ing in the afternoons, drinking in the evenings. There were of course rumors that he eventually spent a little time in Paris with Kristian Haas and Alex Petty.

It was also said that after a few months in Paris, Alex Petty simply returned to Berlin. There, he was often seen with Kristian Haas, or waiting alone at a bar. His relationship with the secret world continued to remain undefined.

There were rumors, of course, that Petty eventually met with Rose again, but there were always such rumors. Year after year, over and over, there was always someone who claimed to have spent an afternoon with Harry Rose.